A CONSPIRACY
OF RAVENS

A **CONSPIRACY** OF **RAVENS**

TERRENCE McCAULEY

Copyright © 2017 by Terrence McCauley
Cover and jacket design by 2Faced Design
Interior designed and formatted by E.M. Tippetts Book Designs

ISBN 978-1-943818-71-6
eISBN 978-1-943818-72-3

First trade paperback edition September 2017 by Polis Books, LLC
1201 Hudson Street
Hoboken, NJ 07030
www.PolisBooks.com

POLIS BOOKS

To Melissa Gardella
For all the years of support and friendship

ALSO BY
TERRENCE McCAULEY
FROM POLIS BOOKS

Prohibition
Slow Burn

<u>James Hicks series</u>
Sympathy for the Devil
A Murder of Crows

CHAPTER
1

2:00 A.M.

JAMES HICKS WAS two hours south of Manhattan, driving to a meeting he didn't want to attend in Washington, when his dashboard screen flashed red. It was a Proximity Alert from OMNI.

POSSIBLE SURVEILLANCE IN PROGRESS

"Goddamn it." Hicks pounded the steering wheel. "Not this shit again."

Surveillance was the whole reason he was driving to Washington, D.C. in the first place.

The Optimized Mechanical and Network Integration System (OMNI) was one of the most advanced computer networks in the world, giving the University one of the few advantages it enjoyed over the larger, federally-funded agencies. OMNI's access to satellites, data systems, and communications networks collected more data in a millisecond than any human mind could ever comprehend, and saw more than any human eye could see.

Since being selected as Dean of the University weeks ago, the network now dedicated part of its impressive bandwidth to constantly scan his immediate area for patterns and signals that may constitute a threat to Hicks.

He had refused the security measures at first, finding it intrusive for a man who had spent most of his life in the shadows. He had managed to stay alive this long without babysitting. He had seen no reason to allow it now.

But the protection came with the job and could not be refused, not even by the Dean. Given the number of people who had tried to kill him in the past few months, Hicks decided an extra set of eyes watching his back might not be a bad idea.

The automatic alert he was reading now proved he had made the right choice.

He tapped the dashboard screen for more information.

TARGET CAR: BMW 750i

TAIL TIME: 30 minutes and counting

SPEED: Matching 70 miles per hour

ERROR: New Jersey license plates do not match VIN on black box

The fact that a car had been behind him for thirty minutes didn't bother him. People often popped on the cruise control and let the car do the driving in light traffic like this.

It was the problem with the plates that bothered him. They didn't match the Vehicle Identification Number OMNI detected from the signal on the BMW's black box. That *was* unusual. Too unusual for it to be written off as a mistake.

Hicks had been checking his mirrors constantly during the

drive south. He hadn't detected anyone following him, but it was difficult to track a car in the middle of the night.

Hicks tapped a button on the Buick's steering wheel, accessing the OMNI network. "Get me an Operator."

"Contacting an Operator," the female electronic voice answered as it connected him to one of the dozens of technicians located throughout the world who constantly monitored OMNI's field operations.

A man's voice, betraying a slight British inflection, came over the Buick's speakers. OMNI may have been a secure closed network operating entirely on its own bandwidth, but University Operators still answered using a standard protocol script. "You've reached the switchboard. How may I help you?"

"This is Professor Warren." It was the signal that he was not in any immediate danger and free to talk. If he had given them any other name, the Operator would have assumed he was in trouble and activated necessary security measures. Even with twenty-first-century technology, old tricks like code words still had a place. "Looks like I've become pretty popular. I need more information."

"I'm sorry to hear that, sir." Hicks heard the Operator's fingers work a keyboard as he accessed OMNI to find his location and the alert that had flashed on the dashboard screen. "I see the nature of the problem now. The plates match the exact make, model, and year of the BMW following you, but the VIN is completely different."

Hicks knew that ruled out any government agencies following him. They would not need to steal plates for a vehicle.

But someone did. "Who owns the car, according to the VIN?"

He heard the Operator typing. "Records show it was delivered to a BMW dealership in New Jersey late last week." More clicks. "No record of sale. No stolen car reports with the police, either. It's possible they stole the car tonight from the dealership after it closed."

Convenient timing. "Who owns the plates?"

More clicks of the keyboard. "Michael Spatola of Franklin Lakes, New Jersey. Zooming in to get eyes on his address now." More clicks on the keyboard. "Satellites show his BMW is still parked in his driveway, but the license plates have been removed from the vehicle."

Hicks kept his eyes on the road. Someone had been smart enough to steal plates matching the same make, model, and year of the vehicle they had just stolen. Even if a cop decided to run the plates, they would be close enough to match and the cop would probably let them go. Both the car and the plates would be reported stolen eventually, but not for several hours.

That kind of pairing took planning and access. It took effort that common car thieves wouldn't have gone through. And the odds that common car thieves just happened to be following him this long by accident were astronomical.

Everything about the car and the plates showed intent. It showed planning.

Hicks didn't like it.

He needed answers and, under the circumstances, there was only one way to get them.

"Check traffic and toll cams based on my route. I'm looking for a visual of the driver. Send anything you get to my screen."

Thirty seconds later, the Operator said, "Sending an image to you now."

4

Hicks glanced at the screen while keeping his eyes on the road. A blurry image of two white males at a toll booth in the BMW appeared on his dashboard screen. Judging by the way they filled their seats, he guessed they were each over six feet tall and powerfully built.

The Operator explained, "That picture was taken as they blew through an EZ Pass station without an EZ Pass. I'll keep looking for a clearer image, but that's all I have for now."

Hicks didn't care about clearer pictures. He needed to find out who was driving that car.

"I'm in a generous mood tonight," Hicks told the Operator, "so let's do Mr. Spatola a favor. Enter the theft of the plates and the vehicle into the police network. Say the suspects should be considered armed and dangerous and are believed to be heading for the D.C. area."

More keyboard clicks. "Doing it now, sir."

Another idea came to him. "Show me the closest patrol unit on my map."

A few more clicks. "I've just posted the location of the closest unit to your position on your map, sir. The blue icon is the closest police car—a county sheriff's deputy manning a speed trap approximately three miles and closing from your current position. The tail car is the red icon on your map, while your car is black."

Hicks would have preferred a state trooper, but at least a county cop wasn't some local Barney Fife looking to be a hero.

Hicks pulled the gloves tighter on his fingers. "Plot the nearest off-ramp between here and the speed trap. Something that gives me easy access back onto the highway."

A blue line appeared on the map of his dashboard screen.

5

"There's an off-ramp approximately two miles ahead of you, sir, but be advised: you may not be able to outrun the BMW. It's got a twin 445 horsepower V8 engine. With all due respect, sir, that's a tough engine for an old Buick to beat."

Hicks smiled. *That's why I've got an Aston Martin V12 engine under the hood.* "Consider me advised. Since the alert is already on the system, send a message directly to the deputy's onboard computer. Tell him the vehicle is heading his way. Let's see what he does."

"Doing it now," the Operator replied. "And good luck, sir."

Hicks killed the connection. He never believed in luck. Only in himself.

HICKS GLIDED INTO the left lane to pass the slower traffic and floored it. The V12 engine came to life, hurtling the old Buick south at a speed it hadn't been meant to go when it left the factory all those years ago. But thanks to some alterations by the technicians in the University's Varsity Squad, the vehicle was an older car only in appearance.

In addition to installing the new engine, the techs had also replaced all the windows with bulletproof glass, reinforced the frame, installed armor plating, and upgraded the electronics so the old La Crosse was tied in to the OMNI system.

He glanced at the map on his dashboard screen. The red icon of the BMW quickly disappeared at the bottom as Hicks sped out of range. He cut the wheel to the right and moved across two lanes of traffic to the exit lane, coasting up the off-ramp and stopping at a red light.

The on-ramp to take him back on the highway was well

marked and straight ahead of him. Since no cars had followed him up the ramp, he decided to stay where he was when the light turned green. He wanted the BMW to pass him before he made a move. He wanted to wait for that cop to pull the car over and start asking questions. He could always find out what the cop found out by accessing the police records later. Anything to get that BMW off his back.

He watched the dashboard screen. The red icon of the BMW remained on the highway, continuing south without changing speed.

Hicks tapped the screen, expanding the map to show how close the BMW was to the speed trap. Only a mile out.

The traffic light turned green again and Hicks checked his rearview mirror. Still no cars behind him. He stayed where he was.

The red icon moved past the blue icon of the speed trap. The blue icon pulled out and fell in behind the red.

A good start.

He watched as both icons moved across the lanes of traffic to the highway shoulder. The tail car was in front, while the sheriff's car remained several yards back.

Hicks tapped the screen to switch the view from a map to the green hue of the night vision lens from the satellite miles above the earth.

He zoomed in and saw the BMW had pulled over. The sheriff's car was just behind it, high beams on and lights flashing.

Hicks liked what he was seeing. *Follow your training, Ace. It's an Armed and Dangerous call. Don't be a cowboy. Stay in the car. Call for backup and wait for the cavalry to show up.*

The sheriff's car door opened and a large deputy stepped

out from behind the wheel.

"Goddamn it!" Hicks punched the steering wheel. "Stay in the fucking car!"

That was when Hicks saw the BMW's passenger door open as well.

He tapped back to the map view and widened the search area for additional police units. No other cars were in range.

Hicks hit the gas and bolted for the on-ramp.

The deputy might not have needed any help.

He was going to get it anyway.

A GUNFIGHT WAS ALREADY under way by the time Hicks reached the scene.

The deputy was on the ground between the BMW and his patrol car, firing at the passenger side. The rear window was shattered. The passenger was out of the car and firing down at the cop, while the driver gestured wildly at him to get back in the car.

Hicks cut the wheel to the right, screeching to a stop at an angle in front of the BMW. Horns blared at the new obstruction in the right lane of the highway.

The passenger glanced back at Hicks as he reloaded.

The driver began getting out of the car.

Time to move.

Hicks pulled his Ruger .454 from his shoulder holster as he opened his door.

Hicks aimed at the passenger as he stepped out of the car and fired. One round from the powerful pistol caught the passenger in the top of the forehead. Red mist appeared behind his head as he dropped to the asphalt.

From the cover of the BMW's door the driver fired three times, all three shots hitting the bullet-proof glass of the Buick's side windows.

Hicks fired twice, each round punching through the driver's window, catching the shooter in the center of the chest. The man dropped his pistol as he fell.

Hicks kicked the driver's pistol under the BMW as he rushed to the deputy. He found the cop on the ground, trying to keep blood from spurting out of a bullet wound in the left side of his neck while trying to cover the scene with the gun in his right hand. The slide was locked back, proving the gun was empty.

Hicks ignored the gun as he knelt beside the wounded deputy. "Relax, Ace. I'm one of the good guys." He saw the cop's mic was clipped to his bulletproof vest. So was a body camera. Hicks hit the squawk button and spoke into the radio. "Officer shot." He read the name from the deputy's name plate. "Deputy Hass needs assistance at the Armed and Dangerous stop on the highway." He read off the license plate number of the car and ignored the dispatcher's demands for him to identify himself.

Hicks holstered his Ruger and pulled the cop to his feet. He walked him to the backseat of his patrol car. He found a towel on the ledge of the rear window, balled it up, and stuck it over the wound. "You got hit in the shoulder, not the throat. It's a bad wound, but if you keep pressure on it, you should be okay until the cavalry gets here. Stay sitting up straight; that will reduce the blood loss and you'll stay alive."

Hicks left the deputy in the backseat and pulled his OMNI handheld device from his pocket. Since he was wearing driving gloves he knew he hadn't left any prints on the mic, not that prints would tell the police much, anyway. The cop's body camera had probably caught images of his face, but OMNI could take care of that later. He had work to do first.

Horns blared and rubberneckers slowed, drawn by the flashing lights and awkward angle of the Buick off the shoulder. Hicks kept his face turned away from the traffic in case anyone was taking pictures.

Hicks raised his handheld and took a picture of the driver's corpse so OMNI should get a good match on his identity. Then he placed four of the dead man's fingers on the screen and scanned them.

The wail of sirens in the near distance began to grow louder as Hicks went to the passenger side of the BMW. The top of his head was completely gone, but he took his picture anyway and scanned his fingerprints. The approaching sirens were growing louder by the second.

Time to go.

Hicks slipped the handheld back into his pocket as he climbed into the Buick and pulled out into the slow flow of traffic. In his rearview mirror, he could see dozens of pairs of red-and-blue lights from several patrol cars race across the median to help their fallen comrade.

He eyed his mirrors for the next few miles, watching for a police car that might be chasing him.

He decided he was in the clear five miles later. He hit the call button on his steering wheel again and called Jason, his second in command at the University. The position had been dubbed the Dutchman because, like the boy in the story, he kept plugging leaks in the dam.

Despite the late hour, Jason picked up on the first ring. "I woke up when I heard you had received a proximity alert. I tracked the whole thing via OMNI. Are you hurt?"

"No, but we've got a problem. The deputy I helped was wearing a body camera. I know he got my face, maybe even a couple of shots of the car."

"I know," Jason said. "But fortunately, the county doesn't have a live feed from their officers in the field. We'll alter the dash and body cam footage as soon as they download it from the devices. OMNI is already running print analysis and facial recognition searches on the men you killed. No solid hits yet, but preliminary scans of their features say they're of Slavic origin. Probably Russian, definitely not Farmhands."

Farmhands was the University's term for people who worked at the *Barnyard*, which was another University term for the Central Intelligence Agency. This didn't feel like a government op gone wrong. If they had been feds, they would have called it in and had the deputy ordered to back off. They wouldn't have gone to the trouble of stealing a car and license plates in the first place.

"Try tracing their movements from the time OMNI realized they were tracking me. Might help figure out how the hell they found me."

"I'm already on it," Jason said. "I should have something within an hour. But there's something else." He hesitated before saying, "I know how important tomorrow's meeting is for the University, but after this incident I think you should consider postponing. Since those men weren't agents, we should know who they were and how they found you before you meet with people like this."

Hicks hadn't always agreed with Jason, especially back

when Jason had been his boss. But he agreed with him now and, unfortunately, it didn't make a damned bit of difference. "The Trustee had to pull a lot of strings to get this meeting to happen. If we call it off now, we might not get this chance again. And if the clowns who were following me turn out to be Russian, then they're probably with the Vanguard. That's why we're meeting with Langley in the first place."

"Just wanted to voice my concern. I'll make sure you're notified as soon as OMNI finishes the search on the two dead men, but don't get your hopes up. You know OMNI's reach gets weaker the further east we go, so if they're Russian, we may not get positive identifications."

Hicks didn't need a computer to tell him what his gut already knew.

The dead men had been working for the Vanguard. And the University would need all the help it could get.

"I'll be in the car for the next few hours. Let me know if you find anything. And keep an eye on how the deputy is doing. Give me updates as you get them."

Hicks killed the connection and continued driving south.

Traffic was flowing easily again and no one seemed to be following him. He kept checking his mirrors for flashing lights, but didn't see any.

He wondered how many of the other drivers on the road beside him remembered the scene they had witnessed only a few miles ago. He figured most of them had probably already forgotten it and had gone back to listening to the radio or thinking over their own problems as they rolled along to wherever they were going. Their world extended as far as the headlights of their respective vehicles and no further.

Hicks wished he had the luxury of ignorance, of complacency. He wished the woman he loved had loved him back. He wished he knew for certain if she was actually carrying his baby.

He wished he had the same concerns as his fellow drivers about taxes and which party to go to and whether they were going to get a house down the shore that summer. He wished he had to worry about little Billy's braces and about the boys teasing Mary for being taller than them.

In a few hours, he would have a meeting that wouldn't just decide the future of the University. It was a meeting he might not walk away from.

Since he couldn't do anything to stop it, there was no reason to delay it.

He hit the gas and sped toward D.C.

CHAPTER
2

Washington D.C.

HICKS HAD ALWAYS hated meeting in public areas. His run-in on I-95 earlier that morning hadn't made him like them any better.

Meridian Hill Park in Washington, D.C. was as public as it got.

It was the first real day of spring and lived up to the billing. The sun was warm, the birds were singing, and the sky was postcard-perfect blue. Green shoots of flowers had begun to break through the soil after a long winter's slumber, eager to bask in the growing warmth of the sun. Another sweltering summer was soon to follow, but days like this almost made up for it.

Hicks might have enjoyed the scenery if he wasn't so worried about being captured or killed. Not just by the Vanguard, but by the CIA.

The perfect weather seemed to have drawn half of Washington to this green oasis among the concrete landscape of the nation's capital. The paved pathways of the park were jammed with parents and toddlers, and nannies with strollers. Serious joggers and amateur jigglers in various states of fitness moved along at varying paces, both attempting to rid themselves of winter flab before beach weather arrived. Couples of all ages strolled through the park, too, along with office workers who seemed to have decided their lunch hour would last a little longer that day.

Hicks knew most of them were completely innocent, or at least as innocent as anyone who lived in Washington could be.

He also knew any one of them could have been sent to watch him. The crowded conditions in the park made it easy for government operatives to pose as civilians. Outdoor meetings such as this were particularly dangerous, as the Agency could just as easily observe them from the next bench or from a satellite parked miles above the earth.

Hicks reminded himself that he hadn't been given a choice in selecting the venue, a fact that bothered him most of all.

He glanced at the elegant older woman seated next to him one bench over. She was close enough to be within earshot, but not close enough for anyone to think they were together. That was the point. They looked as if they were from two different worlds, which was by design.

Hicks hadn't shaved in days and couldn't remember the last time he'd combed his hair. He'd changed his clothes since the drive down to D.C. and now wore faded jeans and a hooded gray sweatshirt over a Kevlar vest. The Ruger .454 tucked in the pouch of his bulky sweatshirt was his only other protection.

He looked so close to homelessness that none of the park patrons looked at him for very long. No one wanted to be put in the awkward position of denying his request for a handout. Anonymity had always been one of Hicks's greatest assets.

In contrast, the older woman on the next bench wore a tailored blue suit cut to match her thin frame. Her silver hair was cut fashionably short and her pearl necklace made her look more like a wealthy donor to the Smithsonian than what she really was—a spy, just like him.

Hicks made sure no one was within earshot before asking, "You sure love meeting in parks, don't you, Ma?"

The woman he knew only as the Trustee didn't break cover. She continued thumbing through the magazine on her lap. "At least I don't have anyone aiming a high-powered rifle at your chest like I did in Savannah. A decision I'm likely to regret if you continue to call me Ma or Mom, or any of the other colorful nicknames you've invented for me. I may not be as young as some of the chippies trotting around here in Spandex tops and yoga bottoms, but I'm not old enough to be your mother."

Hicks thought about that as he watched two young women in tank tops and shorts jog past them at a good clip.

He knew almost nothing about the Trustee except that she had once been the Dean of the University and was now his liaison to the University's Board of Directors. During their last meeting in a public square in Savannah, she had threatened to have him shot if he disobeyed the demands of her fellow Trustees. He didn't even know her real name or how old she was. But Hicks had never allowed his own ignorance to get in the way of a good dig. "You won't tell me your real name, so..."

"My name is of no importance and has no bearing on

today's meeting. You should be more concerned about how you'll handle Carl when he gets here instead of superfluous details like my name."

Hicks knew Carl was Charles Demerest, head of Clandestine Services at the CIA. He was rumored to be in line for the recently-vacated position of Director of National Intelligence, a spot that could either help or hurt the University...depending on how the meeting went.

Hicks had already planned how he'd approach Carl when he got there. He had more pressing issues to discuss. "You got the report on what happened to me on the ride down here?"

"I did," she admitted, "but don't mention it to Carl right now. We need to ease him into our confidence slowly. Approach him from a position of cooperation and strength. Informing him of your run-in with a couple of thugs who may have been working for the Vanguard might alarm him, so let's keep that to ourselves until we know more, shall we?"

Hicks didn't have enough information to alarm anyone. OMNI had run the prints and faces of the men he had killed through virtually every database in the western hemisphere and didn't get a single match. Jason had broadened the search to include Russian and Middle Eastern databases, but systems in that part of the world were fractured and inefficient, making it difficult to access the right information. He might not be able to prove the men were with the Vanguard, but he knew it.

"If it's any comfort," the Trustee said, "I think you handled the entire situation perfectly. I understand the deputy will pull through, due in no small part to your quick action."

Hicks wasn't so sure. Maybe if he had gotten there earlier, he could have stopped it. Maybe he should have handled it

17

entirely himself and kept the deputy out of it. But it was too late to second-guess himself now. "The cop got lucky. So did we. I dodged a couple of bullets last night. I hope I'm not walking into one now."

"Ye of little faith." She thumbed through her magazine. "I'm not a rookie, you know. I've known Carl for years and he's a man of his word. He told me that he's prepared to allow us to make our case and, things being what they are, we have no choice but to believe him. Remember, his organization is as besieged as our own."

Hicks knew that was true. The entire American intelligence community had been bogged down in oversight committee hearings since news of their black site in New Jersey broke. News that Hicks had made sure broke at just the right time to get them off his back as he hunted down leads on Jabbar and, ultimately, the Vanguard.

He looked around the park as he waited for Carl Demerest to show up. Old people, young people, toddlers, and teens. Any or none of them could have been a threat. That's what the Barnyard did best. That's what worried him most.

The Trustee cleared her throat. "Stop looking so pensive, James. You're supposed to be enjoying a beautiful day in the park, remember?"

"Guess I'm just not used to giving my enemies a free shot at me."

"Stop calling them the enemy, damn you. Carl and his group are an important part of our operation against the Vanguard and..." She clenched her jaw as she let a long breath escape through her nose. She composed herself as she appeared to refocus on her magazine. "I wish your predecessor had warned me about your insolence when he recommended you for Dean."

Hicks eyed a young couple strolling toward them. They were arm in arm and checking their iPhones as they walked, oblivious to the beautiful day. Modern lovers in the technological age, or agents scouting out the area in advance of Carl's arrival? They didn't look like CIA operatives, but the best ones never did.

He waited until they passed out of earshot. "What you call insolence some might call prudence."

"You're only a couple of months into your tenure," she pointed out, "though I'll admit you're off to an impressive start. The idea of seeing the evidence you secured from Jabbar is the main reason Carl agreed to meet with us at all. He's showing a considerable amount of trust in us. The least you could do is reciprocate."

"Sorry, Ma, but I have trouble trusting anyone after they try to kill me, and Carl's buddies tried pretty damned hard. Twice."

"Carl wasn't involved in that nonsense and you know it. Besides, Jabbar's evidence will help take some of the heat off the agency just when they need it most. The fact that it will help Carl's career is a bonus for the University. I think you'll find him and his colleagues much more receptive now. Mutual vulnerability can be a unifying concept."

"Maybe," Hicks allowed, "but I haven't lived this long by believing in 'mutual vulnerability.'"

Hicks took his handheld device from his pocket and tapped the icon for Mark Stephens's phone. "Cosmo, you reading me?"

The Trustee's head snapped toward him. "Who the hell are you talking to? We were supposed to come alone. That was part of the agreement."

Hicks ignored her as Mark's voice came over the tiny

19

Bluetooth device in his ear. "I told you to knock off that Cosmo shit, man. I hate that nickname."

Hicks loved making the University's newest Faculty Member uncomfortable. Stephens had been part of the joint taskforce that had tried to kill him a few weeks before. But after the black site story hit the media, Stephens and his taskforce quickly became liabilities. The fact that Hicks had made it look as though Stephens had leaked the information made his revenge that much sweeter. Being able to recruit the disgraced Stephens to the University had been a trifecta for Hicks's ego.

"I need a situation report," Hicks told him, "not a heart-to-heart about your call sign preferences."

"All is status quo, amigo," Stephens replied. "Varsity Squad throughout the park report nothing out of the ordinary. No suspicious vehicles or obvious listening posts. Just normal foot traffic in and out. No one's queuing up or mustering anywhere near you except for Frisbee games and picnics. No one's paying attention to your location from anywhere in the park. If your new friend brought any playmates with him, they're split up and good at blending in."

Hicks knew if the CIA had sent in an advance team, they would be better than good. They'd be almost impossible to spot. He felt better knowing he had his own people in the vicinity watching his back. "What does our eye in the sky tell us?"

Stephens said, "OMNI's satellite scans confirm there's nothing out of the ordinary. No non-commercial comm signals, nobody lurking in any bushes or on rooftops around the perimeter of the park. Shit, if I knew you people had this kind of technology when I was hunting you, I would've just shot you instead."

"You tried, remember? Didn't turn out so well for you. I'll be maintaining radio silence from here on out, but my earpiece will remain active. If you see anything, don't be shy about letting me know."

Hicks slipped the handheld back into his sweatshirt pocket. He tried to avoid the Trustee's glare. He didn't have to look at her to feel her anger.

And it didn't take long for her to express it. "You've positioned a Varsity Squad in the park against my orders?"

"You're a Trustee, but I'm the Dean. You give advice. I give orders. If this meeting goes sideways, I want our people on-site to handle it."

Her slender fingers gripped the magazine until it crinkled. "How many do you have?"

"Twelve."

She raised an eyebrow. "Quite a number. I assume they're armed."

"What do you think?"

The Trustee's narrow jaw tightened again as she looked back down at her magazine. "I had to call in a hell of a lot of favors to get Carl to even consider this meeting, much less agree to attend. If he spots your teams, he'll walk away and we'll be in a worse position than we already are."

"Don't worry." He nodded toward a man making his way toward them through a group of slower walkers at the edge of the park. "Looks like our date is here."

HICKS HAD NEVER heard of Charles "Carl" Demerest until the Trustee had emailed his file two days before. His official employee photo had been a standard Agency shot of a fleshy, balding man in his sixties, wearing a blue suit next to an American flag. The blue tie was equally bland.

But on this day, Hicks saw the man as a whole. He was just above medium height and build, though he was soft around the middle. He didn't look like a man who was about to be named his country's chief spy, but that's who he was. His faded red windbreaker and khakis hadn't seen a washing machine in a long time. His shoes were from a camping catalogue and had seen too many miles to belong to a fat man.

Hicks noted the thin sheen of sweat on Demerest's bald head, showing he had walked some distance in the warm spring weather. It was a good sign that he had come alone and entered from the north entrance of the park as per their agreement.

Yet, despite the warm day, Demerest had kept the windbreaker on, probably to conceal a gun or a Kevlar vest. Hicks couldn't blame the man for being careful.

After all, he had twelve of his own men stationed throughout the park.

The Trustee closed her magazine and rose to kiss Demerest on the cheek. "Carl, you made it." She sounded as if they were old friends. Hicks wondered if they were. "How long has it been?"

"At least ten years, though you wouldn't know it by looking at you," he replied. "You haven't aged a second since we last met, Sarah. What's your secret?"

Hicks caught the name. *Sarah.*

She nudged the Agency man with her shoulder. "You always were a horrible liar. I only wish we were meeting under more pleasant circumstances."

Demerest sat beside her. "We only meet when things are dire, don't we?"

"It wasn't always that way." She shrugged. "But, alas, here we are."

Hicks didn't know what history these two had, but whatever it had been was enough to get a shrug out of Sarah. He'd barely seen her smile unless she was threatening to kill him.

Demerest leaned forward just enough to look past her at Hicks. "I take it this is the rookie you've been telling me about?"

Hicks casually looked around to see if anyone had followed Demerest into the park. No one had. "That's right, Ace. The same rookie you assholes failed to kill twice in the same week. The same rookie who also burned your black site in New Jersey and got your agency dragged before two congressional hearings." Hicks winked at the older man. "Not too bad for a rookie."

"My people didn't try to kill you, son. Two rogue agents from the Defense Intelligence Agency ran an unauthorized mission on their own. Got themselves drummed out of the service for their trouble. If anyone from my shop wanted you dead, Sarah and I would be chatting at your gravesite right now." Demerest smiled. "We don't miss what we aim at."

"That's catchy," Hicks said. "You should put that on a t-shirt in the gift shop at Langley. Might help you raise some money now that your funding is coming under fire. How are those hearings going anyway? What is it the press is calling it? Black Site-gate? Heard your director is getting the shit kicked out of him by the Senate Intelligence Committee as we speak."

Demerest's smile didn't fade. "A bump in the road. We've been through this sort of thing before, and we'll be around long after two-bit stringers like you are dead and forgotten."

Sarah leaned forward just enough to break the men's view of each other. "I'm so happy that I'm biologically unequipped to participate in this dick measuring contest. And since I'm afraid I left my measuring tape in my other handbag, let's call this one a tie and get down to the reason we're here today, shall we?"

Hicks had to hand it to her. She knew how to handle the male ego. He imagined she had gotten plenty of practice back when she had been the Dean of the University.

"Fine by me." Demerest sat back on the bench like he didn't have a care in the world. Just another citizen on a park bench, enjoying the beautiful day with his lady friend, ignoring the bum on the next bench over. He spoke loud enough so Hicks could hear him. "Last night, Sarah told me all about you and the University. She even showed me that executive order from Eisenhower that she believes gives your group authority to operate independent of government oversight. I think my lawyers would beg to differ, but…"

"A great many of your lawyers have begged to differ with the order over the years," Sarah said. "Some attorneys general and presidents, too. The last president who tried to bring us under his heel was forced to resign in disgrace. Of all the avenues we should be exploring here today, the legality of the University's authority shouldn't be one of them."

Demerest closed his eyes. "I forgot it's impossible to win an argument with you." He looked at Hicks. "Sarah told me that you were the one who grabbed Bajjah in that motel in Philly. I saw the footage, son, so I know you're not just another one of Sarah's policy geeks writing white papers on foreign affairs."

"Damned right I'm not."

Demerest went on. "She told me you had an interesting

story to tell me in exchange for cooperation between our two organizations. Since I've been hunting Bajjah for over a decade, you've got exactly five minutes to tell me where he is before I bring the wrath of God down on your head. If I like what I hear, we can talk about cooperation."

Hicks stole a quick glance down at his handheld to see if Stephens had sent him any security warnings. He hadn't. OMNI hadn't detected any secure signals in the immediate area, either. For all intents and purposes, Demerest had lived up to his end of the bargain. Hicks saw no reason that he shouldn't live up to his.

Hicks tapped the jamming icon on his device, tucked it away, and started the abbreviated script he and Sarah had agreed upon beforehand. "A couple of months ago, one of my top operatives infiltrated a cell of suspected Somali zealots working out of a cab company in Queens. After being there a few months, we agreed they were probably harmless. I was about to shut down the op and reassign my man somewhere else, when he sent me an emergency message requesting a meeting ASAP. Since he was one of my best people, I knew he wouldn't hit the panic button unless it was important. When I showed up at the meet, I found he'd not only been drugged, but had also been forced to set me up for an ambush. He died in the resulting shootout, along with two of the men who'd brought him there."

Demerest surprised him by asking, "What was his name?"

"What do you care?"

"I've had good people turn on me in the field, too, son. I never forgot their names, even after they died. I'd like to know his."

Hicks hadn't expected such sincerity this early in the

25

conversation. Maybe it was part of his plan to establish a rapport. Maybe it was just a way to throw him off balance. "His name was Colin."

"Colin," Demerest repeated. "It's never easy losing anyone, especially in a situation like that. I hope you got the bastards who turned him."

"That's the reason we're here," Hicks went on. "I tracked a third man who fled the scene. Turned out he was working for the same Somalis who Colin had infiltrated at the cabstand. I caught up to them just as they launched a biological attack on New York City later that week. I know the cover story was that it was a Legionnaire's disease outbreak but…"

"No one in the community really believed that," Demerest said. "Our sources at the CDC told us someone had infected about two dozen Somali illegals with an amalgamated contagion of the SARS, MERS, and Ebola viruses. It was exactly the kind of attack our sources reported Bajjah had been plotting for years. You deserve a lot of credit for catching him. Now it's time to step aside and let the grownups handle this. Hand him over."

"Not much to hand over," Hicks said, "unless you brought a baggie with you."

"You mean he's dead?" Demerest's left eye twitched. "You fucking killed him? Why?"

"Dead and cremated. Happened during questioning." Hicks decided the details would have only made him angrier, so he skipped them. "Don't worry. We got enough out of him before he died. You play nice, maybe we'll tell you what he told us."

"You son of a bitch." Demerest's face reddened. "Why didn't you hand him over to us? Why did you have to kill him? You stupid—"

Hicks cut him off. "I needed to find out if he was planning another wave of attacks and I needed to know fast."

"In case you haven't heard, my people are pretty good at getting people to talk."

"Which people?" Hicks asked. "The NSA? CIA? DIA? Don't forget the FBI since the son of a bitch was taken on American soil. Hell, by the time you people decided which agency would talk to him first, another outbreak could've happened in Chicago or San Francisco or Los Angeles. We decided bureaucratic red tape was a luxury we couldn't afford, so we interrogated him ourselves."

"Based on an executive order a paranoid old man signed back in the fifties." Demerest looked at the Trustee. "You disrespect the Constitution one minute and hide behind it the next. You people are something else."

The Trustee said, "But he's got a point, Carl."

Demerest looked like he wanted to argue, but didn't. As a career Agency man, he knew Hicks was right. The American intelligence community had some of the most talented people in the world on its payroll, but it had many stakeholders...and stakeholders all wanted a say in how things were done. And if Bajjah had lawyered up, it might have been months before they got anything out of him. "So, what did he tell you?"

"In broad strokes, he confessed he was behind the entire bio-attack. Smuggling the Somalis into the country, paying for the safe house where he kept them before he injected them with the toxin. He even paid for the scientists who manufactured the virus. The only real question was who funded him and why."

"Jabbar's organization funded him," Demerest said. "Bajjah is his best fighter. Or at least he *was*. Jabbar wouldn't trust anyone else to lead an attack of that magnitude."

"Except Jabbar kicked Bajjah out of the organization a year before the attack was even finalized. He'd grown too radical, even for them. They were afraid he'd do something stupid and bring even more heat on their organization, so they cut him loose. Cut all funding from him, too, hoping that would shut him down and make him listen to reason."

"We never heard about that," Demerest admitted. "Are you sure?"

"As sure as I can be. Jabbar told me directly. Gave me proof, too."

The Agency man grew very still. "Careful, son. Jabbar is nothing to joke about."

"This isn't Comedy Central," Hicks said, "and I'm not laughing."

Demerest looked at Sarah. "Is this real? Are you telling me this guy caught both Bajjah *and* Jabbar?"

Sarah placed a thin hand on Demerest's arm. "Hear him out, Carl. Believe me, you're going to want to hear what he has to say."

Demerest jerked his hand away. "Enough fucking around, damn it. No more hints or maybes or talking around things. If you have Jabbar, I want him. This isn't one of your academic exercises, asshole. I want him right now."

Sarah folded her hands on her lap and looked at the ground. "I'm afraid that won't be possible."

"What the hell are you talking about? Of course it's possible. In fact, it's mandatory. If I don't have that monster in custody by...."

Demerest stopped. His eyes narrowed, looking first at

Sarah, then at Hicks. "Holy shit. You mean he's dead, too?" The redness drained from his face as quickly as it had appeared. "Jesus Christ. You killed them both, didn't you? Why in the hell would you...?"

"We didn't kill either of them," Hicks said. "Bajjah's heart gave out during questioning. But before he got his forty virgins, he gave us enough to find Jabbar."

"Died during questioning," Demerest repeated. "How fucking convenient. And what about Jabbar? Slip in the shower? Fall down an elevator shaft?"

Hicks was beginning to lose his patience. "The Mossad shot Jabbar when they tracked me to our meeting in Toronto. A little over a month ago."

Demerest eased himself back on the bench. A group of teenagers sharing a joint skittered by while the Agency man digested the information.

Hicks figured it might have been the biggest news Demerest had ever received. It wasn't every day that a complete stranger from an organization he'd barely heard of told him two of the most wanted people in the world were already dead.

Demerest waited until the teenagers were further down the path before saying, "You expect me to believe you managed to single-handedly find someone who has evaded the entire intelligence community since the late eighties, but the Mossad killed him without telling anyone about it? After all he's done against Israel?" Demerest shook his head. "They'd never keep something like that quiet. They'd have a fucking parade. Sounds like you've been had, son." He looked at the Trustee. "I expected better of you, Sarah." He began to stand up. "This conversation is over and you're both in custody as of right now."

Sarah stammered a response as Hicks made one last stab at salvaging the entire thing. "Your own people can validate everything I've just told you."

"Excuse me?"

"I'm sure at least a few of your analysts have reported a change in the Jabbar chatter in the past month. Subtle things like a difference in tone or slight variations in syntax. Maybe details of the types of orders given. Someone in your shop must have raised the possibility that a completely different person might be in charge of the Jabbar network. There *is* someone else in charge since Jabbar was killed by a Mossad sniper at the CN Tower over a month ago."

The details seemed to be enough to get Demerest to remain seated on the bench. "Congratulations, son. You're finally making sense. I've received reports speculating there may have been a change in the Jabbar organization." He leaned closer. "But you're shit out of luck on the CN Tower shooting. The Canadians reached out to us when the victim was a young Pakistani woman who'd been killed with a high-powered rifle. She didn't have any ID and her fingerprints had been burned off, so the Canadians thought we might have a line on who she was. We didn't. And we sure as hell don't think she was Jabbar."

Sarah said, "The original Jabbar died of natural causes a few years ago. This young woman was a niece who took his place and continued her uncle's work in anonymity. Since Islamic extremists aren't exactly feminists, I'm sure you can understand why she operated in secrecy. Quite clever of her, actually, in an evil sort of way."

But Demerest hadn't gotten past the part about Jabbar's death. "How the hell did the Mossad find out about the meeting?"

"I'm still trying to find that out," Hicks lied. There was no point in telling him that the Mossad sniper was not only a Faculty Member of the University, but his lover, Tali Saddon. Telling him she might be carrying his child may have given him a coronary, so he skipped that part, too. He kept it simple. "All I know is that they somehow tracked us to the meet and listened in. As soon as they realized the girl was Jabbar, they took her out."

"So why haven't the Israelis made a bigger deal about it? They've wanted Jabbar dead longer than we have."

"Maybe because they don't want to get the reputation of executing people on foreign soil?" Hicks had brokered a deal for the Mossad's silence, but that part could wait. "It doesn't matter how the Mossad found out about the meeting. Jabbar's death doesn't even matter. What matters is the reason Jabbar wanted to meet me in the first place. She wanted to give me evidence that proved neither she nor her group had anything to do with Bajjah's attack on New York. Evidence that proves her group had ruled out a bio-attack like Bajjah's because they didn't think it would work."

"So Jabbar gave you evidence that exonerated her organization," Demerest observed. "Another convenience. You believe it, of course."

"Everything she gave us checks out," Sarah told him. "We didn't just want to hand you a hard drive full of files and PDFs and reports from a dubious source. I'll admit I was skeptical at first, but I wouldn't have asked to meet with you today, much less put my own freedom at risk, unless I was absolutely convinced that Jabbar's information proves we are facing a new threat from an enemy we barely knew existed."

"And down the rabbit hole we go." Demerest considered that for a moment. "Okay. I'll play along for a bit. If Jabbar wasn't pulling Bajjah's strings, who was? And if the next words out of your mouth aren't specific, I swear to Christ I'll have both of you in a cell within the hour."

Hicks ignored the threat. He knew the facts would stick better if Demerest arrived at his own conclusions. "Someone who had the resources to help Bajjah obtain access to a bio-weapon, smuggle two dozen people into the country, and house them while he put his plan into place."

Demerest had a ready answer. "I can think of about half a dozen wealthy families in the Middle East who'd be more than happy to bankroll an op like that, especially with someone who had Bajjah's pedigree. He was one of Jabbar's best people."

"But none of those families would bankroll an operation without Jabbar's blessing," Hicks said, "Any time Jabbar blesses an attack, it sets off an increase in chatter overseas. Since you didn't hear any increase, that means Bajjah received funding and support from somewhere else."

Sarah removed a thumb drive from her purse and placed it in Demerest's hand. "Jabbar told us who was funding Bajjah right before the Mossad killed her. She gave us a laptop that contained proof her organization had nothing to do with it." She looked down at the small plastic device in Demerest's palm. "This thumb drive is a summary of the evidence we've spent the past month vetting. It provides enough information to prove the Jabbar group had nothing to do with this. And it tells us who did."

Demerest didn't close his fingers around the drive. He just

let it sit there, as if it was a bird that had landed on his shoulder. As if the slightest movement might make it chirp, shit, or just fly away. "I'm going to ask this just one more time. For the very last time. Who supported Bajjah?"

Hicks felt sweat break out across his back. This was the moment he had feared since becoming Dean of the University, the moment when his actions and his judgement would decide the future of his organization.

If Demerest believed the evidence, he would become an important ally in the fight ahead. As Director of National Intelligence, Demerest would oversee every intelligence agency in the nation. If he became an ally, he would give the University more influence than it had ever had before.

But if Demerest didn't believe the evidence, then the University would find itself squarely in the crosshairs of every intelligence organization in the western hemisphere.

Hicks swallowed hard. "A group of ex-Russian and ex-Chinese intelligence officers that calls themselves the Vanguard."

Given OMNI's access to some CIA files, Hicks knew Demerest was at least aware of the Vanguard. He hoped that would be enough to convince him to keep listening.

It wasn't. "The Vanguard? Are you kidding me? That's your bogeyman? They're a bunch of mercs and arms dealers and drug runners spread throughout Asia and the Baltic. Our people have infiltrated their organization dozens of times over the years. They're businessmen, not ideologues. They're certainly not radicals. Hell, we haven't even been able to prove they're actually a group, much less looking to attack a nation."

Sarah said, "You barely had any proof that the University existed until I handed you the executive order last night. Why is it out of the question that an organization like the Vanguard could have more sinister aims in mind? It could only take a small change in operations to make them political instead of criminal."

"There's a big difference between running guns and running a proxy war against the United States," Demerest said. "You know that."

"And what if it's a mixture of both?" Hicks asked. "If Bajjah had lived long enough to claim responsibility for the attack in New York, we would've had no choice but to re-double our military presence in the Middle East. That would've pulled our focus away from Russian expansion into the Ukraine and Syria, not to mention China's expansion into the Pacific. That means more weaponry flowing into the region while their mother countries continue their expansion at will. The Vanguard could profit financially and politically at the same time."

"That's one hell of a big if, son."

"Which is why we wanted to make sure Jabbar's evidence was solid before we contacted you." Sarah placed her hand over Demerest's again. "I've never wasted your time before, Carl. And believe me when I promise you that I'm not wasting it now." She tried a smile. "Read the evidence on the thumb drive and you'll see we're right. Work with us, Carl. I promise you won't regret it."

Hicks could almost see the machinations of the Agency man's mind working. He now had a complete understanding of why they had scheduled the meeting. He knew the players, he knew the game, and he knew he had been given clear evidence to review. But he still needed a clearer picture.

"If you were smart enough to bring this to me now,"

Demerest said, "then you're smart enough to have people on the ground digging around for information about the Vanguard. And if you deny it, I'll get up and walk away right now."

Hicks decided to tell him the bare minimum. "I have small teams in place in the field."

"Where?"

"Berlin, Moscow, and London."

"Why there?"

Hicks shook his head. "Not until you agree to cooperate. You read over the information on the thumb drive and you'll understand why. If you agree to work with us, the kimono opens all the way. Until then, the obi stays tied. That's more than fair."

Hicks watched Demerest mull it over. He was like the dozens of other community men he'd worked with and against in his time at the University. Demerest was a career company man who had spent his life in clandestine services. Experience like that was worth its weight in gold in the private sector. The fact that he was still the lead choice for the Director of National Intelligence spot even after the black site scandal proved he was well respected and capable in the community.

Hicks imagined Demerest had been offered several chances at the brass ring over the years, a cushy private sector consulting gig with a salary nestled deeply within the six-figure range, with an annual bonus that might push it into the seven-figure range. All he would have needed to do was write a couple of white papers a year that told trade organizations a region was stable enough for investment. Tell the shareholders what they wanted to hear. Shake hands and close deals. Paper cuts and carpal tunnel syndrome would have been the biggest threats he faced each day.

But Demerest hadn't jumped ship and Hicks knew why. It wasn't out of love for God, country, and the CIA, though that was part of it. It wasn't fear of failure in the private sector, either.

People like Demerest stayed because nothing else could compare to The Life. He wasn't just a spectator in the stands, or worse, a talking head the news networks brought in when some asshole blew up a bus or hijacked a plane or shot up a nightclub somewhere in Europe. Charles Demerest was still in the field and in the game, making plays and making a difference, no matter how small that difference might be. The Life was the only life he knew or had ever wanted to know.

Hicks knew the feeling well. He felt the same way.

And it was why he knew this company man would take the offer Sarah and he had given him.

Demerest surprised them by suddenly standing up as he put the thumb drive in the pocket of his windbreaker. "You two are free to go for now. I'll review what's on the thumb drive, but if I like what I see, I'll want my people digging into Jabbar's laptop as soon as possible. And don't tell me you don't have it because I know damned well you do."

Hicks showed him the handheld again. "All I need is an e-mail address and you'll have the contents of the hard drive in seconds. We can send the laptop to you for verification whenever you're ready."

Demerest finally looked impressed. "I assume you'll be sending it from a secure server, so tracing it will be pointless."

"The server will go off-line as soon as it sends the information, and will never be used again," Hicks said.

Sarah stood next to her friend. "You've made a wise decision, Carl. Really."

Demerest pulled his windbreaker over his belly. "If this evidence is as good as you claim it is, we'll have a deal. If I get the DNI spot, I'll give you your autonomy and our cooperation in working against the Vanguard."

His fleshy face reddened again. "But if either of you ever lie to me or try to use me or hold anything back in any way, you're both dead. No meetings in the park, no disagreements, no renegotiation of terms, and no warning. Just a single bullet in the brain for each of you before I pull your organization apart like warm bread and bring it under my control."

Sarah took a step back. "Carl, I—"

Demerest looked down at Hicks. "You were right, son. The University has only lasted this long because no one has ever taken the time to connect the dots to see exactly what you are. But now we know and that changes everything. You play games with us this time, the Vanguard will be the least of your concerns. A couple of DIA hotheads tried to kill you with our equipment, son. If I do it, we won't miss."

He handed Hicks a plain business card with an abnormally long IP address on it. "Upload everything you have to that server. If I don't have everything by the time I get back to my desk, the deal is off and you're back in the crosshairs." He looked at Sarah. "Both of you."

Demerest turned and headed back the way he'd come in, leaving Sarah standing alone to watch her old friend walk away.

"Poor thing," she said. "His ego is bruised worse than I had expected. But don't worry, James. He'll come around when he sees the kind of evidence we're giving him."

"Who's worrying?" Hicks was already typing the server address Demerest had just given him into his handheld. "If he agrees to work with us, great. If not, we'll keep doing our thing like we always have. Our way."

"And if he lives up to his threats?"

"Then we start making some of our own."

After entering the lengthy address, Hicks hit the upload button, sending the hundreds of encrypted ZIP files Jabbar had given him to the secure Langley server. Bank records, surveillance footage, technical information on the contagion Bajjah had paid to have engineered, and the like. All of it proving Bajjah had been financed by members of the Vanguard to carry out biological attacks against the United States.

Once OMNI confirmed the files had been uploaded, Hicks ordered OMNI to erase the hard drive of the server and deactivate it. The Langley systems were probably already running an automatic trace, but all they'd find was a dead spot somewhere in cyberspace.

Hicks looked up and saw Sarah was still looking in the direction where Demerest had headed.

Hicks normally didn't give in to sentiment, but he did now. "We just handed him the case of his career. Look on the bright side…at least now I know your first name."

If Sarah heard him, she didn't show it. "I hope he doesn't allow his pride to foul this up. For his sake, as much as our own. He's a very dangerous man, James, and doesn't make idle threats."

Hicks put his handheld back into his sweatshirt pouch as he stood to leave. He readjusted the Ruger so it didn't bulge in his pocket. "Neither do I."

"I know," she said. "That's what worries me."

Hicks quickly walked eastward, out of the park. Too many

people could have noticed them talking, especially after one of Demerest's outbursts. No sense in making more of a spectacle by saying goodbye. Besides, Sarah looked too lost in her concern for her old friend to notice.

He took out his handheld as he walked and tapped the same icon as before, opening a line to Stephens. "Have everyone stand down, Cosmo. Field trip is over. Get everyone back to New York and get plenty of rest tonight. We've got a lot of work to do."

CHAPTER
3

A S PER HIS agreement with Sarah, Charles Demerest exited the park the same way he had entered. He reached the corner of Sixteenth Street and Florida Avenue NW, where a black Ford Expedition was waiting for him, engine running. The windows of the SUV were tinted darker than the legal limit, but the official federal plates kept curious police at bay.

After climbing into the backseat and pulling the door closed, Demerest yanked the windbreaker over his head. "Goddamned thing made me sweat like a pig, Williamson. Remind me to fire the idiot who told me to wear it."

"It was your idea, sir," Williamson said from behind the wheel. "You didn't want to wear a vest, so the windbreaker was as bulletproof as we could make you. The Kevlar lining made it warmer than it should've been."

"Never let the facts get in the way of a good complaint." Demerest threw the sopping windbreaker aside and took the thumb drive out of the pocket. "I left my phone on the entire time. Tell me you were able to record everything."

"Unfortunately not, sir." Williamson pulled the Expedition out into southbound traffic. "The snipers had a visual on you on the whole time, but no audio. I think Hicks was blocking the signal somehow, though we don't know that for sure. I'm sorry, sir."

"Don't apologize for something that's not your fault. Did our people find out if Hicks had anyone else in the park?"

"We pegged twelve possible targets, but none confirmed. If they were working with Hicks, they were both subtle and good. Facial recognition scans on each of them came up blank, leading us to suspect they were working for Hicks. The Go Team leader wanted to grab them when your audio went dead. I kept them at bay because you didn't give us the signal to move in."

"You made the right call," Demerest said. "I got more out of the son of a bitch on a park bench than I would have in a cell at Fort Meade, anyway."

When they stopped at a red light, Demerest handed the thumb drive to his aide. "I want this analyzed on a secure machine in case he put a virus or a tracker on it. No internet or network connections, understand?"

"Consider it done, sir." Williamson slipped the thumb drive into his jacket pocket, flush against the nine millimeter holstered on his left shoulder. He glanced at his boss in the rearview mirror. "May I ask what's on it?"

"An executive summary of a much bigger package. I gave Hicks an old server where he could upload additional information. I want every byte of every file scanned and rescanned before anyone clicks on anything. I wouldn't put it past the son of a bitch to hide a Trojan horse to try to access our systems. He told me he'd kill the server after he sent it, but have our people run a trace on it anyway."

"I'll make sure your orders are followed to the letter, sir." Williams hesitated a moment before asking, "May I ask your impression of the man, sir? Hicks, I mean. I know you had reservations about meeting him in a public place."

Demerest considered his answer as he watched people flow past on the crosswalk. Williamson was a good aide, capable with a quick mind, but he was still only an aide. He was neither a confidant nor a peer. Shutting him out too much might crush his spirit and render him useless. But too much familiarity often bred contempt. In their business, contempt often led to disaster.

"He's smart," Demerest allowed. "A lot smarter than Sarah led me to believe. Cocky, too. Normally I'd see that as a flaw we could exploit, but I get the feeling that son of a bitch is every bit as good as he thinks he is."

"He looked like a bum to me, sir." The light changed and Williamson let the Expedition move with traffic. "If he was that good, he'd be working for us, or would have at one point."

Demerest looked out the window. "If there's one thing I learned a long time ago, Williamson, it's that appearances don't mean much. That's certainly the case with James Hicks."

If it was a lesson he had forgotten, Sarah had reminded him of it during their phone call the night before. He knew she had worked for the University in the past, but had no idea the organization was anything more than a think tank. He certainly never knew she had once been its Dean. That revelation alone had caused him a sleepless night, wondering what else he may have missed over the years. *I was married to the woman for three years*, he thought, *and I had no idea. Was that why the marriage failed? Were we both too good at keeping secrets?*

He had also had no idea about the extent of the University's activities. That troubled him even more, especially with his appointment as Director of National Intelligence about to be announced within the next few days. He had heard whispers about the University over the years, rumors and stories of assets around the world claiming to be part of the CIA or NSA or an independent contractor, only to find out later that they didn't exist.

But now that he knew about the University, he would have his people start connecting some dots. James Hicks was the first dot on the sheet.

Until his conversation with Sarah, all Demerest had on Hicks was a screen shot from the security camera in Philly and a few ATM photos snapped in Manhattan before someone spiked their surveillance.

Once she'd given him Hicks's name, Demerest ran it through every system at his disposal, including military personnel records of all NATO countries. The search hadn't yielded much more than photos. A few references in dozens of debriefings from overseas case officers and agents offered a general description of a man who could have been Hicks. Blurred images taken by field operatives working in Egypt, Iran, Turkey, and half a dozen African countries had tagged a man fitting Hicks's description as James Hilts, John Hicks, John Hilts, Jeff Hayes, and other derivations of his name.

Demerest was sure James Hicks was an alias, too, but a good

one. Facial recognition comparisons of every picture from the motel security camera and the ATM shots from the DIA fiasco came up as possible matches at best. He was confident Hicks had received some level of military training at some point, but had covered his tracks well. That meant he was careful and technologically proficient.

Tracking down two of the most wanted terrorists in the world and leaking information that led to a congressional hearing of the Agency also made him very dangerous.

But if the Jabbar information Hicks was providing him turned out to be solid, Hicks might prove useful in the near future.

But that was a huge if. *The Vanguard?* He absently rubbed his finger along his chin as he stared out the window. *Gunrunners going political? It was certainly possible. But was it probable?*

Demerest decided all he could do was speculate until his people had a chance to review the information. He chose to give his busy mind a rest and look out the window at the passing city. Washington, D.C. His city. The capital of the greatest nation the world had ever known. Unlike most people who worked in Washington, he was a true native in every sense of the word. He had been born there, raised there, and had even gone to school there.

Yet, even after a life spent there, the beauty of the place still never failed to reach him. He often wondered how a city so beautiful, built on the promise of the best of human endeavors, could be so comfortable with its own darkness. Dichotomy had always intrigued Charles Demerest. Dichotomy was what troubled him now.

James Hicks and the University could either be the greatest

weapon in his arsenal or the greatest danger to his career. And only time would tell him which it would be.

Williamson brought him out of his thoughts by clearing his throat before asking, "What are the next steps concerning this Hicks and Mrs. Demerest, sir?"

"That depends on the validity of the information he sent us." There was no reason to tell Williamson more than that. He'd know about it soon enough.

"And if the information proves to be correct?"

"Then James Hicks just got a whole lot of new friends."

"And if it proves to be a ruse?"

He caught a glimpse of the National Mall in the near distance. The cherry blossoms were about to bloom. *Beautiful.* "Then we take Hicks down."

CHAPTER
4

BEFORE DRIVING BACK to Manhattan, Hicks had OMNI's scanning parameters broadened to include anything that might be a government signal. Demerest hadn't risen to consideration for Director of National Intelligence by being careless, so he expected some surveillance. Even though he'd just been handed a treasure trove of information, people like Demerest always wanted to know more.

But OMNI hadn't detected any significant anomalies during the entire drive home. Nothing from a federal agency. Nothing from anyone tailing him, either. Hicks was relieved to make it back to his 23rd Street facility without incident.

He had never thought of the facility as home, but it was the closest thing to a home he had.

Just after becoming head of the University's New York office several years before, Hicks had blackmailed a young real estate developer into allowing him to build a large concrete bunker beneath the foundation of three townhouses he was rehabilitating on West 23rd Street.

The University had arranged for secure contractors to work quietly and quickly. Some creative manipulation of the city's building department's records had allowed the extra construction to occur without government interference or knowledge.

The garden apartment on street level looked convincingly cozy to any of the thousands of people who walked or drove past the townhouses each day. There were curtains on the windows, furniture in the living room, and a bookcase crammed with books. Renters on the upper floors paid market rates for rent, which brought in a nice sum each month to fund the University's Bursar's Office.

Once inside the garden apartment, Hicks took the stairs down to the basement, where a working boiler served the two apartments above. But the basement's real function was to serve as a stopgap space for Hicks's sub-basement facility.

The facility was secured by a plain wooden door with an ordinary-looking doorknob and lock. But there was no key to the lock and the knob didn't turn. The door could only be opened when a scanner in the knob read the biometrics of his left hand while a hidden camera scanned his facial features. When the two results matched, a section of the wall hissed and the steel-reinforced hatch opened inward like an airplane hatch.

The sub-basement facility was a large, steel-reinforced concrete vault that slowly bled power off the city's grid, storing it in its three massive batteries. An independent HVAC unit had filters and radiation sensors to detect any poisonous emissions

47

from the outside world. Three gas-fueled generators could be used in an emergency if the power grid went down for good.

The facility had been designed to withstand a nuclear blast. Even if the three buildings above him were obliterated, Hicks would still be able to operate for weeks on generator and auxiliary power before he would need to venture outside. He made sure the facility was always stocked with enough food, gas, weapons, and equipment for that eventuality.

The previous Dean had originally called the facility overkill. But in a post-9/11 world, Hicks saw it as a wise investment. *Semper Paratus* had been his motto earlier in life. It still was. Always Prepared.

Hicks knew a fixed location could never be fully secure, but the 23rd Street facility was as close to secure as anyone could hope to get.

When he reached his desktop computer, Hicks checked OMNI to see what he had missed during his journey to Washington.

As Dean of the University, Hicks was now responsible for reviewing and approving all activities of dozens of University offices throughout the world every day. The University had Department Heads in every major city in the world where Professors engaged in Field Work and ran Assets who fed them information. Every day, his inbox was full of reports from various operations looking for his review and approval. That afternoon was no different.

A Faculty Member in France wanted to blackmail a trade minister looking to cut a deal with Somali insurgents looking to purchase weapons. A Faculty Member in Manila was tracking a non-government organization in the Philippines attempting to import guns for Muslim rebels rather than food for the needy. A Faculty Member in London had discovered a financier who was hiding cash for the Taliban. Another Faculty Member in Ankara believed an opium dealer was trying to influence a member of the Turkish parliament.

All of it was too much information for one individual to track on his own, which was why Jason served as his Dutchman. In addition to handling all of the dozens of minor details that sprang up in the course of a day, he also compressed all of it into a single report twice a day for Hicks's review and comment.

Most of the information they tracked and logged into OMNI might be trivial at first, but it often led to something more important further down the road. Every detail of every case had become important now that the Vanguard was on their radar screen.

And if the men he had killed on the highway were working for the Vanguard, then Hicks was on the Vanguard's radar screen, too.

Before he could find out how they had found him, he had to figure out who they were. Since the initial searches on the dead men had come up empty, he'd need a lot of help fighting the Vanguard. Help that Demerest could provide.

Jabbar's evidence showed that the Vanguard mirrored the University in many ways. The group didn't have a central location, preferring to operate out of various scattered mobile areas throughout Russia and Asia. The Vanguard also used laptop computers and burner phones and carefully encrypted messages back and forth between their operatives and "straw men" tied indirectly to their organization. Most of their business was done through third-party personnel, many of whom didn't seem to know who they were really working for.

OMNI hadn't been able to detect any active devices on any networks, but communications systems grew more difficult to crack the further east they extended.

Jabbar's evidence showed Bajjah's plot had been financed by several withdrawals and deposits made in a small bank in central Berlin. Bank records and security cameras could only tell so much of the story.

That was why Hicks had sent a Faculty Member to the city; the one man he knew who could prowl the shadows of Berlin, digging up information through rumor, innuendo, and vice. Someone who could mine the underground of Europe for more information than even OMNI could.

An alert window popped up on his screen, reminding him of his scheduled video conference call with his man in Berlin. He clicked on OMNI's secure videoconference application and opened the connection. A new window opened, showing a disheveled Roger Cobb coming into frame.

The University's chief interrogator was wearing a spiked orange wig and a matching lightning-bolt stripe painted over the right side of his face. Muted techno music thudded in the background.

"Sorry, boss," Roger said as he struggled to pull the headphones and mouthpiece over his wig. "The club is doing a Bowie tribute tonight and I opted for the Ziggy phase. I should've gone for a more muted look because everyone in the place showed up in an orange wig and face paint. You know how much I hate to blend in. Unimaginative krauts. No wonder they lost the fucking war."

There were about a dozen or so Faculty Members who Hicks

could have sent to Berlin, but Roger was the perfect choice to establish an intelligence beachhead in the city. His Jolly Roger Club on the west side of Manhattan was one of the best-known vice dens in the world, catering to the carnal, forbidden vices of wealthy clients from all over the world. They paid a high price to satisfy their dark desires with complete discretion day or night, twenty-four hours a day, seven days a week.

Roger drew the line at pedophilia and bestiality, but as he liked to say, "Everything from cocaine and the profane are my métier."

His clients' indulgences at The Jolly Roger Club came at a higher cost than the price of admission. Every sex act committed and every drug used was done under the watchful eye of dozens of OMNI cameras strategically placed throughout the building. The resulting extortion, when necessary, was often the most effective way to persuade some of Roger's influential patrons to act on behalf of the University without knowing the institution existed. After all, sharing secrets on a business deal or a murder plot or allowing a friend of Roger's to use your house on Lake Como for a month seemed a small price to pay to avoid your wife or investors seeing footage of you getting spanked by a sex worker.

Hicks had sent Roger to Berlin under the guise of possibly opening a branch of The Jolly Roger Club. As Roger was often fond of saying, "Vice is the true international language; the common bond that unites us all." A nightclub in Berlin allowed him to be in residence as he got the feel for the German nightclub scene. It was perfect cover for his investigative work.

It wasn't the most orthodox way of gathering information, but it was as good as anything Hicks could come up with to crack the enigma of the Vanguard.

"Looks like your cover is holding up," Hicks said, "even if your makeup isn't."

Roger straightened his wig. "Don't let this get-up fool you, honey. Partying with Euro-trash every night isn't as much fun as it sounds. They all drink like fish and get nasty when they do. But the dirt I'm digging up on some people could prove very profitable later on. These boys love their parties, and—"

"Skip it." Hicks knew Roger would dish dirt for hours if he let him. He had more pressing business. "Did you get my message about what happened to me last night?"

"That highway thing? Yes, I saw it. That's part of the reason I scheduled this call. I've run into a lot of people here who I thought might be linked to the Vanguard, but your incident made me cull the list down quite a bit. There's one gentleman in particular I think we should focus on."

For all his eccentricities and oddities, Roger Cobb was still one of the best operatives Hicks had ever worked with. If he said he had something, it was solid. "Tell me."

"Quite a few people are excited about the possibility of a Jolly Roger Club opening here in Berlin. I've been approached by several unsavory characters about investing in the enterprise. I'll sift through OMNI's override of the club's security cameras and send you some images to go along with the names in my report. But, in light of your run-in on the highway last night, I think we should focus on one character in particular. Calls himself Boris, but I'm almost sure that's a lie."

A Russian named Boris. "Go on."

"He's like a lot of the other goons who come in here. A big Cro-Magnon Russian bastard with a penchant for expensive leather jackets and bathes himself in obnoxious cologne. He makes a point of wearing a different Rolex every night and wears more jewelry than an Arab whore. Drives a white BMW with all the bells and whistles, too. Loves Asian women, which makes him unique. His type usually goes for the blondes."

"Wow," Hicks said. "You've found a gaudy Russian hood named Boris. Hope you got pictures. No one will ever believe it. Biggest thing since Bigfoot."

Roger didn't laugh. "Well, this particular gaudy Russian hood, you sarcastic bastard, happens to be sporting a *Spetsnaz* tattoo. And not just any *Spetsnaz* tattoo, either. His is from the Forty-Fifth Guards."

Hicks's interest ticked up a notch. The *Spetsnaz* were Russia's Special Forces, and the Forty-Fifth Guards were their airborne unit. Men with that level of skill usually made better money as mercenaries, not common street thugs.

"What makes him interesting besides the ink?"

"He's taken something of an interest in me," Roger said. "Not sexually, unfortunately, but a business interest. He says he wants to be a silent partner in opening a Jolly Roger Club here in Berlin and maybe Moscow. I didn't pay him much attention until I got your email."

Hicks's interest ticked up another notch. "Who does he work for?"

"That's what makes him so interesting," Roger explained. "He said he wants to be my exclusive partner in the club. He's adamant that no one else can be involved or know he's my silent partner. He said he'll give me complete control over the operation and he's willing to pay all in cash up front. All he wants is to profit from the deal. And he wants to get started as soon as possible. The sooner the better."

That was odd. Many people had approached Roger about being partners in his club over the years. Most of them had been serving as a front man for someone else, claiming they represented important clients. Boris wasn't claiming access to capital. He *had* the capital. "Why is he so concerned about secrecy? And why the hurry?"

"I decided to prod him a little when he showed up at the club tonight. He said he's been saving his money for years and wants to get in on the ground floor of something profitable, fast. He said his boss disapproves of his lifestyle and has ordered him to cut back. He also said his boss is beginning to branch out into some operations our friend doesn't like."

"What kind of operations?"

"The kind that made him get out of the army in the first place," Roger said. "He looked scared when he told me this, James, and when you see what Boris looks like, you'll see he's not the type who scares easily. Look."

The screen changed to a shot from one of the Berlin club's security cameras showing a man well over six feet tall, broad-shouldered, with only a hint of belly flab beneath his leather coat. He had a diamond earring in his left ear and a large Byzantine cross on a thick gold chain around his neck. He had a buzzed haircut and a broad, sloping forehead above deep-set eyes.

He looked like a Russian mafia hood straight out of central casting, but if Roger said there was more to him than that, Hicks had no choice but to believe him. "If this clown has enough money to blow on BMWs and Rolexes, he can buy a plane ticket to Costa Rica and disappear."

"That's exactly what I told him," Roger said. "But he's convinced there's no place on earth he could go where his boss couldn't find him. And when he did find him, he'd make an example of him. That's why he wants to get something started now. He wants to disappear. Fast."

Hicks's interest in Boris was growing by the minute. If Boris's employer was getting involved in something that made a *Spetsnaz* veteran anxious, there might be a connection with the Vanguard. Maybe. Or maybe his employer's activities might lead to the Vanguard somehow. The long and winding road of intelligence work was rarely quick and never a straight line. "Have you tried to ID this guy through OMNI yet?"

"No," Roger admitted. "I'd written him off as another one of the desperate hoods who've rolled up on me since I got here. But your email made him stand out. I think we need to dig into him further, James. If he turns out to be a dead end, I'll keep looking."

Hicks wasn't ready to do any cartwheels yet, but it was the first promising lead Roger had gotten on the Vanguard since he'd been in Berlin. "I'll run him through OMNI and let you know what I find. In the meantime, I want you to go old school on Boris. Get him drunk and get him talking. Have someone get his license plate number and see if you can't get someone to follow him when he leaves the club tonight. Let's find out where he goes and who he knows, and maybe we can see if he's worth our time."

The screen switched back to Roger's crooked wig and ruined makeup. "I'm way ahead of you. I've already hired an ex-cop from Bonn to babysit Boris when he leaves the club tonight. He's working for next to nothing, so don't worry about him asking any awkward questions."

Hicks didn't like the idea of using non-University personnel on something like this, but he didn't have much of a choice. If Boris turned out to be tied to a key player, he could always send Stephens or someone else to do the heavier work. "Keep me posted on what you turn up." He decided he couldn't end the call without at least one dig at Roger Cobb's vanity. "And you really do look beautiful tonight, Roger."

His friend gave him the middle finger from over four thousand miles away. "Fuck you, darling. Talk to you tomorrow." Roger killed the connection from his end.

Hicks smiled at the blank screen. *Fucking Roger.*

CHAPTER
5

HICKS CLOSED HIS eyes and dropped his head in his hands. The events of the past several hours finally settled on him. The Carousel of Concern was spinning full tilt in his mind.

Demerest. The Vanguard. Roger's lead: Boris. The dead men on the highway. Tali in Berlin. The baby she may be carrying.

Not to mention all the dozens of other concerns he had as Dean of the University.

He hadn't taken a break in over twelve hours, and decided to take one now. It would be easy to allow everything to blend into a single overwhelming wave, but he couldn't let that happen. So, he removed the Ruger from his holster, took his cleaning kit from the armory, and began cleaning the weapon. It was the most mindless activity he could do while actually getting something done. His daily yoga routine would have to wait.

He hoped Jabbar's evidence would be enough to convince

Demerest to work with the University. He could use their resources now more than ever to help fight the Vanguard. The University's limited resources could only do so much. The more eyes and ears looking out for the Vanguard, the better.

The Carousel in his mind began to slow as he cleaned the barrel, stopping on Boris. It was a slim lead, one more likely to lead to a brick wall than to the Vanguard, but it was a starting point. He wished he'd had the time to check the dead men on the highway for tattoos or other markings, but the sirens had been too close. Did they have *Spetsnaz* tattoos like Boris?

He'd have to wait until OMNI was able to access the coroner's reports to see if they had any distinguishing marks. But the report probably wouldn't be available until the following morning at the earliest. Hicks didn't want to wait that long. The dead men hadn't decided to follow him on a whim. They'd shot at the cop because they had wanted to get away. Someone had ordered them to follow him. That someone undoubtedly knew their people were dead and were covering their tracks accordingly.

Time, as always, was his enemy.

But Roger had given him Boris, so Boris was where he would start.

He finished cleaning the Ruger, reloaded it, and put the cleaning kit back in the armory. He went back to his computer and directed OMNI to run the image of Boris through databases all over the world. Since Roger thought he was Russian, Hicks knew getting a positive identification of facial recognition scans would be a long shot.

A search that might take OMNI a few minutes to scan government systems in the West could take over an hour or more in the eastern part of the world.

Hicks refused to sit in front of the computer like a teenager waiting for his girlfriend to text him back. OMNI would hack databases whether he was at the desk or not. He decided to do something useful instead, like make a fresh pot of coffee.

He had just pushed himself away from his desk when he heard a familiar tone through his computer's speakers. He was surprised to see that OMNI had already found one record that matched the Boris image.

It was a mug shot from an arrest record from the previous decade on a police database in Bonn, Germany. Boris had been born Yulian Vasiliev in Moscow forty-three years before the date of his arrest, which put him at fifty-three now. Some mental math conversion from the metric system helped Hicks place Yulian at six feet four inches tall and two hundred and ten pounds. Judging by what he had seen of him in Roger's footage, Yulian weighed closer to two fifty now.

The arrest record showed a picture of the military tattoo on his left arm, which matched the *Spetsnaz* insignia Roger had described. The report also noted evidence of massive scarring on his body. That fit the profile of a *Spetsnaz* veteran. The Russians didn't use those boys for parades or light gardening around the grounds of the Kremlin.

Hicks's German was good enough to translate Yulian's arrest record. He had been arrested multiple times during his time in Bonn for assault, grand larceny, menacing, promotion of prostitution, armed robbery, attempted murder, and a variety of drug charges. German courts weren't known for their leniency, so Hicks didn't understand why Yulian wasn't serving hard time in Stadelheim Prison.

A few more clicks into Yulian's record told Hicks part of the story. Each case brought against him had been ultimately dropped before trial, due to insufficient evidence.

Yulian had friends in high places.

Maybe friends like the boss he had told Roger he feared.

A search of Yulian's known associates turned up several felons with longer records than Yulian. None of the names or faces meant anything to Hicks, so he began clicking on the various names to get a sense of the kind of people Yulian knew. They were all either Russian or East German thugs who had been arrested for the same kinds of offenses as Yulian.

The last name on the list turned out to be the most interesting. It was the only name linked to every one of the other known associates in Yulian's file: Willus Tessmer, also known as Wilhelm Tessmer. Given his connection to the other hoods on the record, Hicks pegged him as the ringleader. But was he *still* Yulian's boss?

Tessmer's arrest record might have been worthy of a crime boss, but he certainly didn't look like one. He'd been arrested for the same variety of crimes as Yulian, with a few white-collar crimes thrown in. Money laundering, stock manipulation, drug trafficking, and the like.

Tessmer's mug shot showed a balding man with a crown of close-cropped dark hair. One set of pictures showed him with rounded spectacles while the other didn't. He had blue eyes and a narrow face more befitting a banker than a felon, though the line between the two blurred more each day.

His arrest record said he was five feet ten inches tall and one hundred and forty pounds. He had been born fifty-five years earlier in East Berlin under the old Soviet regime, putting him at around sixty-five now. Given Yulian's claims that his boss hated the excesses of capitalism, maybe some of the old Soviet philosophies had stuck with him even after the Berlin Wall fell.

Hicks clicked on Tessmer's record to find out more about him.

Nothing happened. Not even a 404-error message of a bad link. *Interesting.*

He clicked on other items on Tessmer's record. Biography, nature of his charges. None of the links worked.

One dead link might have been a technical glitch or a clerical error.

But a page full of dead links meant someone had gone to great lengths to hide something.

Mr. Tessmer was becoming more interesting by the minute.

Hicks backed out of the Bonn police database and had OMNI do a broader search on Willus Tessmer and Wilhelm Tessmer, complete with a facial recognition scan of his mug shot. The search took several minutes. Of all the databases and resources OMNI could access all over the world, the only file OMNI could find was the police record from the Bonn database.

No aliases. No bank records. No news articles. No records in the German court system on any of the dozens of charges leveled against him. Not even a social media account. Even the facial recognition scan of Tessmer's mug shot came up blank. None of the law enforcement or intelligence agencies in the world had an image of the man, save for the single forgotten file on the police servers in Bonn.

Hicks slowly sat back in his chair. Mr. Tessmer had secrets, and he had a lot of help to keep them that way.

The kind of help a group like the Vanguard might be able

to provide.

He looked at the dead-eyed man on the screen. He didn't know anything about him yet, but he was going to find out.

HICKS PICKED UP the phone and called Ronen Tayeb's encrypted cell phone. He knew the Mossad's new section chief in Moscow was probably sleeping, but the Tessmer anomaly was worth the call.

Tayeb sounded appropriately groggy when he answered the phone on the fourth ring. "I'm glad to see you haven't lost your knack for calling at the worst possible times, my old friend."

The two men were, indeed, old friends. Tayeb had been a fine field agent in his day, but found himself out of favor when a bureaucrat named Emanuel Schneider rose to power within the Mossad. Since Schneider saw field personnel as tools to be used to further his own career, it wasn't long before Tayeb found himself behind a desk in an obscure office in Tel Aviv.

But with Schneider out of the way, thanks to Hicks, Tayeb was back in the field where he belonged. The Mossad had been understandably angry with Hicks's involvement in Schneider's plane exploding over the Atlantic, but their anger quickly subsided when he explained Schneider's role in assassinating Jabbar on foreign soil without clearance from his supervisors in Tel Aviv. Killing the most wanted person in the country was bad enough, but to do so without permission could prove to be an embarrassment if word got out.

So Hicks did what he had been trained to do. He brokered a deal. He agreed to share the Jabbar evidence with the Israelis on two conditions. The first was that they were not to share the information with any other intelligence agency. The second was that they send Tayeb to Moscow to help hunt for the Vanguard. It was an arrangement he had neglected to mention to Demerest. If he agreed to work together, Hicks would tell him eventually, but for the moment, what the CIA didn't know couldn't hurt him.

"Sorry about the hour," Hicks told Tayeb, "but I've found something that might be important."

"Sleep is important, too," the Israeli said, "especially if I'm going to continue doing your job for you."

"Easy, Ronen. The University is footing the bill for all your extra work. I take it the equipment I sent to your safe house is working?"

"It works perfectly and its reach is impressive, though the security measures are a bit ridiculous."

"But necessary," Hicks said. To help with their hunt for the Vanguard, he had sent Tayeb's team a pair of University laptops with very restricted access to the OMNI network. He could always widen their access if they found a lead on the Vanguard, but for now they needed thumbprints and face scans each time they logged on to the OMNI features on the equipment. Any attempt to hack the equipment or broaden their authorization would lock up the system and fry the hard drives.

The measures were necessary. Part of the reason Hicks had ordered Emmanuel Schneider's plane destroyed was because he had taken Tali Saddon's handheld OMNI device. He had no intention of allowing the Israelis to have an open door to the OMNI network then. He trusted Tayeb, but only to a point. "I took a big risk sending you those laptops in the first place, so for now the security measures stay in place."

"You may be risking technology, but my men are risking their lives."

"They're only your men because I talked your bosses into giving you a field command again. And I've told you my people will be on the ground right beside yours as soon as we get actionable intelligence on the Vanguard."

"I was behind a desk too long," Tayeb yawned. "I have forgotten that it's almost impossible to win an argument with you. I will save time by admitting defeat and ask again why you are calling at this unholy hour."

"I have a lead on someone who may be part of the Vanguard."

"It is too early in the morning for maybes, James."

"Maybe is the best I've got," Hicks said, "and the best either of us have had since we began searching for these bastards."

"Who is it and how did you come by this information?"

"The lead reached out to Roger about being an investor in his club in Berlin." Hicks began typing on his keyboard. "I'm sending you the information via OMNI as we speak. Yulian Vasiliev, ex-*Spetsnaz*. When I began digging into his background, I found police records indicating he worked for Willus or Wilhelm Tessmer in Berlin."

Tayeb was quiet for a moment. "Never heard of either man. What makes the *Spetsnaz* man so interesting to Roger? And please don't tell me it's because he has a crush on him."

Hicks ignored the jab about Roger's proclivities. "It's Yulian's boss, Tessmer, who interests me. I can't find anything on him anywhere in any database we can reach."

Hicks could hear Tayeb get out of bed and maybe turn on a light. "Nothing on any of the networks?"

"Other than an old arrest file on an ancient police

department database in Bonn, nothing. No arrest records or newspaper accounts or court papers about his arrests. Not even dismissals. Even raw facial recognition searches of his mug shot came up empty."

"Sounds like someone worked really hard to turn this Tessmer into a ghost," Tayeb said. "Send me whatever information you have on both men. I'll have my people begin digging into them as soon as possible. Perhaps we have something on him in our files back in Tel Aviv. We may have to go back to paper on this one." The Mossad agent laughed. "There's a novel concept. I'll also do some digging here in Moscow. There's bound to be someone who knows something of them here."

"Take a light approach first," Hicks said. "This Vasiliev could be another aging gangster looking to get out of The Life while he's still got a few good years left. And for all we know, Tessmer could be a skeleton by now."

"Or they could be the lead we've been looking for," Tayeb added. "I'll give you daily reports on our progress and let you know if we find something solid."

"My Adjuncts can be in Moscow within twelve hours if you need them."

Tayeb laughed once more. "The Deans of the University may change but the efficiency remains the same, eh, James? You will hear from me in a few hours."

Hicks couldn't explain why, but felt the need to add, "Just be careful, Ronen. There's something about this that doesn't feel right."

"We are always careful, my friend. Now, at least one of us should get some sleep. It won't be me. It might as well be you."

CHAPTER
6

CHARLES DEMEREST HAD lost complete sense of time. He didn't know if it was the middle of the night or early in the morning. He didn't care. The only thing that mattered to him was the document he was reading on his desktop computer.

He used his mouse to slowly scroll through the Agency's preliminary analysis report of the Jabbar information Hicks had given him. The analysis was in: the Jabbar evidence was pure gold.

It was perfect in that it wasn't too perfect. His analysts would have been suspicious if the information had been a neat narrative, leading them down a clear path to where the terrorist had wanted the reader to go.

But it wasn't a narrative. Billing records. Travel records. Financial transactions. Meetings recorded on a cell phone camera. Only perspective could allow the viewer to see it in whole. Even then, only a practiced eye could appreciate the importance of what they were seeing.

Demerest had one of the most practiced eyes in the community. And what he was reading now filled in a lot of blanks in what, up until that exact moment, had been the Agency's passive understanding of what the Vanguard truly was. The information Hicks had given them would start a full-blown investigation into the Vanguard, into what it had been up to all these years, and what it was planning for the future.

He eased back in his chair and looked up at the ceiling. *The goddamned Vanguard.* The Agency had been studying them for years, but they'd been elusive as hell. They would hear them, the way one hears millions of crickets in a forest without ever seeing a single one.

Thanks to Hicks, they not only knew they were there, but what they looked like.

With all the scrutiny the Agency was facing on Capitol Hill, this windfall of information was exactly what it needed to turn down some of the heat.

It was also what Demerest needed to seal the deal on his appointment as Director of National Intelligence. There had been some in Congress and in the administration and even in the community who said Demerest might not be ready for the post. They wondered if he had been tainted by the black site scandal and other intelligence failures over recent years. Snowden and Assange, those little shits.

The Jabbar information would give even his harshest critics no choice but to support his elevation.

The only problem was the timing. People would question where this windfall of information came from. Demerest could dodge publicly, but the same question would haunt him privately. James Hicks and the University were still an enigma to him. The man and the organization had been operating outside the intelligence community for so long, he had no idea if they could really be trusted. Hell, they'd never really been *in* the community, not since the early days of the Iron Curtain.

If Hicks could be trusted, the man and his University could be an invaluable tool to him as DNI.

But Hicks had proven to be a dangerous man in a short time. He had beaten the DIA taskforce at their own game. He had caught two of the most wanted people in the world entirely on his own. He had turned the tables on the community and brought the wrath of the legislature down on their heads. Demerest remembered the Mossad had lost one of their spymasters, an insufferable prick named Schneider, in a plane crash over the Atlantic a few weeks ago. He re-read the clips. It was the same day Hicks said the Mossad killed Jabbar. It could be written off as a coincidence, but the community didn't believe in coincidences, and neither did Demerest.

He'd bet his pension Hicks had something to do with that crash. He had caused a lot of trouble for some of the most powerful people in Washington. He had pulled the community out of the shadows and into the light of public scrutiny. A lot of people who weren't used to being asked direct questions were being forced to answer such questions now. All because they had crossed James Hicks.

A man like that could either make or break Demerest's career. Could he afford to roll the dice on Hicks?

He picked up his phone and made one of the most important calls of his life.

CHAPTER
7

An unfamiliar chirping from his desktop computer and handheld device snapped Hicks awake from a half-forgotten dream. He knew it wasn't his regular alarm. He always woke well before it sounded. This was a sound he had never heard before.

He grabbed the handheld from the nightstand and looked at the screen. It was an automatic emergency message generated directly by the OMNI system.

MOSCOW: CROATOAN

He sat up in bed and rubbed the sleep from his eyes. He must have read the message wrong. It didn't make any sense.

He blinked his eyes clear and read the screen again. The message remained the same.

MOSCOW: CROATOAN.

He threw aside his blankets and got to his desktop.

CROATOAN was University code for a facility that had gone completely off-line, derived from the North Carolina settlement that had mysteriously vanished without a trace in 1590.

OMNI was programmed to automatically generate the message if all communication devices for a particular facility suddenly went off-line without warning. A preliminary alert would have sounded if there had been a blackout and all devices went to battery power. He searched the log for such a warning, but didn't find anything.

The message didn't make any sense. Ronen Tayeb had ten Mossad in the Moscow office. The CROATOAN warning meant the entire unit had gone completely dark without warning at the same time.

Something was wrong.

He called Tayeb's phone, but it went straight to voicemail. Tayeb's phone never went to voicemail.

Hicks had OMNI begin checking the international wires for reports of blackouts in the Moscow area. He ran a search for reports of disturbances in Moscow overnight, a reported terrorist attack or a massive power outage, anything that might explain why the entire Mossad facility had suddenly gone off-line.

But the city of Moscow had enjoyed a quiet evening. Nothing on any news sites or the municipal sites hinted there was any trouble, just the usual news about local developments, national politics, sports, and the weather.

He toggled over to the duty roster of the Mossad's Moscow office. Ronen Tayeb and the names of his nine support staff members were listed in alphabetical order. The word **INACTIVE** blinked in red next to each of their names.

All their University equipment was off-line. So was every cell phone Tayeb had reported using, including his own.

He wasn't surprised when his phone rang and it was Jason.

"I just got the CROATOAN message," Hicks told him. "Something definitely happened. I'm not finding—"

"Sir, you've got to get the hell out of there," Jason said. "Now."

Back when Jason had been his boss, he always made it a point to cut Hicks off, dismissing his reports and belittling his findings. But since Hicks had become the Dean, Jason had never cut him off. He had never been one to overreact, either.

If he was telling Hicks he had to move, it was for a damned good reason.

He put the call on speaker as he began to get dressed. "What's going on?"

"NORAD has just detected an unknown aircraft entering U.S. airspace over Long Island, heading straight for New York City. They're treating it as an armed incursion and are scrambling jets to intercept. Every air traffic controller on the East Coast is diverting flights away from the city airports. OMNI detects that it's making a beeline for your location."

Shit. Hicks pulled on his Kevlar tactical vest, then his sweatshirt, and shrugged into his holster with the Ruger. "Projected ETA?" He buttoned his jeans.

"OMNI predicts it's exactly four minutes out from your position, but closing fast."

He slipped into his boots and then pulled on a black Kevlar tactical jacket from the armory. "Any idea what it is?"

"NORAD and OMNI confirm the radar signature matches a Valkyrie-class drone," Jason reported. "They're assuming it's armed."

Hicks grabbed the black knapsack that served as his bug-out bag from the armory and threw it over his left shoulder. It contained an M4 with a collapsible stock, several dozen rounds of ammo for the rifle and the Ruger, a tactical knife, and a battlefield first aid kit complete with anti-coagulant, water, and protein bars. It wasn't enough to survive an apocalypse, but it would be enough to keep him alive for the next day or so. "*My position? How the hell does it know where…?*"

His handheld and desktop began blaring a proximity alert generated by OMNI, the same alert that had sounded in his car when the DIA had used a Valkyrie drone to try to kill him two months before. The drone's weapons system had just locked on to his location.

"Drone's weapons system just went hot," Jason reported. "Jets are still scrambling, but won't be there in time."

Hicks pocketed the handheld and slipped the tiny earpiece into his ear as he opened the hatch and moved up to the apartment. A Valkyrie-class drone could carry anything from a Hellfire missile to a biological weapon. The scrubbers on the bunker's ventilation could neutralize a bio-attack and the bunker had been designed to withstand a nuclear bomb detonating somewhere in Manhattan. But it wouldn't withstand a direct hit from a Hellfire missile.

And if whoever had sent the drone knew where he was, they would know enough to arm the drone with a bunker-busting payload.

He heard the hatch hiss shut behind him as he reached the apartment above. "Any idea if it's ours? Can you hack the drone's system? You've done it before."

"Not this time. This guidance system is something neither

OMNI nor NORAD has ever seen before. Even the weapons signature is reading odd, like it's a two-part system. NORAD didn't respond like this during the drone attack on you a couple of months ago, so this is definitely not an American operation. You've got less than three minutes now, sir."

Two-part weapons system? Why were they using a two-part weapons system? Was someone guiding the drone from the ground?

Hicks knew time was running out, but he stopped by the side door to the apartment. He pulled out his handheld and accessed the facility's external cameras. He wanted to make sure someone wasn't trying to flush him out of the bunker and into a trap.

All he saw was the endless flow of cars and people moving along 23rd Street. No one seemed to be watching the building or waiting for him outside. None of them seemed aware that a missile was about to ruin their day.

Jason said, "You have to get out of there, sir. I'm implementing the Scorched Earth Protocol now. All I need is your authorization code."

Hicks gave him the code that would fry the hard drive of every system in the bunker, just in case they survived the blast. Anyone sifting through the rubble would only find busted computer equipment.

He heard Jason's fingers on the keyboard. "Enacting protocol now. Keep moving, sir. OMNI's latest analysis of the radar signature gives a high probability that it's definitely carrying something heavy, probably a Hellfire. I'll track your movements from here, but you've got to move now."

Hicks reached for the doorknob, but stopped. "How long

before impact?"

"Seventy seconds and closing, sir. It looks like they're going to drop this thing right on top of you. You've got to move, sir!"

But Hicks didn't move.

The bits of information were coming together fast.

Of all the buildings in all of Manhattan, someone had targeted his precise location. He knew why.

But how? A Hellfire missile's targeting system could easily get confused in a densely-populated area like Manhattan. With so many targets, it might strike a similar building or land in the middle of the street. Someone was keeping it on course.

Jason had said it was a two-part weapons system. That meant someone *was* guiding it from the ground. And he had to find out who it was.

Hicks said, "Have the satellite zoom in on my location. Someone's guiding the missile, probably by lasing my building from someplace close. Check the rooftops. Someone will be manning the laser to keep it from getting knocked over or keep the light from being blocked by something."

He heard Jason's fingers work the keyboard again. "Sixty-five seconds, James. You need to go!"

Hicks gripped the door to the outside world tight. "Keep working."

Time was his enemy, but it was also his friend. The closer it got to impact, the more likely it was that the target team would start to move out. Even if it was only one man, the satellite would detect the movement. And Hicks would have a target of his own.

While Jason looked, Hicks scanned the streetscape from his window. It was another sunny morning in Manhattan, and the street was full of people walking back and forth in both directions, going to the store, jaywalking across 23rd Street. Kids going to school and people tapping away on their cell phones, not watching where they were going. None of them had any idea they were in the middle of a war-zone. Most of them would either die or be seriously injured from the blast radius of an incoming missile.

But there was nothing he could do to save them. He just hoped Jason could find the target within the next five seconds or...

"I have contact!" Jason yelled. "Three men on the roof of the building directly across from your position. A five-story walk-up..."

Jason kept telling him details, but Hicks was already out the door and running across the street.

CHAPTER 8

"**S**IXTY SECONDS, JAMES."

Hicks threaded his way through the taxis and buses and vans stuck at a standstill in the snarl of cross-town rush hour traffic.

He drew his Ruger as he burst through the outer door of the walk-up and shot the lock on the interior door. Hicks barreled into the building, taking the stairs two at a time as he raced up to the roof. He heard various parts of the information Jason fed him as the blood roared in his ears. "...three men...tripod setup...backing away from the laser...making their way to adjoining roof facing 22nd Street..."

Hicks didn't stop when he reached the door to the rooftop. The lock had already been broken, the door tapping lightly against the frame in the slight morning breeze.

The Ruger led the way as Hicks ran out onto the roof. The

ancient door hinges squealed.

Thirty seconds to impact.

Time slowed.

Hicks knew taking out the laser was pointless. It might send the missile into a more populated area of midtown, maybe an office building, where it would kill thousands instead of hundreds.

But he still had a play for the bastards who had guided it in.

The three men were on south side of the roof.

Target One was already over the low, crumbling brick wall that separated the two buildings.

Target Two was halfway over the wall.

Target Three turned when he heard the roof door hinges squeal.

Hicks shot him first. The round struck Target Three just below the throat, splattering his blood on Target Two. He fell back against the brick wall before collapsing to the roof.

Hicks aimed at Target Two and fired just as the man flopped over the edge onto the 22nd Street building. The .45 caliber slug kept going, striking Target One in the pelvis instead. The impact sent the man sprawling.

Target Two was still somewhere behind the short brick wall, but Hicks knew he wouldn't stay there for long, not with a Hellfire with enough ordinance to level a city block less than half a minute out. He would need to move and soon.

The weight of Hicks's bug-out bag on his back slowed him down as he ran at a crouch toward the brick wall, the Ruger still in front of him. He hit the deck when he saw a gun barrel pop up over the top of the wall. Automatic-rifle fire filled the air as Target Two fired blindly. All the rounds went high, sailing high over 23rd Street.

Flat on his stomach, Hicks aimed at brickwork and fired. The slug punched through two layers of the crumbling masonry and struck the man on the other side. The rifle disappeared.

His internal clock: *twenty seconds.*

Hicks scrambled to his feet and ran to the wall. Target Three was out of commission, gurgling blood as he clutched at his throat wound. He looked over the wall and saw Target Two clutching at the bleeding hole in the center of his chest. Hicks grabbed the man's rifle and threw it to the other side of the roof. Both men were dying. They were useless from an intelligence perspective.

Hicks hopped the wall and saw Target One lying spread-eagle on the rooftop, bleeding from the pelvic wound. His arms were flailing but his legs were useless. The bullet had probably severed the spinal cord at the base.

But he was still alive.

His internal clock: *fifteen seconds.*

Target One kept flailing his hands and yelled in Russian, "I don't have a gun. Don't shoot!"

Hicks grabbed the man by the collar and dragged him toward the roof door. The man was smart enough to stop flailing and hold his arms close to his chest, making it easier to drag him. This man had been in combat before.

Hicks pulled the door open and dragged Target One inside, pulling him down the stairs to the top floor of the building, his dead legs flopping against the treads.

His internal clock: *ten sec…*

A sickening crack filled the air, followed by a powerful explosion that seemed to rise from deep within the earth.

The Hellfire missile had hit its target.

The blast wave shook the entire building, making it feel as if it had bounced off its foundation. Hicks lost his footing and tumbled down the remaining stairs to the top landing, losing his grip on the wounded Russian as he fell.

The lights in the hallway blinked out as chunks of plaster fell from the ceiling and walls. The sound of shattering glass was everywhere.

Hicks landed hard on his stomach, knocking the wind out of him. It had happened to him more times than he could count, so he knew enough not to panic. It still took a moment for him to catch his breath. The cloud of thin plaster dust in the air didn't make breathing any easier and stung his eyes. His ears rang from the blast wave, but he could already hear the telltale sounds that always followed an explosion.

Panic.

People screaming, yelling, and cursing in the streets, in the building.

Car alarms blaring.

He finally caught his breath and did a mental check of his body. He moved his arms and legs. Nothing was broken. The Ruger was still in his hand. His chest hurt from the impact. He might have cracked a couple of ribs from the fall, but at least he could move.

And he had to move. Now.

He rolled over on his side and saw that the only light was coming from the entrance to the roof. The door was gone. Thick, darkening smoke began to waft inside.

He felt a fleeting sense of pride that he'd managed to hold on to the Ruger through it all.

A CONSPIRACY OF RAVENS

The ringing in his ears began to die away as he heard the Russian scream from somewhere behind him. He turned in time to see the wounded man stab at his leg with a tactical knife, narrowly missing Hicks's thigh.

Hicks rolled, planting a knee on the man's prone forearm. The resulting crunch of bone and cartilage made the Russian scream just before Hicks cracked him across the temple with the butt of the Ruger. The wounded man's body went slack. Hicks pulled the knife from his hand and stuck it in his belt. No sense in letting a good knife go to waste.

Even through the fine plaster cloud, Hicks saw the man was bleeding heavily from the pelvic wound. He shrugged out of his bug-out bag, opened it, and dug out the XStat. He plunged the syringe into the bullet hole and hit the plunger, injecting several anti-hemorrhagic sponges into the wound to slow down the bleeding. It was better than the bastard deserved, but he was no good to Hicks if he bled to death before Hicks could question him.

Hicks slung the bag back on his shoulders and got to his feet, shaking off the bits of plaster that had covered him. The ringing in his ears cleared enough for him to hear Jason calling to him via his earbud: "James. Are you okay?"

"No, but I'm alive. Two hostiles down and I kept the third one alive. Give me a status report. How bad was the blast?"

"Satellite feed shows a hell of a lot of smoke, but it looks like the missile was rigged for a deep impact. The bunker seems to have absorbed most of the blast. All three buildings above it have imploded, but the surrounding buildings are still standing. Vehicles on 23rd Street are covered in debris, but the street is filled with people. OMNI's initial estimates are that it was a

Hellfire II, a bunker-buster, but I can't confirm that. Emergency services are streaming into your area. Two F-16s are already in the air and emergency services are closing in on your position. NYPD has helicopters in the air. What do you want me to do?"

Hicks grabbed the unconscious Russian by the collar, pulled him onto his shoulder, and began to fireman-carry him down the stairs. "Get Stephens to bring a Varsity Squad with him to the site. Tell him to use his old DIA credentials to lock down the site if he has to. Get the Trustee to clear it with the local agencies. I want our people in command of the site before anyone else starts digging around."

"Consider it done. What else?"

"Contact Scott at the Annex." The Annex was the University's secondary facility, located in Alphabet City, that served as the University's detention and medical facility. "I want his people on full alert and to get the med unit ready. I'm coming in with a target with a gunshot wound to the pelvis and a possible fractured spinal column. We need to keep the son of a bitch alive long enough to question him about this."

"They'll be ready by the time you get there," Jason said. "Do you need Varsity transport to get you there?"

"Negative." Hicks had to shield his eyes as more plaster began to fall from the stairwell ceiling. The powder and the extra weight of the Russian made it difficult to keep his balance on the narrow stairs, but he kept moving. "Have Scott order a security sweep of the area around the Annex. If these bastards knew about 23rd Street, they might know about that one, too. If they find anyone, they are to detain if possible but kill if necessary."

"I'll let them know. Anything else?"

Hicks skirted around the dazed building residents who were beginning to fill the halls, asking each other what had happened and if it was another terrorist attack. They barely paid any attention to Hicks or the man he was carrying. They weren't panicking yet, but that was temporary. He had to get out of the building before they did. "Alert all Faculty Members everywhere to go dark until further notice and be on the lookout for any suspicious activity."

"I'll do that right after I have the Annex up and running," Jason said. "Anything else?"

Hicks paused at the top of the second landing, ignoring the shoves and curses of the people behind him who suddenly had to get around him.

Something Jason said struck him.

Transport.

"I know the smoke cover is thick, but have OMNI zoom in on 22nd Street in front of my location. Do a thermal reading for any parked vehicles that might have an engine running."

He heard Jason's fingers working the keyboard. "I just alerted Stephens and sent a message to the Trustee. I'm working on the thermal imaging now, but why?"

"Because these bastards brought a lot of equipment with them and they sure as hell didn't take the bus. I'll bet they had a driver and he's probably waiting for them right outside."

Hicks CONTINUED TO lug the wounded Russian out into the chaotic scene on 22nd Street. It was easy to blend in with the crowd of confused, frantic people darting in all directions. It was the same kind of scene Hicks had witnessed following every bomb attack he'd survived all over the world. No one knew what had just happened. No one knew what might happen next. And more than a few of them were anxious to see the carnage for themselves.

He spotted the black Chevy Tahoe exactly where Jason had told him it would be, parked half a block away on the north side of the street, facing east. Dark-tinted windows made it impossible to see inside, though OMNI's thermal scan registered only the driver inside. A smart move. The fake diplomatic plates made it less likely that a cop would bother them.

Knowing the driver was looking for the three Russians to come out of the building, Hicks put on a show, limping as he lugged the wounded man across his shoulder. The driver would be looking for three men in a hurry, not a wounded stranger carrying a friend to safety.

Hicks limped alongside the driver side door before pulling the Ruger from his jacket pocket and firing once into the window at near point-blank range. The glass wasn't bulletproof, and shattered on impact. The driver slumped over to his right.

Already frightened people screamed as they ran away from the sound of gunfire. Hicks reached through the shattered window, unlocked all the Tahoe's doors, opened the rear door, and dumped the unconscious Russian into the backseat.

He unbuckled the dead driver and dragged him onto the sidewalk. He slipped his bug-out bag from his shoulders and used it to sweep the broken glass off the seat. He tossed the bag onto the passenger seat and climbed up behind the wheel. He used the sleeve of his jacket to smear away some of the blood that had hit the windshield. It wasn't spotless, but enough to pass casual inspection.

With the motor already running, he put the SUV in drive and pulled away from the curb, heading east. The passenger window had caught most of the splatter and had been punctured by his shot. Hicks lowered it to avoid suspicion. Every cop in the city would be on edge. He didn't need one of them pulling him over to ask a lot of questions he didn't want to answer.

He heard Jason in his ear as he gunned the engine to beat a red light. "Did you kill the driver?"

"What do you think?" He hit the gas and made the SUV cut through a narrow gap that had opened in northbound traffic. Traffic was already beginning to thicken and he needed to get to Alphabet City as soon as possible. "Status report."

"Stephens said he's on his way to the blast site. The Trustee said she's already making the necessary phone calls to make sure all public statements are cleared by federal authorities first. I also alerted all Faculty Members to go dark until further notice. Scott is prepping the Annex as we speak. What else do you need me to do?"

Hicks saw the Tahoe had been outfitted with a police package: full lights and sirens. *Christ, these bastards thought of everything, didn't they?* He hit the cherry lights and siren to help clear the traffic that was beginning to slow in front of him. He'd have to get south before he got caught up in a traffic jam. It was only a matter of time before the NYPD started shutting down streets, if they hadn't already.

"Have a Varsity team pick up the two bodies I left back on the roof. I want their prints and pictures run through OMNI as soon as possible. Then contact the field team in Europe. Tell them to lock down but get ready to mobilize. We're activating Moscow Protocol."

Jason wasn't typing. "Jesus."

The sirens were working. Traffic was beginning to move out of his way.

Hicks floored it. "That's right, Ace. We're going to war."

CHAPTER
9

HICKS TOOK THE turn into the underground garage too hard, throwing sparks as the bottom of the SUV scraped over the speed bump on the ramp.

The garage door automatically closed behind him as he pulled the SUV to a screeching halt at the bottom of the ramp.

Scott and members of his Varsity Squad were already waiting. Hicks unlocked the doors and the Varsity members gently pulled the Russian onto the gurney and wheeled him inside. Far more gently than Hicks thought he deserved.

He called after them as they moved. "Tell the doc he's paralyzed from the waist down and is losing a lot of blood. Tell him I don't need him alive for long, just long enough to question him."

Scott fell in behind Hicks. "Jason called it in already. Doc Fischer is ready to work on him as soon as he gets him on the table."

"Good. Our perimeter secure?"

"I've got men stationed two blocks out in every direction," Scott said. "If something comes our way on ground or in the air, we'll know about it. Nothing out of the ordinary so far."

Hicks wasn't done. "I want your people to take apart that SUV for any signs of a tracking device. I didn't pick up any signals from my handheld, but we need to be sure."

Scott pointed at two of his men, who went back to the vehicle. "We're on it."

"You get the message that I activated Moscow Protocol?"

"I did. Oohrah."

"I guess that's Marine talk for approval."

"You didn't have a choice," Scott said. "I didn't think you had it in you."

"Today is full of surprises."

They walked down a short tunnel that led into the building that had come to be known as the Annex.

At some point in the 1970s—for reasons lost to history— the University had acquired a dilapidated three-story walk-up in the lower east side section of Manhattan known as Alphabet City. Hicks's predecessors had used it as a temporary hideout for Assets and Faculty Members who needed to lie low for a couple of days.

But when Hicks had become head of the University's New York office, he decided to put the building to use. The Dean of the University, who had always resisted having actual facilities or campuses of any kind, surprised him by agreeing to fund it. Over time, it had been nicknamed the Annex.

The building had long been deemed an eyesore in the

neighborhood, and for good reason. Layers of graffiti marred the building's masonry, while the doors and windows had been boarded up for years. It had served as a squatters' den for the homeless, a shooting gallery for junkies, a flop house for runaways, and a den where crack whores brought their johns.

Hicks had decided to put the building to good use the day he took over. Knowing any activity in front of the building would only bring unwanted attention, he purchased the old tenement building behind it and had University contractors enter through a common basement both buildings shared. This way, work could go on inside the original dilapidated building without drawing unwanted neighborhood attention. The University had always emphasized secrecy at all costs. The other building also had a garage, which made it easier for vehicles to come and go without being seen in front of the main building.

Contractors had worked around the clock to secretly reinforce the decrepit building's interior. Steel plating was installed behind the wooden boards. All other access points had been sealed, save for an old door at the back of the building that could only be accessed through a dim, grimy service entrance. Here, a state-of-the-art security portal was welded to the newly-reinforced infrastructure.

Security cameras and motion detectors were subtly installed at the perimeter to make sure no one tried to gain access. No one could get in or out of the building without biometric permission.

Except for extensive rewiring and a few improvements to transform part of the safe house into a holding area, the Dean's funding ended there. Few of the old apartments had been gutted, and much of the abandoned furniture had remained as the junkies and vagrants had left them.

Periodically, neighborhood activists still called for the building to be revitalized or turned into a homeless shelter or school. Hicks saw to it they were subtly—but effectively—convinced to turn their attention elsewhere. Over the years, several developers had tried to buy the property but were told the owner had no intention of selling. Few had taken no for an answer. Hicks hadn't been as gentle in changing their minds. Drug dealers still tried to gain entrance to the building. They were dealt with in a far more permanent manner.

Once they closed the armored door between the garage and the Annex, the Varsity men pushed the Russian into the elevator and took him up to the third floor. Since there wasn't enough room for Scott and Hicks, they stayed behind.

Scott handed two pills to Hicks as they waited for the elevator to come back down. "Doc Fischer wants you to take these. Says they'll dissolve in your mouth. Help with your nerves."

Hicks ignored them. "What nerves? Christ, Scott. I've been through worse."

Scott's hand didn't budge. He was ex-Marine Recon and looked the part. He wasn't much taller than Hicks, but broader and more muscular. He had short-cropped silver hair, a lopsided jaw that had been broken at least half a dozen times, and a nose to match. He would have made a lousy clandestine operative, but he excelled as the leader of the University Varsity Squad.

"Take the pills, boss."

"I don't need them."

"You just had a missile dropped on your head, shot four men, drove cross-town at high speeds in the middle of a war zone, and your hands are shaking like leaves. Take the fucking

89

pills."

Hicks looked down and saw both of his hands were, indeed, trembling. He hadn't realized it until now.

He decided to reach for the pills, but his hand began shaking even worse. He balled his hand into a fist as he pulled it away.

Hicks tried to laugh it off. "Guess I'm not as tough as—"

Scott cupped his hand over Hicks's mouth, depositing the pills inside. "Remember not to chew them. Let them dissolve. They work better that way. They work quickly, too." He wiped his hand on his pants leg. "Had to take them once or twice myself."

The pills had dissolved by the time the elevator returned to the basement, leaving a bad taste in his mouth. "Oohrah."

CHAPTER 10

THE PILLS DID their job. Hicks's hands had begun to stop shaking by the time he sat at the table of one of the dilapidated kitchens in the Annex. He'd even managed to light a cigarette from a pack he'd found on the table. He normally preferred cigars, but hadn't had time to grab any before the proximity alert had sounded. Beggars couldn't be choosers, and since the place he lived had been obliterated, he was technically homeless.

The cigarette was stale, but the tobacco still felt good. He drew it deep into his lungs before letting it escape slowly through his nose.

Homeless. He winced at the thought of a missile destroying his facility. The idea of it didn't make sense to him. *How had they known where to find me?* He had never allowed himself to think of the place as anything more than an office with a bed in it. He had never decorated it with family pictures. He would have needed a family to photograph, and everyone who qualified was long-dead. He didn't believe in reminding himself of the people in his life who had passed on. He lived with enough ghosts as it was.

Other than his selection of weapons in the armory, the only personal touch he had allowed in the facility had been his humidor. The loss of the facility, its armory, and technology was bad enough, but it wasn't until that first drag on a stale cigarette that he remembered he had just filled his humidor with a full box of vintage Padron cigars. He could always get another box, but it was the waste that bothered him.

Waste had always angered him and the destruction of 23rd Street was just about the biggest waste he could think of. Anger wouldn't do him any good. Anger made things personal, and personal matters led to mistakes.

He didn't know who he was fighting. The CIA? Demerest? The Vanguard? Someone else? He would need a clear head if he was going to find out who and why. And not just for himself. Not even for the University. But for Tali and the life she was carrying inside her.

For the first time in his life, he was thinking of someone else outside mission parameters. Someone he hadn't even met yet, but wanted to.

He wanted to call Tali. He wanted to spill his guts and tell her everything that had happened. He wanted to tell her he was okay. But he decided to text her instead. His ego had taken enough of a beating for one day. He didn't want to risk hearing indifference in her voice. Tali wasn't known for her compassion.

He pulled out his handheld and sent her a direct message: **STAY INSIDE. VERY DANGEROUS. STAY AWARE.**

He was surprised when her response was immediate: **I'M GLAD YOU'RE OKAY. WAS WORRIED.**

His mood brightened a bit. *At least I've got that going for me.* He allowed himself another drag on the cigarette before calling Jason. It was time to get back in the game.

"I'm glad to see you arrived at the safe house, sir," Jason said. "I had OMNI track your route and no one followed you. No signals from your vehicle, either. Did the prisoner survive the trip?"

"For the moment. Fischer has him on the table right now. Have there been any other attacks on us?"

"Negative," Jason said. "All other Faculty Members, Adjuncts, Assets, and Affiliates have reported in and seem to be unharmed. The entire team in Europe is gathering at the rendezvous point in Berlin. Tali is already there, so…"

Hicks already knew where she was. He couldn't think about her now. "Is she following protocol? Has she gone off-line?"

"Negative," Jason said. "She's still observing the bank in Berlin. Remotely, of course, but she hasn't cut the feed yet. There's no signs that OMNI has been compromised, of course, but she's still violating the protocol. Do you want me disconnect her remotely?"

He had assigned Tali to set up the safe house and monitor everyone who went into and out of the small boutique bank the Vanguard used to make cash deposits. Everyone who entered and exited the building was photographed and run through OMNI's facial recognition software. The system looked for common depositors, times of when deposits were made, and other patterns. When someone appeared to be of interest, Tali did a deeper dive into their background and began investigating

93

them in the hopes one of them would lead to the Vanguard. It was a shot in the dark, but when chasing ghosts, one had to stalk the shadows.

"Leave her alone for now. What about Roger?"

"He responded to the alert and is in the process of packing now. He should be out of the nightclub within the hour."

Hicks's jaw set on edge. *Fucking Roger was never on time.* "Ping him back and tell him he's got only ten minutes. I need him mobile, not trapped in a nightclub in the middle of Berlin."

"I'll tell him to get moving, sir."

"Good. Give me a situation report on what's happening at the attack site."

"I was talking to Mark Stephens when you called. He's still on the line. I'll patch him through now."

Stephens skipped the pleasantries and began his report. "I don't know who you called, James, but whoever it was has some serious juice. Every agency on the ground deferred to me as soon as I got here. The media ran with the gas explosion story I fed them without question. They didn't even blink an eye during the fire department press conference."

Many people mourned the death of investigative journalism. James Hicks wasn't one of them. "Any federal agencies on site?"

"The whole alphabet soup. ATF, FBI, NTSB. Our friends in Langley sent some people, too, but they're playing it cool and hanging back. Everyone is following my lead like the fear of God has been put into them."

Hicks could hear a glint of pride in the former DIA man's voice. It was understandable that he liked his detractors kissing his ass for a change, but Hicks didn't have time for indulgences. He made a mental note to keep Stephens's ego in check before the call ended. "What's the real death count? Don't sugarcoat it. The media is reporting zero fatalities."

"They're not sugarcoating it," Stephens said. "No one was home in any of the apartments at the time of the blast. A couple of cats may have bitten the dust, but no human casualties. Some people got hurt by debris, but nothing life-threatening. The media is calling it a miracle. Lots of wrecked cars on the street, but that's what insurance is for."

Hicks didn't believe in miracles. At least they wouldn't have a lot of victims' families being interviewed on the news, demanding answers about how this happened. "Is the facility secure?"

"Completely destroyed," Stephens reported. "Looks like whoever it was dropped a Hellfire II on you. A bunker-buster set for ground detonation."

"I know what a fucking Hellfire II is," Hicks snapped. "I want a damage assessment."

Stephens complied. "It crashed through the buildings like a rock through water, but didn't detonate until it hit the sub-basement. Most of the blast was contained by the bunker. Probably vaporized everything. Absorbed a good portion of the blast, too. Some of the neighboring buildings might need structural support, but—"

Hicks didn't care about real estate. "I want verification on total destruction of the facility as soon as possible. Remove anything that even resembles technical equipment as soon as it's safe. There's an armory down there, so be careful of exploding ammunition. I want all of that cleared out before the firemen get in there with cell phones and start posting images on Instagram. If anyone remarks that it looks like someone was living down there, write it off as squatters or some damned thing."

"Okay, James. Jesus, you don't have to be so—"

"Did you grab the three packages I left across the street?"

"A Varsity Squad already removed the driver and is in the process of getting the two men on the roof as we speak. They'll run their prints and faces through OMNI before they move them."

"Good. Stay on-site and report back every hour on the hour until further notice. If you need a break, I'll send Scott over to spell you. I want a command presence on-site at all times, especially when they begin clearing the debris. Keep an eye on the feds, too. We still don't know whose side they're on."

Stephens paused for a moment. "Hold on a minute. You don't think Demerest could be behind this, do you?"

Hicks found that rich, coming from Stephens. "You and your friends tried killing me with a drone once, remember? You tell me."

"Damn," Stephens said. "You don't give an inch, do you?"

"I'm not paid to be nice," Hicks reminded him. "Report back in an hour. And keep your ego in check. Don't throw your weight around unless it's absolutely necessary. I don't want anyone making phone calls just because you're feeling yourself. Understand?"

Hicks killed the connection, but Jason called right back.

Jason said, "Stephens deserved that dressing down, sir. I'll monitor the situation from here just in case I need to step in."

"Quit kissing my ass," Hicks told him. "I can take people trying to kill me, but I can't take people brown-nosing me."

Jason was silent for a beat. "Okay. What do you want me to do?"

"I need you here in New York as soon as possible. Report to the Annex and be ready to jump in to help Stephens if I need you."

"But I thought you said Scott would spell him if—"

"I've got other plans for Scott. And I need you here while I'm in the field."

"Understood," Jason said. "In the meantime, the Trustee contacted me a few minutes ago. She said she needs to speak to you. It's urgent."

Of course it is.

He groaned as he ran his hand over his face. The hand was rock-steady now.

Normally, he could picture his Carousel of Concern spinning at an orderly pace, each priority clearly presenting itself to be dealt with in an orderly fashion.

Now the goddamned thing had been blown to bits and he didn't have the time to try to put it back together again. Now wasn't the time for contemplation. It was the time for action.

But contemplation edged its way in anyway. He'd only been concerned about the attack. He hadn't the time to think about why it happened until that very moment.

The facts began coming into focus on their own.

Roger had given him a lead on a Russian thug who called himself Boris.

OMNI showed Boris was tied to a mysterious thug named Wilhelm/Willus Tessmer.

Hicks had called Tayeb to start digging into Tessmer.

Tayeb's facility went CROATOAN hours after that.

Then someone dropped a missile on his facility. A Russian squad had lased his building for it.

All of it was related. Only question was if the Vanguard or Russian contractors were working for Demerest.

Jason snapped him out of it. "Are you still there? The Trustee is waiting."

"I'll call her in a minute. In the meantime, find out what happened to Tayeb and his men. Look at media accounts, police channels, everything. I know OMNI's reach is weak in that part of the world, but try it anyway. Call me if you get something definitive. Send me a report in an hour no matter what."

"God," Jason said. "You think all of this is related, don't you?"

"I don't know, and that's what bothers me. And by the way, sorry for snapping at you just now. You saved my ass today."

"No need to thank me. It's my job."

Hicks killed the connection. He took a long, final drag on his cigarette before he flicked it into the ancient sink behind him. His hands were finally as steady as they normally were.

Time to see what Ma wants. He dialed the Trustee's extension on his handheld.

"Asking how you're doing would be a stupid question," she said. "Were you injured?"

"I got out in plenty of time, thanks to OMNI and Jason." Hicks felt his temper begin to spike and fought to tamp it down. "I'm going to ask you a direct question. I want a straight yes or no answer from you. No hedging. No stalling. Did Demerest do this?"

"Absolutely not," she answered. "I was on the phone with him discussing the Jabbar information. He was over the moon about it, James. We were actually talking about how we could work together when he got word of the attack."

"Sounds awfully convenient."

"We were already on the phone for an hour," she said. "And he's not the type to use a drone on American soil against an American target. Definitely not with all the heat on the Agency at the moment. I didn't even know we had a facility on 23rd Street. How did they find it?"

"I don't know," Hicks admitted, "but I'm going to find out. I'm hoping my friend upstairs can give me some answers."

"I hope he does," she said. "I know you still blame Carl for the drone attack on the highway last year, but that wasn't him. He's not above ordering you killed, but he would have done it a lot cleaner than this. It's simply not his style. And based on my conversation with him this morning, he was looking to work with you, not kill you."

Hicks didn't know her well enough to believe her. But he knew sincerity when he heard it, and he heard it now. "Then that means it was the Vanguard. I'll confirm that after I talk to the asshole I captured. They're working on stabilizing him now. In the meantime, I need you to check on Ronen Tayeb's people in Moscow. They were working on a couple of leads for us."

"I already checked," she said. "They're gone, James. I'm sorry. I know you and Tayeb were close."

Hicks felt weak. All signs had pointed to them being dead, but hearing it was different. "How?"

"The media is reporting it as a gang war," she told him. "But it was one hell of a firefight. Someone attacked Tayeb's safe house with an awful lot of fire power. My sources in Moscow tell me the street was covered in shell casings, but the only bodies they found were in the safe house. It looks like the Vanguard took their dead with them, because there were no corpses on the street. At some point, someone got desperate enough to launch an RPG through the window. That accounts for the CROATOAN message. Everything went down at once."

The Trustee kept talking, but Hicks took the phone away from his ear. He and Tayeb had never been especially close. He couldn't even honestly call the man a friend. But he knew his abilities. He knew he wouldn't have gone down without putting up a hell of a fight. He knew it would take a hell of a lot of effort to take him down.

After seeing what they had done to his facility and to Tayeb's people, one thing was certain: the Vanguard was much more than just a bunch of arms dealers. They were capable of more than just waging war by proxy.

They were capable of waging war directly.

And although he hated to admit it, the Vanguard seemed too big for the University to fight on its own.

The Trustee was still talking when Hicks said, "I need to talk to Demerest. Now."

"Haven't you been listening?" she asked. "He wants to talk to you, too. I'll make all the arrangements and get back to you as soon as I have them. In the meantime, get what you can out of that prisoner. Anything he says will help. And make sure your people in Europe are ready."

"My people are always ready. Let me know when you hear back from Demerest."

He killed the connection and dumped the phone onto the table. He ran his hands through his shaggy hair as he looked up at the ceiling. His entire world was turning to shit and his best people were all in Europe.

He almost jumped when Scott knocked at the door. "Doc

says the patient's ready for you now."

Hicks gathered up his phone and headed upstairs. Roger had high praise for this new doctor. He'd even called him a protégé. He hoped he was at least half as good an interrogator as Roger. And he hoped Roger was already long gone from that nightclub in Berlin. He'd already lost too many people today. He couldn't afford to lose him, too.

CHAPTER
11

BY LUNCHTIME, THE media had taken the cover story and ran with it.

BREAKING NEWS: GAS EXPLOSION ROCKS NYC

A powerful gas explosion ripped through the heart of the Chelsea district of Manhattan this morning, causing the collapse of three brownstone buildings on West 23rd Street. Dozens were wounded, some seriously, but there were no fatalities, a fact that some city officials are calling a miracle. Every tenant of all three buildings was either at work or at other appointments throughout the city.

While the investigation is still ongoing, sources say a slow gas leak was the most likely cause of the explosion. They claim natural gas from a cracked line had leaked slowly into a small sub-basement all three brownstones shared. Officials have stated there is absolutely no evidence of terrorism in this instance, something that has helped quell the fears of many New Yorkers in a city already on edge.

Other items caught the media's interest as well.

MOTHER NATURE SPARKS FEAR

A flock of migrating birds sent air traffic controllers into a frenzy this morning when civilian and military radar systems mistakenly identified an abnormally large flock of geese as an unidentified aircraft entering American airspace. Scientists say the odd migration pattern was most likely caused by changing environmental conditions caused by global warming.

VIOLENCE IN MOSCOW

On the international front, escalating gang violence is being blamed for a bombing in Russia's capital city today. At least ten people were confirmed killed in a blast at an apartment complex. Moscow police officials say the attack was attributed to rising tensions between local crime factions involved in the city's growing heroin trade.

CHAPTER
12

Berlin, Germany

ROGER COBB GAVE his handheld device the finger when another message from Jason came through. "Of course I'm moving, you fucking idiot," he said to the empty room as he packed his gear. "I'd like to see you move any faster with all the shit I have to pack."

The phone sounded again and he was about to fire off a nasty message to Jason when he realized it was a different sound. It was the security alarm. He looked at the red screen.

PROXIMITY ALERT: ARMED PERSONNEL NEARBY

He tapped the screen and an image from the club's external security camera showed five large men in long leather coats at the mouth of the alley on the north side of the club. OMNI's green crosshairs highlighted the outline of a M4 rifle under one man's coat. He bet all of them were similarly armed.

He was mildly flattered. A hit squad. And these boys had

come to party.

Even before he received the Moscow Protocol alert, Roger knew something was wrong. The ex-cop he'd sent to follow Boris hadn't called or shown up to get his money. The man lived on vodka and tobacco and was always broke. If he didn't show up for his payment, something was wrong.

He figured the hit squad in the alley was probably that something.

Roger watched as four of them kept an eye on either end of the alley while a fifth man jammed a crowbar into the side door.

Roger cringed. Zev, the owner of Der Underground, would have to get a new one, as well as repair all the other damage that was undoubtedly about to happen within the club. Roger made a mental note to leave him an extra ten thousand euros to cover the incidentals.

A cold mixture of fear and excitement spread through Roger's belly. He tucked the nine millimeter Glock into the holster on his hip, then dug into the bottom of his bag and removed the sheath holding the KA-BAR fixed-blade combat knife. It might not have been the most intimidating-looking knife in the world, but it had never let him down.

He checked the camera feed on his handheld as he moved out into the hall and closed the door to his room. The man with the crowbar almost had the door open, and it wouldn't be long before all five men were inside.

Roger ran down the maze of halls to the discreet door that led to the stairway to the club's control room, where all the club's music and strobes and lighting could be activated from a single console. He didn't have to see his handheld to hear the steel door finally giving way to the crowbar. The squad had breached the club.

Roger looked at the bank of monitors that showed a live feed of every camera in the club. For insurance purposes, Zev made sure they ran twenty-four hours a day, seven days a week, recording on a daily loop. Roger saw all five men had clustered near the coatroom, each of them holding the M4 carbine they'd been concealing beneath their coats. It was a lot of hardware to capture just one man, Roger thought, but Russians weren't known for their subtlety.

One man with a crew cut was pointing in various directions, telling each man where he wanted them to go. This man was obviously their leader.

Roger decided to kill him first.

Roger watched the squad fan out. They were obviously professionals, moving low and fast through the darkened building.

As soon as each man was alone in a section deep within the club's maze, Roger shut down the breaker that powered the emergency lights. The windowless building was plunged into complete darkness.

The club's security camera feed automatically switched to night vision, installed to give security staff the ability to see what was going on in the dark reaches of the club. Roger watched all five men stop in place and drop to a crouch, M4s at their shoulders. They knew they'd been discovered. And none of them had brought night vision goggles to the party.

Roger focused on the monitor showing the team leader, who had just reached one of the several bars off the club's main dancefloor. He was the only member of the team talking, probably via a throat mic.

Time to bust a move, boys. Roger flicked a switch.

Techno music began blaring through the club's speakers. He raised the volume above standard levels, to the point where it was impossible for the intruders to hear anything in their earpieces.

He watched the green images of the men react to the loud music, each of them pushing the ear buds deeper into their ear canals in an attempt to hear their team leader's orders. Each man was deaf and alone in the pitch-blackness of a maze, against a target they didn't understand. They weren't panicking yet, but they weren't exploring, either. They were holding in place, trying to figure out what to do next.

Roger threw another switch on the console, activating thousands of tiny white strobe lights throughout the club. The pulsating, blinding light combined with the deafening music disoriented the team even further. The camera feed went back to normal mode and he saw the team leader backtracking toward the alley door.

Now that the rest of the squad was blind, deaf, and isolated, Roger decided it was time to start improving the odds.

He slipped out of the control room and down the stairs to the main body of the club. The music thudded as the pulsating lights revealed a microsecond of brilliant clarity before going dark again.

Roger kept his eyes shut to avoid being blinded by the strobes. He knew the place like the back of his hand and moved across the wall, tracking the team leader who had just managed to find the alley door and made it outside.

Roger pulled the combat knife from his belt and burst through the door. The team leader was slumped against the brick wall of the alley, shaking his head to try to get his bearings.

From behind, Roger wrapped his left hand around the much larger man's head as he slid the knife up into the base of his brain.

The team leader was already dead, but his body didn't know it. It tensed and twitched as the electrical impulses of his brain slowly died.

Roger shoved him behind one of the dumpsters lining the alley, bringing both hands down on the M4 to keep him from firing it as he twitched.

Roger pried the larger man's hands away from the weapon and fell with him as he slumped to the ground, the rifle hanging slack from the shoulder harness beneath his coat.

As the leader's body went slack, Roger withdrew the blade and rolled the dead man onto his belly. He wiped the blade clean on the leader's pants and tucked the knife back into his belt. He yanked down the man's leather coat by the collar until it was completely off, then pulled the M4 free from his shoulder. He patted the coat's pockets and the dying man's body for extra clips for the rifle. All he found was a nine millimeter Glock in a holster on his right hip. No extra rounds.

Roger checked the coat and saw he'd been wrong. No Kevlar lining. No Kevlar vest, either. Interesting. If the leader wasn't wearing one, his men probably weren't either. Why would they? This was supposed to be an easy job. *Bag the fag*, right? *Sink the twink* and be on their way. Ten minutes, tops.

Roger allowed himself a smile as he heard the leader gurgle free whatever oxygen was left in his lungs. He playfully tapped the team leader's face. "Wasn't quite so easy, was it, love?"

Roger ejected the magazine from the M4, saw it was full,

and slapped it back in. He stood flat against the wall and dug his handheld out of his pocket to check the feed from the club's security cameras.

The team leader would have been proud of his men. They had found each other in the pulsing darkness and were making their way downstairs via an auxiliary stairway. No strobes in the stairway meant they were in pitch black, though the music ensured they were still deaf. The men moved as a unit, using the wall to guide them in the darkness. Their rifles led the way as they moved in a tight cover formation.

Easy targets for Roger's new M4.

Roger pocketed the handheld as he ducked back inside and ran for the staircase. He crouched in the darkness, eyes closed against the strobes, stopping where he knew the stairway door would be.

He checked his handheld and saw the men had just rounded the turn for the final landing. He poked the M4 around the doorway and raked the group with withering fire at point-blank range, low and tight. The techno music drowned out the gunfire. The muzzle flashed even faster than the strobes, showing Roger the outlines of the men as they fell.

Roger kept firing until the magazine ran dry. He pulled back into the club and checked his handheld again to make sure they were all dead. All four men were down. All of them had been hit in the upper body several times. None of them was moving. Roger watched for another minute in case one of the men was playing possum. They had obviously been trained, so they might be smart enough to lie in wait for a target to present itself. After a good five minutes without even the slightest movement, he decided it was safe to check the scene himself.

Using the flashlight mode of his handheld, he stripped each man of his weapons. They'd all been carrying the same load as their leader: an M4 and a Glock. He tossed all the guns out into the club before checking each man's throat for signs of a pulse. Only one of them showed even a glimmer of life. A quick plunge of the knife put an end to that. He also took pictures of each man's face and scanned their fingerprints. All of it would be uploaded to the OMNI system, where it would automatically attempt to identify each of the men. He made a mental note to do that to the team leader, too, before he placed him in the dumpster.

His preliminary work done, he shined his cell phone's light around the stairwell. There was blood, of course, but his aim had been true. Most of the rounds had found their targets and hadn't nicked much of the building at all. The stairs and walls were chewed up by the bullets, but not enough for clubgoers to notice. A little bleach, a dab of paint, and it would be passible enough for the club to open that night.

Loading the bodies into the dumpster outside one at a time would take some effort. Doing it discreetly even more so, but it had to be done. He'd use one of the plastic sheets from the S and M chamber upstairs to slide them through the club and into the alley one at a time. That should minimize the blood left in the more public areas of the club.

He couldn't expect Zev to do that for him.

He'd been such a gracious host. Expecting him to clean up five dead bodies would've been rude.

He tossed his empty rifle with the others and sagged against the stairwell wall.

All this work and he still hadn't finished packing.

CHAPTER
13

The Annex, New York City

THE MEDICAL FLOOR was the only clean room in the entire
Annex.

Roger had insisted that the suite, in addition to the Cube
interrogation chamber, had all the features of a modern
operating room, including a full complement of drugs needed
to either dull or magnify pain. A surgeon could either patch
up a gunshot wound or perform open-heart surgery should the
need arise. Hicks had balked at the cost at first, but eventually
gave in. He was glad he did. Roger was nothing if not thorough.

Doctor Fischer stood at the bedside of the man he had just
spent several hours working to save, only for Hicks to question
and most likely kill. If Fischer felt any irony, he hid it well.

Hicks listened to the cacophony of the various machines
monitoring the Russian's vital signs as the patient's chest rose
and fell in ragged breaths. The entire left side of his face and

skull was black and swollen, his left eye completely shut due to the blow from the Ruger. A steady drip from an IV sent medicine directly into a port in his right hand.

"Any tattoos on him?" Hicks asked the doctor.

"Left arm," Fischer said. "Looks like *Spetsnaz*. I saw a few when I was in Afghanistan."

Hicks checked it himself and saw he was right. "What's his status?"

"Barely alive," Fischer said. "The XStat kept him from bleeding out, but he had a hell of a lot of internal bleeding in the intestines. I did what I could, but I'll have to go in again if you want him to last the night. A good portion of his lower vertebrae is gone, so he'll never walk again, assuming he lives long enough to try. His left wrist is crushed and several bones in his left arm are fractured. If I don't tend to them, they'll become infected. There's a good chance I'll have to amputate everything below the elbow in a day or so. The left side of his skull is broken and he'll probably lose that eye if he lives long enough. I'd bet he has a concussion, too, but..."

Hicks looked at him. "You asking me to feel sorry for him, doc?"

Doctor Fischer's bland expression held. "No, but the concussion and the anesthesia, combined with the shock he's going through, will make him less responsive than you expect. There's also a possibility of a bone fragment hitting his lungs or heart, which would kill him instantly at this point." He looked down at the broken body of the patient in the bed. "I've seen what you do to people who displease you. I'd like to avoid the same fate."

Hicks couldn't argue with him there. "Can you wake him

up?"

"I can try, but no guarantees on what will happen when I do. He could go into cardiac arrest or die."

"Do it anyway."

Fischer took a vial from the medicine cabinet, loaded a syringe, and injected it into the port in the Russian's hand. The patient's eyes fluttered open as he gasped awake.

Fischer left the room as Hicks leaned over the bed. In Russian, he asked the man, "Who are you working for?"

The man tried to lift his head and cried out from the effort. "Where am I? What happened?" he gasped in his native tongue.

"You're paralyzed from the waist down. Your left arm has been shattered and we'll have to amputate it. Your left eye is gone, and you're probably going to die within the next few hours if I let you."

The Russian looked away as a tear streaked from his right eye. "Be merciful. I am a soldier. Kill me."

"Not until you tell me who sent you. If you don't, I'll keep you alive for weeks. I'll make sure you suffer every minute of pain and every indignity you've got coming. But if you tell me who sent you to light up my building, and you're truthful, this will end quickly and painlessly." He leaned in closer, close enough to smell death approaching the man. "The choice is yours."

It took a couple of tries for the Russian to get enough breath to say, "A man sent us. I don't know his name…gave us your photo…your address…the laser. Told us to shoot you if you came out of the house…but you didn't. Not in time for us to get away from the blast."

"Where did the order come from?"

"From…Berlin. We…" The man's body went rigid as he

seized up, and the machines began to beep wildly.

From the doorway, Fischer called out, "He's going into cardiac arrest!"

The Russian's body slumped as the machines emitted a steady tone, and all the lines on all the screens went flat.

Fischer walked back into the room, his hands behind his back. "Do you want me to try to bring him back?"

Hicks watched the last breath escape the Russian's body. "No. I got enough." The tattoo told him a lot. The fact that he was Russian told him more. Berlin only made him certain.

The Vanguard had tried to kill him.

The only question was how they had found him in the first place.

He pulled out his handheld, took a picture of the dead man's face, and then scanned his fingerprints from his ruined left hand. He doubted OMNI would turn up anything, but he had to try. Every corpse was another link in the chain leading back to the Vanguard. Every lead had to be explored, even dead ones.

After he was finished, Hicks told Fischer, "Follow standard protocol. Dump him in the incinerator downstairs. Analyze his effects to see if we can find out where they were bought. Clothes, shoes, everything. Run a toxicology report, too. Anything could help."

He looked at the doctor until Fischer looked back. "Then get some sleep. You've earned it. I wouldn't have gotten anything out of him if it hadn't been for you. You did a hell of a job today, Fischer."

The doctor looked down at the Russian's corpse. "All of that effort to save a dying man's life for a single name. We are sons of bitches, aren't we, James? The both of us."

Hicks was already on his way out the door. "We have to be."

H E FOUND SCOTT in one of the living rooms downstairs, seated on a faded couch, thumbing through his handheld. The Varsity man didn't look up when Hicks walked in. "Your Russian dead?"

Hicks dropped onto an equally dilapidated overstuffed chair. "Yeah."

"Get anything out of him?"

"I got enough. Your men get anything off the SUV?"

Scott kept looking through his device. "Nope. Stolen from a garage in midtown about a week ago. Belonged to a dentist. The security cameras in the garage were miraculously on the fritz that day, so nothing on who stole it. We stripped it down to the steel and didn't come up with anything. No tracking devices, no modifications. Just a stolen vehicle with phony diplomatic tags. Good fakes, though. Would've fooled a cop on a traffic stop. Whoever did it has resources and knows what they're doing."

"I know. That's why I want you to pack a bag. We're going to Berlin."

Scott's eyebrows rose as he looked up from his device. "How did I get so lucky?"

Hicks ignored the sarcasm. Scott and he had always had a terse relationship. Scott had always been a field man. He saw Hicks as management, a sellout who'd given up the field for a cushy desk job. *If he only knew.*

"Why me?" Scott went on. "You've got your new playmate Stephens to help you with those kinds of things. I just do what I'm told, remember?"

115

Hicks closed his eyes. Scott's ego was still bruised from when he'd ordered him to take Rahul Patel to the airport a few weeks ago. The simple task was an affront to his skills, and he was still holding on to the grudge all these weeks later.

"Stephens has a role to fill here as head of the New York Office, at least until things settle down. I need you on the ground with me because things are going to get dicey over there. Now, if you'd prefer to stay here where it's nice and safe, I'll get someone else."

"How dicey?"

"Your kind of dicey."

Hicks couldn't swear to it, but he thought he saw Scott smile. "Well, count me in."

It was the closest thing to good news Hicks had heard in a long time. "Good. Be ready to go in thirty minutes. Then be ready to pick me up within the hour."

Scott watched him stand up. "Where are you going?"

"To see a man about a phone."

CHAPTER 14

St. Mark's Place, New York City

S T. MARK'S PLACE was one of the last sections of the city that had successfully fended off gentrification. Times Square had become an amusement park. SoHo had devolved from quaint local shops to little more than an outdoor mall for high-end retail chains. Even the Meatpacking District had swapped out hookers and junkies to become a binge-drinking Mecca for Millennials and aging Generation X-ers who lied to themselves about still being hip.

But St. Mark's Place had managed to dodge modernity. Technically, it was just another street on the map, a section of 8th Street that ran between Third Avenue and Avenue A. In reality, it was one of the last places on the island of Manhattan where people who didn't fit in anywhere else could find a home.

Populated by bars and restaurants, small shops and tattoo parlors, St. Mark's offered something for everyone looking to either lose themselves or find themselves, be it for a few hours or a lifetime. The inked and the pierced, the androgynous and the artistic, the punk rocker and the Emo, and even the occasional banker looking to slum.

A few tourists invariably found their way there, of course, but a lack of kitsch left them little to cling to, so they rarely stayed long, preferring the elegant architecture of Fifth Avenue or the bright lights of Broadway. St. Mark's made no pretense of being anything more than what it was, which was whatever you wanted it to be.

It was the perfect place for Hicks to speak to the CIA.

Sarah had texted him that Demerest's contact would be waiting for him on the steps of the old brownstone at 80 St. Mark's Place. It had been a speakeasy at one time but now housed a small theater and museum.

The weight of the Ruger in the holster beneath his left arm gave Hicks a measure of security when he spotted a homeless man on the brownstone stairs half a block away. The black man's shaggy beard and filthy clothes would have made him stick out in any other part of the city, but on this street he blended in. That was the point. Just another member of New York's forgotten class.

The man made eye contact with Hicks for a full second longer than a homeless person normally would. Hicks knew this was Demerest's man. He watched the vagrant pick up a brown paper bag from between his feet, drain the bottle hidden inside it, and set it down on the step. He let out an epic belch that Hicks heard from half a block away.

He watched the man stand up, straighten out his filthy coat, and stagger off in the opposite direction. Hicks eyed the street as he approached the stoop before sitting down next to the bag. He spotted a black flip phone wedged between the bag and the concrete stair.

He looked around as he picked up the phone, finding it thicker and heavier than most cheap burner phones.

The phone began to buzz. He flipped it open and the connection was made. The voice on the other end belonged to Charles Demerest. "This is an encrypted phone, so we can speak freely."

"How comforting."

"Make sure you keep it with you at all times," Demerest said. "It's got an international calling function on it. Don't worry. It's not an official agency device so I can't track you on it. It used to be my daughter's phone. This is how we'll communicate from here on out."

"From here on out?" Hicks repeated. "Sounds permanent. We going steady now, Ace?"

"Maybe," Demerest said. "Sarah already told you the Jabbar information you gave us was golden. That means we need to work together, especially after today's attack. I know we don't trust each other yet. That's understandable. Trust has to be earned on both sides. But we're in this together whether we like it or not. We'll win a hell of a lot sooner if we're both pulling in the same direction."

Hicks felt his breath catch. Because, just like that, the CIA had agreed to work with the University.

Every action Hicks had taken for the past several weeks had led up to that moment. It was something the University had fought for and against numerous times over the decades since Eisenhower's executive order in the fifties. From the moment

Colin had died in the snow in Central Park all those weeks ago, through the Bajjah mess, and right up until the previous night, Hicks had been pushing for CIA cooperation. Now he finally had it.

It should have been one of the finest moments of Hicks's career. He'd proven the previous Dean wrong and now had the full support of the most powerful intelligence agency in the West.

And it didn't mean a damned thing to him.

Because his facility had been destroyed and his people had been killed and the University's entire operation was frozen in place. All because he asked Tayeb to investigate a man who no longer existed except on a forgotten server in a police station in Bonn.

Tessmer.

Demerest snapped him out of it. "You still there, son?"

"Yeah," Hicks said. "But after what happened this morning, I don't want anyone being able to track me."

"We won't be tracking you. You have my word."

On any other day, Hicks would have laughed. The word of a spy was worthless. But this was no time for laughter. "How about you start building good will by telling me how Washington is responding to the attack?"

"The gas leak story seems to have satisfied the media," Demerest explained, "but none of the department heads are buying it. Everyone from NORAD right down to the NYPD know it was a missile attack, but no one wants pandemonium so they're keeping a lid on it for now. Every member of the cabinet is scrambling to find out how this happened and why. I wouldn't count on that lasting, though. With the Agency under investigation, it's only a matter of time before someone at Langley tries to curry favor with the committees and leaks the truth about the attack."

Hicks caught that. "Maybe someone who's already depending on those committees for a cabinet post. Someone who's up for Director of National Intelligence, maybe."

"That's not funny, son. An attack on the homeland was exactly the last thing I needed right now. And any information I pass along to them will only reinforce their idea that we must have missed something here at the CIA. Besides, my confirmation is the least of our worries now."

"Meaning?"

"Meaning international relations were strained in the last twenty-four hours or so, even before this attack. The State Department reports relations between Russia and Israel are devolving at a rapid pace. The Russians are furious that a Mossad unit was operating in their hometown. The Israelis are blaming the Russians for the massacre of their people. Some members of the Knesset are beginning to grumble about the mysterious plane explosion that killed Mossad chief Schneider a few weeks ago. They're grumbling that maybe the Russians were involved. If you had come to me later, a lot of people might be looking at you in a whole different light. You would make a convenient scapegoat for a lot of people right about now."

"Yeah," Hicks said as he lit another stale cigarette from the pack he'd found at the Annex. "Lucky me."

"I've opened my kimono," Demerest said. "Now it's your turn. Sarah told me you grabbed one of the guys lasing your building. Have you gotten anything out of him yet?"

Since Hicks didn't have much to tell him, he decided not

to hold anything back. "He had a *Spetsnaz* tattoo on his arm and said he received his orders from Berlin. He didn't live long enough to give me a name."

"Shit, Hicks. We've got to teach you boys how to keep your prisoners alive."

"He was half dead when I brought him in." Hicks didn't tell Demerest that OMNI hadn't been able to find their identities in any databases in the Western world. The less Demerest knew about the University's abilities, the better. At least for now. "But I've got pictures and prints of all the men who took a run at me. I'll send you everything in a few minutes. Maybe you can identify them. I don't have any proof, but based on the ordinance and the coordination these boys had, it makes me think this was a Vanguard show."

"You and I know that," Demerest said, "but it's not that simple. One of the F-16s we scrambled was about to blow the drone out of the sky over a field in New Jersey when the damned thing exploded on its own. Whoever was piloting the drone had rigged it with a self-destruct proximity sensor. That explains why the drone had to fly so high that it showed up on our radar systems. It would've self-destructed if it got too close to a building. Fortunately, we were able to map the debris field immediately and our people have managed to find a few things. The wreckage is almost identical to Valkyrie knock-offs we've recovered in Syria and Iraq. Our people think the drones have been supplied by—"

"Iran," Hicks said. "Which buys similar systems from people working with the Vanguard. Just like Jabbar's evidence proves." He took a drag on the cigarette. "Sometimes I hate being right."

"You can take a victory lap later," Demerest said. "The Joint

Chiefs and several Agency brass are looking to pin this on Iran. I'm doing what I can to keep that idea from getting traction, but until I can produce solid evidence of Vanguard involvement, Iran's looking like the villain here. And you know what that means."

It made sense to Hicks. Iran had been denouncing the United States for decades. They had been funding the other side in the War on Terror since the beginning. Proof that an Iranian drone had targeted an American city would raise public outcry for a response, probably even all-out war.

The Vanguard would get the Middle East distraction like they wanted. They would also make millions off new arms sales that would spike throughout the region. The mission that had begun with Bajjah's failed biological attack on New York would be complete. "These bastards are smart."

"Which means we've got to get smarter, and fast," Demerest said. "You provided me with a lot of important information about the Vanguard and the biological attack on New York. But I need something to tie them to the attack today, and an Iranian drone only muddies the waters. I can't go to the president or even my director with a hypothetical about a mysterious group of arms dealers firing a missile into New York. They'd laugh me right out of the room and keep blaming Iran for this."

Demerest cleared his throat. "You're not going to like this, but I need to know what kind of facility you had at 23rd Street. They're already wondering why the building was targeted in the first place. They're going to find out when they clear the rubble away in a day or two anyway. If I know what was there, I can explain whatever they find."

Demerest was right. Hicks didn't like it, but he didn't have a choice. Everything was destroyed, but he decided to hedge the truth for the sake of the University. "It was a communications center we were using to run down leads on the Vanguard. A generator and some computer equipment. A small armory, too. I fried the electronics before I left, but the hardware is still there so we'll need to explain it."

He got the sense Demerest was writing this down. "That's fine. I can spin that. I can say it was one of our facilities in use since the Cold War. They'll buy that, especially since it wasn't a debacle like Black Site Friday. No one minded we had the place in Jersey, just that the media found out about it once we torched it. We couldn't get ahead of that story, but we can get ahead of this one. How many people knew it existed? Who else knew it was there? Sarah swears she didn't know about it."

"That's because she didn't," Hicks said. "No one knew about it except me and the previous Dean. I don't even know how the Vanguard knew about it or how important it was, but I intend to find out. In Berlin."

"And I take it you're heading there personally?"

"Within the hour."

Demerest paused. "Any chance I can talk you into waiting a day or so?"

"Absolutely none whatsoever."

"Yeah, I figured you'd say something like that. Look, everything we do from here on out needs to be coordinated if I'm going to be successful in keeping people here from pinning the attack on Iran. They'll act on it very quickly, and I won't be able to stop them unless I have proof the Vanguard did this, not Iran. Now, I can have a hundred people in Berlin by morning. Your group and mine can coordinate with Germany's state police."

"No." Hicks let the cigarette smoke drift from his nose.

"No? What the hell do you mean 'no'? You can't do this on your own. Your group isn't big enough to handle the Vanguard on your own. You said so yourself."

"We're not coordinating with anyone because that's exactly what the Vanguard expects us to do. A rapid response. SWAT teams kicking in doors and rounding up the usual suspects all over the world. That's why we're not going to give it to them. We're going to head-fake them and change the narrative."

Demerest was silent a beat longer than necessary. "Have you been checked out by a doctor? I think there's a good chance you're in shock, because you're not making any sense."

"My people in Berlin and I will keep working the bank lead on the Vanguard we told you about yesterday. We keep the footprint small and the response quiet. I don't want anyone knowing we're there, especially your people."

"What the hell are you talking about? Are you still blaming my people for trying to kill you last month? Christ, Hicks. I already told you that wasn't us."

"I don't care about that," Hicks said. "But I do care about someone in your Berlin office reaching out to the German government to help them run down leads. The Vanguard didn't get this big without having people in the right places who could turn a blind eye at the right time. One call from your people to the wrong person, however innocent, and these bastards will disappear. They probably know by now that they didn't kill me in the attack. They may be shutting down their Berlin branch as we speak. If they're moving, they're vulnerable, so the smaller we keep this circle, the better our chances of finding them and taking them down. And getting the proof you need to keep them from falling for the Iran bait the Vanguard is feeding them."

Hicks waited for Demerest to argue, but wasn't surprised by the silence. The agent in him wanted to assert his people's abilities and the full power of the entire American intelligence complex to bring the Vanguard to heel.

But there was another side of Demerest, the side that was nominated for the Director of National Intelligence position. A position he could not secure if he revealed all Jabbar's secrets to his colleagues. It would raise too many questions about what he knew and how he knew it. And why he hadn't gotten the information sooner. Bad news for the Agency. Worse news for Demerest's career.

Demerest bended. "I'm giving you seventy-two hours."

"A week."

"No way," Demerest said. "I'll be shocked if I can buy you seventy-two hours. Right now half of our people are trying to figure out who did this, while the other half are working to cover their own asses in case they missed something. The Israeli and Russian friction complicates things and will keep the State Department clowns busy. That confusion won't last long, and POTUS is going to want to kick somebody's ass for this. I need proof that the Vanguard was behind this as soon as possible, before someone orders a strike on Iran and the Vanguard gets the distraction they want. I know neither of us wants that."

Hicks couldn't argue with the man's logic. He knew Washington better than Hicks did. He knew Demerest could have just assumed control of the entire Berlin operation and shut the University out of it, but he hadn't. He was giving them a chance, which was more than the Vanguard had given them.

Demerest was also giving himself deniability. The less he knew about what Hicks was planning, the less he could testify about under oath should the need arise.

"I'll agree to seventy-two hours," Hicks said, "but the clock doesn't start until this time tomorrow. Deal?"

He could practically hear Demerest frown. "Why do I feel like I've just made a deal with the devil?"

Hicks didn't have a good answer for that one, so he simply closed the phone.

He pulled out his handheld and called Jason. "You get all that?"

"Most of it," Jason said. "His encryption is pretty good. I missed the beginning but OMNI broke through and we got most of it."

"Good. The recording might come in handy somewhere down the line. Can you ghost the phone he gave me?"

"OMNI's doing it as we speak. It shouldn't be hard. You're not going to keep the phone, are you?"

"For now, but I'm taking precautions. Are the jets ready?"

"They're gassed up and ready to go as we speak. Are you sure about this, James? It's a risky proposition, not to mention an expensive one."

"I'm not sure of anything, but it's worth the risk. Where's Scott?"

A few clicks on Jason's end. "Less than thirty seconds from your position."

Hicks looked up and saw Scott's Escalade had just turned on to St. Mark's Place. A goth waif dodged out of the way at the last second and flipped him off from the curb.

God, I love this town.

"I see him. I'll call you from Berlin."

127

CHAPTER
15

SOMEWHERE

THE MAN LISTENED while the German spoke. The Man insisted the German speak in Russian rather than Mandarin, as the Man found his comrade's Mandarin poor to the point of being offensive.

Besides, bad news was unpleasant in any language, even more so in Russian.

"The three-man laser team and their driver have not reported in as they were ordered," the German told him. "There is no sign of the operatives or their vehicle at the site. Because they were not allowed to have cell phones in case they were killed or captured, I cannot confirm their whereabouts. We must assume they are dead."

It was an assumption the Man had arrived at five minutes ago. If his German comrade had any shortcomings, it was that he was not used to failure and did not know how to convey it properly. "The men are of no importance. What about the target? Did he survive?"

"None of my people have been able to get close enough to the rubble to see if the target has been killed. The authorities are reporting that there were no fatalities in the blast, but they are also reporting the explosion was a gas leak, so I do not believe their accounts. My sources report they have members of the ATF, the FBI, and other federal agencies on the scene, so they undoubtedly know this was a missile strike. The drone self-destructed somewhere over New Jersey. We are trying to determine if the debris has been discovered yet. If it hasn't, it is only a matter of time before it is."

The Man gripped the telephone tighter. "If the target is not dead, then he must have received some kind warning about the attack. If he is dead, we should know by now. Since none of your men have contacted you, we must assume the target not only escaped, but killed them as well. You assured me that would not happen. You told me you were aware of how dangerous the American was and that the strike was worth the risk. You said the American would be eliminated and whatever organization he had destroyed. You said Iran would be condemned for the attack, yet I have seen no such condemnation on American media."

The Man felt his anger growing with each word, so he grew silent. He breathed in deeply and exhaled completely three times in succession to regain his composure. His objectivity would salvage this disaster. His rage would only compound the problem.

Besides, the attack had accomplished much. The Americans

were in disarray. Their vulnerabilities exposed once again. The Russian and Israeli tension could lead to further conflict and, therefore, the possibility for them to further their influence in the region. As the Great Leader himself had once said, "In times of difficulties, we must not lose sight of our achievements."

When the Man was ready, he said, "Your failure has exposed our organization and our cause to great risk, without any hint of reward."

"Quite the contrary," the German said. "We have coaxed the rabbit out of his hole. We have—"

"Stop!" The Man slammed his hand on the table, causing the others in the conference room to flinch, but none dared to look over. "Do not cloud your failure with clever hunting analogies. Despite all your protestations against their corrupt culture, I think you watch too many of their television programs and films. The Americans are neither foolish nor inept. Neither are their Jewish allies. You cannot wipe out a Mossad operation *and* attack a major city and expect their intelligence organization will fail to see they are related. I allowed you to conduct this exercise because you convinced me a rapid blow would cauterize the wounds we have suffered and halt their progress in learning more about us."

"You *allowed me*, comrade? Such words speak to a hierarchical structure, one that has no place in our mission. This sounds more like a CEO speaking to an underling, a most capitalistic sentiment. We are equals in service to the Great Cause, are we not?"

The Man was reminded of the German's intelligence. This gift had always been what separated him from the other thugs they employed to further their cause. "An army without culture is a dull-witted army, and a dull-witted army cannot defeat the enemy." The German had proven essential. Pointing out his failures would only serve to make him defensive and possibly lead to further failure. Now was a time for encouragement, not rebuke.

"Of course, comrade. I am simply frustrated by the poor results of our efforts. Let the next words out of your mouth be plain and full of purpose, lest you cause me to lose my patience again."

"I am sorry I offended you," the German said. "However, although the strikes may not have achieved the results we had intended, all is not lost. I have a plan in place to leak word of Iranian involvement in the attack to members of the American intelligence community. This will support the Iranian connection they will find in the wreckage of the drone. We will feed them our Iranian drone pilot and his colleagues in New York if we need to solidify Iranian culpability. These men cannot lead the Americans to us so we will be insulated from further blame. Tensions between the United States and Iran will grow, worsened further still by tensions between Russia and Israel. These tensions will cause Iran to seek more weapons systems from their Russian patrons, a request from which we will profit quite nicely."

The Man frowned. "I think you worry far more about profit than you should, comrade."

The Man heard the German draw a sharp breath. "I meant a profit in influence, not merely in money, comrade."

But the Man wasn't so sure. "And what of the target? Assuming he is alive and your people are dead, he knows he is a target and will act accordingly. He has proven capable enough when he was ignorant of our existence. His awareness will only make him harder to kill."

"Perhaps, sir." The Man could practically hear the German smile over the phone. "And his awareness will make him even more predictable. "In fact, I'm counting on it. I believe I know where he is going and how he's planning on getting there. A past oversight on his account will punish him tonight. And, if I am right, he will cease to be any further trouble."

O F ALL THE University secrets Hicks learned upon being named Dean, the most surprising revelation was that the organization had its own fleet of jets. They were part of a large corporate fleet it had acquired some years ago. Most of the fleet was leased out on a time-sharing basis to corporations, wealthy investors, celebrities, pop stars, and more than a few reality stars. They had all paid handsomely to use the service, unaware they were not only filling the accounts of the University's Bursar's Office, but its intelligence operation as well. Every jet was outfitted with a full complement of surveillance equipment. Everything they said and did on board had been recorded. Some of the information was embarrassing. Some of it was even criminal. All of it would prove useful, if and when the time came for the University to need them.

Only one jet had been held back from service, the newest in the fleet. A Gulfstream G650 ER. At a price tag of over sixty-seven million dollars, it had barely put a dent in the airline company's revenue. Hicks had been shocked at how much people were willing to pay to fly in luxury, but he was glad it was a price they were willing to pay.

The airplane could fly from Hong Kong to New York nonstop, and could fit up to eighteen people. Hicks first thought the idea of the University having its own plane was ridiculous, but slowly came around to seeing how it could come in handy during some select University missions. Like the one he was performing tonight.

Despite the covert nature of the mission, Hicks had seen to it that the plane had registered a formal flight plan from Teterboro Airport in New Jersey to Schonenfeld Airport in Berlin. The manifest listed two people: Professor Henry Warren and Dr. Samuel Jessup. Sometimes even covert missions had to abide by aviation procedures. Sometimes, they even proved useful.

He switched off his overhead light and reclined his leather seat as he tracked the Gulfstream's progress over the Atlantic via his tablet. It was just as secure as his handheld but the screen was much bigger, allowing him to see the plane's various controls and dials as it approached European airspace. The plane hadn't encountered much turbulence and the entire trip over the Atlantic had been uneventful.

Until an angry red bar began blinking at the top of the screen.

PROXIMITY ALERT. RADAR LOCK. WEAPONS INCOMING.

Hicks had forgotten to lower the volume on the tablet, the claxon waking Scott from his sleep on the couch across from him. "What the fuck is that?"

Hicks turned the tablet so he could see it. Scott blinked his eyes clear and looked at the screen. "Oh shit!"

But the warning hadn't been much of a warning at all. The

missile slammed into the center of the aircraft, exploding on impact, incinerating the plane and its occupants, scattering flaming debris into an indifferent Atlantic Ocean like snowflakes on a New York City street.

Professor Warren and Dr. Jessup were dead.

SCOTT GRABBED THE arms of his seat tighter as the claxon continued to sound from the tablet. "Jesus, Hicks. That could've been us."

Hicks winked as he put the tablet into sleep mode and set it aside. With the plane destroyed, he had nothing to pilot remotely. "That *was* us, Ace. At least as far as our pals in the Vanguard are concerned."

He looked up when the co-pilot came out of the cockpit. "Just wanted to give you an update, sir. We're scheduled to land at Vaclav airport in an hour. No need for your seatbelts until we get closer. Looks like smooth skies from here on out."

"Thanks, Ed. And make sure you and Chris take some time to see the sights in Prague. It's beautiful this time of year."

"We count on it, sir. And we'll be ready if you need us."

Hicks waited until the cockpit door was closed before he said, "I envy those bastards. Prague is a hell of a place. Wish we had time to see it."

But Scott kept looking at Hicks. "How the hell did you know they were going to hit the plane?"

"I didn't, but now I do. Schneider had been able to track that same plane when I took it to Toronto to meet Jabbar. If he knew about it, I thought the Vanguard might know it, too. Now we know more about their abilities and that was the point."

"A seventy-million-dollar aircraft is a pretty goddamned expensive way to find out."

Hicks yawned. "Then we'll just have to make sure the bastards pay for it, won't we?" He closed his eyes. "We're still an hour out. Might as well get some sleep. We're going to need it. It's a long drive to Berlin."

CHAPTER 16

The Hotel Delphi
Berlin, Germany

TALI SADDON DIDN'T particularly like The Hotel Delphi, but no one had asked her opinion. After betraying Hicks to Schneider like she had, she was happy to be anywhere above ground. At least Hicks had understood her boss hadn't given her much of a choice. The fact that she was carrying his child only helped him see reason.

At least the view from the hidden penthouse was nice. The coffee she was drinking made it even better.

The Delphi was not as opulent as some of the other, grander hotels in the city. It didn't boast fancy balustrades or refined architecture, or a magnificent lobby or many of the other interesting details tourist guides might rate among the nicest in Berlin.

But The Hotel Delphi had proven herself sturdy, if not remarkable, in that she had lasted through two world wars, several different forms of government, and a Communist wall that cut her city in two. The Delphi even managed to remain untouched during the Allied bombing of the city, except for some scorch marks and shrapnel damage to its unremarkable façade.

No, the old hotel may not have been an architectural marvel, but its capacity for survival had given it a certain respectability that such unremarkable buildings hardly deserved. She smiled as she remembered a line from an American movie that seemed to fit the old hotel best. "Ugly buildings, politicians, and whores all become respectable if they're around long enough."

Tali Saddon wondered if she would live long enough for the same to apply to her.

She had never considered herself a whore, but like any good operative she never fooled herself about what she had done or how she had done it. And like any good operative, she had used the tools at hand to accomplish her mission. Her tools happened to be a good body and a sexuality certain men found alluring. Men who had secrets. Men whose businesses were illegal in most parts of the world.

Men who had information she had been ordered to acquire to protect her way of life.

The University had a nasty term for her kinds of skills. Snake Charmer. She found it quaint, almost British, and far less insulting than other terms used to describe what she had done. Honey trap. Whore.

She knew that life was behind her now that she was about to bring another life into the world, a life she felt growing inside her more every day. She thought every life was a miracle, but this little one even more so.

She wondered if she would miss her old life. Another sip of coffee convinced her she wouldn't. Another sip after that might change her opinion entirely. Such was the mind of Tali Saddon these days.

She was carrying the child of a man she wasn't sure she loved, but whom she knew loved her. Or as close to love as people like James Hicks could know.

Tali wasn't sure she could ever love anyone, not after all she had done in defense of her beloved Israel and for the University. But the idea that a man like Hicks could love her, not the part she had played or the part he wanted her to play, but *her*, after knowing who she was and what she had been, allowed her to believe she may be lovable after all.

She was grateful to Hicks for that. For that and for sparing her life when he had been so close to killing her. She had betrayed him by putting the Mossad above his beloved University. She had killed Jabbar because she had been ordered to, and didn't feel the slightest bit of remorse about it.

The only time she had felt anything was when she saw the pain and anger in his eyes as he wrestled with the notion of killing her for it. She wasn't sure she loved him, but knew she probably could one day. And a sense of gratitude for sparing her life and helping her to create the life she knew was growing within her now was better than feeling nothing toward him at all.

She placed a hand on her flat stomach. *You'll be better than both of us, little one. I promise.*

She took another sip of coffee as she watched the glowing sunset over Potsdamer Platz, the former wasteland barrier between East and West Berlin, between Communism and

Democracy. It had been a dumping ground for almost forty years while the Cold War had raged, but since the Wall had fallen, the city of Berlin had put considerable effort into making it vital again. Skyscrapers and office buildings and nightclubs and other attractions had been built to bring people to the area. People who had no memory of what had come before except for what they read in history books or saw in documentaries.

She didn't blame them. Memories were overrated and often dangerous.

She would see to it that her baby would live in a different world than she had known.

The Moscow Protocol warning had put her on edge since she had received it, even though she had ignored it. It was the first time in her years with the University that she had received such an order, but her surveillance of the PotzdamerBanc was too important to abandon now. Any one of the hundreds of faces entering and leaving the bank could give them the link they needed to find the Vanguard. This was why she ignored the order and let OMNI continue its scans.

She had already been stationed in the safe house for weeks when the Moscow Protocol alert was issued. She had spent the hours since making preparations to activate the facility. Weapons and ammunition had been catalogued and stored. All security measures were checked and re-checked several times a day.

The Penthouse, as it was known within the University, was a relic from the Cold War that had proven useful in modern times. It was accessible only by a converted service elevator that required a physical key to be turned in a lock to access it from the loading bay. A different key must then be used inside the elevator to gain access to the Penthouse, which was located one floor below the actual penthouse.

The elevator was direct and unable to stop on any other floor. All access points for the elevator had been sealed and covered back when the University had first acquired the property in the late 1940s. The elevator was the only point of entry to the suite. The Hotel Delphi was taller than any of the other buildings in the immediate area, so the threat of snipers was minimal. The roof doors were rigged with a silent alarm. Any breach would alert hotel security immediately. None of the staff members were aware of the Penthouse's existence, nor did it appear on any public plans of the building.

Assault by a missile or a helicopter was possible, of course, but the windows were thick enough to withstand fifty-caliber rounds before steel shutters slammed down to protect the structure. Anything larger than a pigeon hitting the glass would bring about the same result.

It was an impressive layout, Tali thought, though with only one way in or out it was both a fortress and a tomb. But in this life, very little could be assured. Least of all life.

Tali looked at the banks of monitors when she heard the alert that the elevator had been activated. She sneered when she saw Roger Cobb boarding, wheelie bag in tow. She knew Roger had been part of Hicks's ground team in Europe. She knew she would have to deal with the disgusting little man eventually, but had successfully blocked the thought from her mind. *Nothing lasts forever.*

She turned back to the window and sipped her coffee, knowing this may be the last time she would be able to savor the view alone for quite some time. Berlin by twilight, a view her grandparents never would have believed possible. A Jew enjoying a beautiful view of Berlin. A woman, no less. The thought made her smile.

Stalin had killed more of her people than Hitler, but Hitler was more reviled. She often wondered why. Perhaps because the footage of Nazi death camps had been readily available, whereas Stalin committed his atrocities behind an Iron Curtain. People feared what they could see and willfully ignored what they could not. Out of sight, out of the collective mind.

The Jews had always been Europe's punching bag, but no longer, not since 1948 and the establishment of a homeland. The homeland she defended even now.

She had always hated Hitler and Stalin and all the beliefs that had allowed both tyrants to rise to power. She knew why it happened. People would run to any light in the darkness, even when that light led them over a cliff.

She remembered her grandmother's tears as she listened to her grandfather's stories of surviving the camps. She remembered her father's stories as a Nazi hunter with the Mossad and her own mother's tears as she waited for him to come home. She remembered his tales of Munich during the Olympics and Entebbe.

And now they were all gone and she had joined the fight in her own way. A fight of her own time in history. Perhaps against the same people who had hunted her ancestors? Yes, she thought, the Jews had been the leftists' punching bag for far too long. No more. Never again.

She shut her eyes when the elevator pinged, sounding its arrival at the Penthouse. A pleasant sound for such an unpleasant event.

"Well, look who's here," Roger said as he pulled his wheeled bag behind him. "My desert rose. It's been a long time."

"Not long enough to suit me."

"What kind of greeting is that for an old friend?" He looked at her coffee. "That won't help with the morning sickness… assuming you're actually pregnant, of course."

"I *am* pregnant, little man. I know I am. The coffee won't hurt the baby. My mother drank and smoked during all her pregnancies and all her children turned out fine." She decided to beat him to the punchline. "Even me."

"Yes, you did."

She watched his eyes move over her, not in a flattering way or even a leering way, but in a cold, appraising manner she did not like. "Yes, I can see why Hicks fell for you now that I can see you in a certain light. You're not beautiful by any stretch of the imagination, but you certainly have an alluring charm about you. The olive skin, the doe eyes, and high cheekbones give you an exotic quality that fits James's profile perfectly. He's always been a sucker for dusky ladies such as yourself. I should know. After all, I'm the one who wrote his profile in the first place. I wrote your profile, too, come to think of it." A smile. "Would you like to know what it says?"

"I'd like you to go to your room and shut the door until James arrives." She set her cup back in the saucer. She no longer wanted it and was anxious to move on. "The first bedroom off the hallway is mine."

But Roger Cobb didn't budge. "I don't blame you for lying to him. About the baby, I mean. You didn't expect him to find out about your treachery with Schneider about the Jabbar business. He had a gun and probably had that look he gets when he's about to do something horrible. I've seen it several times myself. Hell, I would've even told him I was with child, too, if I thought he would buy it." He winked. "But I'm not as good a saleswoman as you. James and I don't share your history, do we?"

"Enough."

"Enough?" Roger laughed. "Oh, my love, I'm only getting started. I know what you said and why you said it. Unfortunately, you've painted yourself into something of a corner, but luckily for you, you've got Uncle Roger to help you get yourself out of it. Because I know you're lying. It was all too convenient, too clever by half to be true. And when James finds out you're lying, he'll get that look again and I don't know what he'll do."

He bent halfway forward. "Oh, I'm not worried about what he does to you. Not for your sake, anyway. I'm worried about what it'll do to him. Finding out he's not going to be a father will crush him. What he does to you after that will only make things worse."

She stood as straight as she could, facing the fair, little man with the dead, gray eyes. She wasn't accustomed to men speaking to her this way. She usually had some charm over them to distract them. But not Roger Cobb. Not because he was a homosexual, or at least she was pretty sure he was, but because he was clinical. His eyes saw everything, and he was every bit as smart as he thought.

Except he was wrong about her pregnancy. She knew he was. She found herself placing her hands on her belly again, where she knew a life must be growing. She knew it in her soul.

But Roger Cobb had no soul. He said, "When you're ready to come clean and tell him the truth, better come to me first. We'll come up with a way to break it to him the right way and at the right time. For all our sakes."

Her mouth suddenly went dry. She pressed her hands against her stomach. "You're a dense little man, aren't you? I'm pregnant and it's his."

"My offer stands for the next two weeks. Come clean by then and we'll let him down easy. He never has to know you lied. I'm pretty good at keeping secrets, even yours." He took a couple of steps toward her and stopped. "But if you insist on continuing this charade, it will break his heart. I'll be very disappointed, and I get very angry when I'm disappointed. For, you see, I don't have any real family anymore and even fewer friends. James is sacred to me. I owe him a lot. I'd do anything to protect him." His eyes moved over her again. "But you? You mean absolutely nothing to me. If you hurt him, I'll hurt you."

Tali wanted to say something clever, but her mouth had gone dry and she found it difficult to breathe. She'd been in dozens of dangerous situations. Her life had been at risk more times than she could count. She had killed men for worse reasons than insulting her the way Roger Cobb just had.

But there was something about this cold, evil man that wasn't just insulting or even threatening. It was more specific than that. He meant every word he said. All she could manage to say was, "I hate you."

"Then you're in good company." Then, as quickly as his mood had darkened, it brightened. "But let's dispense with the threats for now, shall we?" He placed a hand on the handle of his wheelie bag. "Tell me which room is mine. I need to take a moment to freshen up. I've had *quite* a day."

CHAPTER 17

B Y THE TIME Hicks and Scott arrived at the Penthouse, the rest of the team had already gotten there.

Rahul Patel was sitting on the couch next to Tali. Formerly India's top counter-intelligence operative before falling on hard times, he was now in the employ of the University. He had raven-black hair, sharp features, and a natural tan some people spent a lot of time in tanning beds to get. His Bollywood good looks made him too memorable for clandestine work, but he'd killed more of India's enemies than anyone in their service.

Mike Rivas was the only member of the team who had caught a direct flight to Berlin. Since Mike was in a wheelchair, the fewer changes of airports the better. Besides, Hicks doubted even the Vanguard's most thorough operatives, assuming they were watching, would think a man in a wheelchair had entered the country to fight them. The false German passport would only throw them further off the scent. Before losing the use of his legs on an operation in Guatemala, Mike had been one of the most capable Faculty Members in the University. Hicks wanted him to serve as the group's eyes and ears from the safe house while the rest of them were in the field. Jason could help remotely if needed, but he didn't have tactical experience. Mike did.

Roger and Scott stood by the windows in the back.

It wasn't until he examined all five faces looking back at him that Hicks realized he hadn't given a briefing to this large a group in years. All his orders were usually given one-on-one or via his handheld or computer. The whole scene was surprisingly old-fashioned for such a cutting-edge operation like the University. Hicks supposed technology couldn't replace everything. At least not yet.

Hicks avoided looking at Tali for too long. He would only have one chance to get the group up to speed on everything that had happened. He couldn't afford to allow his thoughts about her or the baby distract him. The others would pick up on it and he'd lose their confidence. He needed them to trust he was as focused as they were.

"A lot has happened in the last two days. Some of you know part of what happened, but now you're going to hear all of it. After that, you'll understand why I called everyone to be here in person instead of spread out over Europe."

"I was going to ask about your reasoning for that," Patel said. His crisp British accent added just enough of an edge to his tone to border on insubordination, without actually crossing it. "If we're under attack, isn't it better to present as many targets as possible rather than bunch ourselves together like ducks on a pond?"

Scott answered before Hicks could. "The Penthouse was a forward base of operations during the entirety of the Cold War. No one knows it's here, not even the oldest members of the hotel staff. You saw the security measures it takes to get in here. If you've got any ideas on how they could be compromised or improved, I'll be glad to hear them."

Hicks thought it sounded closer to a dare than a question. Coming from Scott, it probably was.

"We'll get to that in a second," Hicks said. "For now, we've got more important things to worry about. Roger has been working undercover at Der Underground nightclub here in Berlin. Two days ago, he generated a lead on someone we thought might be affiliated with the Vanguard."

Hicks tapped a button on his handheld and the Penthouse's flat screen monitor came alive with the bald, bespectacled mug shot and arrest form of Tessmer. "This led us to investigate this man, a criminal by the name of Wilhelm or Willus Tessmer. I ran his face and name through every database in the Western hemisphere and came up with nothing except this old arrest record in Bonn. All the links you see on this image are dead. No court documents, no arrest records, nothing before or after this record was made. Someone worked very hard to scrub this man's identity from every database in Europe, possibly elsewhere."

Mike Rivas asked, "What about Asia? Didn't Jabbar's information prove the Vanguard was working out of Russia and China?"

"Since Roger's lead had links to *Spetsnaz*," Hicks went on, "I asked the Mossad's office in Moscow to do some digging. A few hours after I spoke with them, the entire Moscow office went

CROATOAN."

"Ronen Tayeb?" Tali asked. "All of his people gone?"

"Taken out by a hit squad we assume were sent by Tessmer's people." Hicks said the words, but still couldn't believe it. He noticed even Roger looked somber.

But Mike didn't. "Did Moscow police get anything from the crime scene?"

"Only that Mossad people were in the office," Hicks told him.

"Impossible," Tali said. "Ronen wouldn't go down without a fight."

"He didn't," Hicks told her. "Moscow cops estimate there were at least three dead on the street, but the hitters took their dead and dying with them."

He paused to let the gravity of that sink in. A group with the ability and presence of mind to take their dead away showed military precision.

"At almost the same time," Hicks continued, "a University facility on 23rd Street was hit by a Hellfire-type missile delivered by a Valkyrie-type drone. This facility was my main base of operations in New York, so we have to assume I was the target and that it was related to the attack on Tayeb's people in Moscow. Digging around about Tessmer must've set off a lot of alarm bells."

He heard all of them begin to ask questions at once and held up a hand to quiet them. "Our facility was taken out by similar equipment used in Syria and Iran. There's evidence that people working with the Vanguard sold it to them."

Mike asked, "Did you make it out okay?"

"No," Roger sneered. "He died, but is risen." He raised his

hands and looked at the ceiling. "It's a miracle!"

None of the others laughed, least of all Rivas, who kept looking at Hicks. "I mean, were you shot? Were you hurt by falling debris? Did you sprain an ankle or dislocate a shoulder or break some ribs? Did you receive a concussion?" He turned his wheelchair enough to glare at Roger. "Meaning did he receive any damage that might affect his capacity to work in the field. I'm going to need to know these things if I'm helping to coordinate the operation, you fucking sarcastic faggot."

Roger blew him a kiss.

"Enough," Hicks said. He had known assembling a team of alpha-types was a risk, but he needed every single one of them. "Doc Fischer checked me out at the Annex, Mike. I probably had a concussion, but I'm okay. A little sore, but I'm fine." He looked at Scott. "He'll vouch for me if anyone needs him to. All of you know he's not exactly president of my fan club."

Scott remained leaning against the wall, arms folded across his chest. "Doc said he's fine, so he's fine."

Tali ignored the banter. "Two simultaneous attacks on two separate continents. Nothing in Jabbar's information led us to believe the Vanguard was this proficient."

"Or aggressive," Patel added. "Funding a proxy war is one thing, but this is something else entirely."

"Which is why I started Moscow Protocol and shut everything down until we knew what we were dealing with."

Mike turned his wheelchair back toward Hicks. "Has OMNI been compromised?"

"No. It would've helped explain how they tracked me down to the 23rd Street facility, but that's still a mystery. None of you knew where it was located and no one else did either. I plan on

asking those Vanguard bastards personally once we find them."
Hicks looked at Patel. "Rahul has been working with our people
in London to track the group's financial activities. Tell us what
you've found so far."

Rahul said, "We used the Jabbar information to analyze all
the suspected transactions associated with possible Vanguard
companies. They're almost impossible to track. The money
flows from one company to another account in microseconds,
then disappears in government securities or other types of
accounts. Whoever they've got working for them knows how
to game the system, and they know how to cover their tracks
almost instantly."

"You must have a list of people behind the accounts," Tali
said.

"Of course I do," Patel told her. "Hundreds, in fact. I wasn't
trying to stop any of them, just find out how they move their
money. And of all the thousands of transactions and accounts
we were able to track, the majority of the cash deposits came
from right here in Berlin, from PotzdamerBanc."

Scott said, "Then they're headquartered here in Berlin, just
like Jabbar told us."

"Not exactly," Patel said. "By a majority, I don't mean fifty
percent or more. I'm talking about just under ten percent. The
rest were spread out from other accounts in other banks all
over Asia. Vietnam, Laos, Moscow, Hong Kong. In fact, a fair
amount of their cash is deposited in a bank in Africa. Senegal of
all places. So PotzdamerBanc isn't a silver bullet, but rather the
most common thread in the Vanguard fabric."

"How quaint," Roger said. "I believe our desert rose has
been minding things over at the PotzdamerBanc, so let's have

her tell us all about that."

Hicks shook his head. *Fucking Roger.* "Go ahead, Tali."

"I was able to use OMNI to access the bank's security cameras both inside and outside the building," Tali told them. "Don't worry. It's an antiquated system that hasn't been updated in a couple of years. I've been running the face of everyone who enters and leaves the building. Employees, bank executives, customers, everybody. I was hoping the bank might be a Vanguard front, but all the executives came back clean. Well, as clean as you could expect a bank executive to be. Some dodgy associations, but none directly tied to the Vanguard. They seem to use it simply as a deposit point, so I have focused on the most frequent customers. And I was able to come up with two who proved to be very interesting."

She tapped her own handheld and changed the image on the television screen to a split shot of two women. They were stills from the security camera located behind the teller counter. Both women were white, of average height and dress. Neither of them looked like they would be working for arms dealers, Hicks thought, but the best ones never did.

"I matched the time of questionable cash deposits with the bank's security footage and came up with these two. You'll notice both women have similar hair color, cut, and dress. I'm sure this is done to make them as unmemorable as possible. In fact, that's what made them stand out to me."

Tali thumbed her handheld again and the screen changed to a Berlin driver's license record. "The woman on the left is Ilsa Bauer, aged fifty, and lives in Berlin. This is the same identification she used when making the deposit into one of the accounts we've been watching. The accounts belong to innocuous shipping companies. Dummy corporations. She makes several deposits a week, never on the same days or times. Always in uneven amounts and nothing over fifty thousand euros."

"Smart," Patel said. "Keeps the bank examiners and the government from getting curious."

Tali showed the driving record for the other woman. "Same goes for this woman. Monica Lange, also aged fifty, also lives in Berlin. Both sets of identification are perfectly legal, with actual addresses in respectable apartment buildings here in the city. I checked both residences personally."

"And?" Hicks asked.

"Furnished apartments, complete with clothes, a full pantry, and stuff in the refrigerator. Except no one lives there. The lights are on timers."

"Who pays the rent?" Patel asked. "The utilities?"

"They're paid by money orders and mailed in from various mailboxes around town. Never the same postage address twice in a row."

"Congratulations," Roger said. "You've found another set of dead ends."

"Hardly." Tali brought up a map up on the flat screen. Various colored lines ran from the bank to other parts of Berlin. "Once I determined their identities were false, I tracked the women's movements via municipal cameras and old-fashioned footwork. As you can see, they always took different routes away from the bank. They often doubled back on themselves, switching for buses or U-Bahn stations. Not exactly the actions of women with nothing to hide, or secretaries making innocent deposits for their bosses."

Hicks wasn't surprised she'd been that thorough. "Where do they wind up?"

"It took me a while to figure it out, but both wind up exactly at the same location." She enlarged one building on the map. A plain, three-story white building on Mohrenstrasse.

Exactly around the corner from PotzdamerBanc.

Tali even smiled. "An awfully long way to go back to the office right around the corner, wouldn't you say, Roger?"

Roger bowed. "My compliments."

"When was the last time you saw them enter the building?" Hicks asked.

"This afternoon," she said, "right before *he* showed up." She gestured toward Roger and muttered, "*Shvantz.*"

Ever the tactician, Scott asked the question before Hicks could. "What do we know about that building?"

Another tap showed a full image of the building on one side of the screen and a copy of the building's blueprints on the other. "I accessed the city's records and came up with this. It's leased to another dummy corporation, which isn't listed with any of the accounts the ladies deposit cash into. As you can see, the glass on the retail space on the street has been painted white and doesn't appear to be in use. The front door has a sturdy lock, but they use a keypad to open it. Other than that, nothing to tell the world about what it is."

Rivas asked, "Did you get close enough to see them enter the code?"

"I did. It changes every time. Some days it's three digits, some days it's ten. It has never been the same code twice."

Hicks looked at the plans on the right side of the screen. "Looks like loft space. Tells us nothing."

"I've got no idea what's inside," Tali admitted, "and I've never seen anyone else go inside the building."

"Security cameras?" Scott asked.

"Several, which makes me think they have something to hide." Tali zoomed out from the image. "Cameras on top of the roof point straight down. Any attempts to access them have failed. OMNI can't even detect so much as a phone line or a Wi-Fi signal coming from anywhere inside the building, even when I know the women are in there."

Patel asked, "Were you able to get a thermal satellite image of the building?"

Tali toggled back to the same overhead shot. All the buildings were in red. The building they were focused on was black. "As you can see, they've got some kind of shielding in there. Nothing gets in or out of the place."

Hicks kept looking at the image on the screen. Someone was hiding something. "What about when they come out?"

"That's just it," Tali said. "They never come out. They only go in."

Hicks had heard enough. "That means there's another way in. Scott and Rahul, I want you two to look at everything Tali has on the building, then dig some more. Look at other buildings next door and behind it. They probably have some kind of back way in, like our Annex back home."

Patel looked puzzled. "What Annex are you talking about?"

Hicks had forgotten that Patel was a recent hire. He had been handling the University's hunt for the Vanguard in London and didn't know much about the New York Field Office. "Scott will fill you in. After you two do your homework, I want eyes on the place tonight. I want to find that second exit as soon as possible, because we're going to hit that place tomorrow."

"Tomorrow?" Patel said. "That's a little soon, isn't it? I'm all for going in guns blazing, but planning a proper breach takes time. A couple of days of planning at least."

Hicks decided he couldn't avoid telling them the bad news any longer. Except it wasn't bad news. Not really. But nothing in this business was ever black and white. Always gray with a streak of blood-red. "We don't have that kind of time. The attack in New York was explained as just another gas explosion, but that's just for the papers. Everyone from POTUS on down knows it was a strike and they're looking to respond fast. I've been able to buy us seventy-two hours before they get wind of Jabbar's information on the Vanguard."

"How did you do that?" Mike Rivas asked.

"I'll tell you later," Hicks said. "But when they find out who the Vanguard is, every agency in Washington will shake all the trees in the jungle looking for them, which will only drive them deeper underground. We've got to hit these bastards before that happens."

Roger actually raised his hand like a kid in school. "What makes you think they haven't already started doing just that? Surely they knew dropping a missile in the middle of Manhattan wasn't going to go unnoticed."

"Tali just told you why," Hicks said. "They're still making deposits. And they already think I'm dead." He looked at Scott. "Don't they?"

Scott went to Tali's computer. "We're on it. You'll have an action plan by noon tomorrow." He motioned to Tali and Patel. "I'll need your help over here."

Both got off the couch and joined Scott at the console,

leaving Hicks with Mike and Roger. Hicks had hoped for the chance to pull Tali aside, but she hadn't given him the chance. He wondered if that was an accident or by design. He decided it was probably better this way.

"What do you want me to do until then?" Rivas asked. "Make coffee?" He looked down at his dead legs. "I'm not much good for anything else."

"Knock that shit off," Hicks said, sharper than he had intended. "We've got enough people gunning for us without self-pity making it worse. You're going to contact Jason and come up with a protocol as to how you're going to work together once we start kicking in doors tomorrow. OMNI's weaker in this part of the world and you're going to make up the difference. Then you're going to go to bed and get some sleep. You're going to need it and we're going to need you sharp."

Rivas turned his chair and began wheeling it toward the rooms. "Sometimes I wish you'd let me die in that helicopter."

"That makes one of us," Hicks said. "Now get some rest."

TWO HOURS LATER, Hicks was sitting alone on the couch in the living room with his eyes closed, attempting to reassemble the Carousel of Concern in his mind while he willed the dull ache behind his eyes to go away. He wondered if it was from the concussion, but decided he didn't care. He had enough to worry about.

Scott, Tali, and Patel were already on the street, doing reconnaissance on the building in question. Mike Rivas was asleep and Roger was doing, well, whatever Roger did behind closed doors. Probably something Hicks didn't want to know.

He decided not to think about it.

He watched Tali as she worked with the others. She lived for this kind of work, just like him. He had hoped to talk to her, to know how she was doing. He wanted to know how the baby was doing, too. She wasn't showing yet, and he doubted she would for some time.

But he shelved that nonsense. There would be plenty of time for sentimentality after the raid tomorrow. For now, nothing was more important than the mission. They both understood that, but at least one of them didn't like it. Hicks knew that one person was him, not Tali.

He had intentionally left his handheld back in his room. It was probably buzzing away with more updates from Jason and questions from Sarah. He had hidden the phone Demerest had given off-site. He knew Demerest probably had a tracking device on the damned thing. No sense in showing all his cards to the company man all at once. The Penthouse may turn out to be the only advantage the University had.

He knew he should be giving them both updates or at least touch base with them, but he didn't. Not until he organized his thoughts first.

The Carousel of Concern was burned and wobbly, creaking as it began to make its slow circuit in his mind once again.

Tali and the baby. The Vanguard. Demerest. Every intelligence agency in Washington's alphabet soup. The CIA. The seventy-two-hour deadline. The University. Tessmer. The building around the corner.

One item gleamed more than the rest. *Tomorrow.* What would tomorrow bring?

He didn't know the answers to any of those questions, but

the building around the corner would be the best place to start. He'd let Sarah and Demerest know what they were doing once Scott and the others came up with a plan. For now, he was the least important member of the team. He had brought these people to Berlin because they were damned good at what they did. All he could do was stay out of their way while they did it.

He smelled the aroma of strong coffee before he heard someone clear his throat.

"For the record," Roger said, "I would like to submit a formal complaint about the prohibition of alcohol on the premises. We should be able to ruminate our troubles over a bottle of rich, aged scotch."

Hicks reluctantly opened his eyes, but gladly took the cup of coffee Roger offered him. "This more of that cat shit coffee of yours?"

"Civet coffee, you uncultured swine," Roger corrected as he sat next to him. "And no, it's not. Forgot to pack it when I left the club. This is some of the stuff our desert rose stocked the place with. Pretty good, actually, but don't tell her I said that. She's already shown me up several times today. No sense in making her head bigger than it already is."

He sipped the coffee and felt his headache dull a bit. "Your secret is safe with me."

"You didn't answer my question. Why no booze? Damned place is as barren as a parson's pantry."

"Patel's on the wagon, remember? I don't want him being more tempted than he already is. I need him calm, not white-knuckling it just because you want to be stylish. You need a drink, go to the bar downstairs."

Roger spoke over the lip of his cup. "My, aren't we touchy

this evening."

"Sorry," Hicks said, even though he wasn't. "Having a fucking missile dropped on my head tends to put me in a bad mood."

"You're entitled." Roger sipped his coffee before setting it on the table. "Though I must admit you've assembled quite the menagerie here in old Berlin. The American thug. The drunken Indian. The embittered, crippled Mexican. Our dangerous desert rose. Christ, all we need is the plucky gay friend and we'd have a fucking sitcom on our hands."

"I figured you had that part covered," Hicks said.

"I'm not gay," Roger said. "I refer to myself as sexually complicated."

The notion of exploring the maze of Roger Cobb's complex sexuality gave new life to his headache. They could spend a week talking about it and get nowhere, so Hicks decided to drop it. "Whatever you call yourself, Mike's not Mexican. He was born in New York and his people are from Guatemala. They hate Mexicans. You'll want to remember that next time you're talking to him."

"What's he going to do, run over my foot with his wheelchair?"

"Might put a bullet in your eye from across the room. Or let someone do it for him on the street when the shit hits the fan. He was a hell of a field man in his day and deserves your respect. I'm disappointed you forgot that."

"I didn't forget." Roger looked down at his coffee. "Just playing that pithy character we were talking about, I suppose."

Another sip of coffee gave Hicks a new thought. "What the hell happened to you today, anyway? You disappeared for a while. You're only cruel when you've killed someone." Hicks started putting things together and set his mug on the table. "What did you do?"

Roger sipped his coffee before he told him. "Someone sent a five-man hit team for me at the club."

Hicks felt his temper spike. "Damn it, Roger. Why the hell didn't you tell me this before?"

"And interrupt the Dean while he's giving his lecture on the Vanguard?" Roger sucked his teeth. "Perish the thought. Besides, there's nothing to be done about it. They're all dead and in a dumpster awaiting proper disposal. None of them had anything of importance on them except the leader, who had a cell phone."

Roger held up a hand to stop Hicks's questions before he voiced them. "Yes, I have it and, yes, I stripped it down before I brought it here so I couldn't be tracked. We can have Mike look it over tomorrow before we begin our great assault against the Vanguard. Had to leave Zeb an extra ten grand, though. Cleaned up the place as best I could, but the five corpses in his dumpster will be an inconvenience."

His headache began to go away. "Tell me you scanned the sons of bitches before you ditched them."

"Their faces and fingerprints have already been run through OMNI. The report was sent to you and Jason right after it happened. As you were in transit, I'm not surprised you missed it. Nothing came up on any of them. Just another group of ghosts. No sign of Boris or whatever his name was, along with the ex-cop I had tailing him. Both are probably dead by now, but I'll bet the ex-cop told them all about me before they killed him. I'm sure that's how they found me. Did him a favor by killing him, really. Poor drunken bastard."

Hicks checked his watch. Nine thirty. Der Underground was already open, so checking the bodies in the dumpster would be foolish. "Give me your handheld. I want to see them for myself."

Roger took the device from his pocket and showed him the photos of the dead men. "The first one's a group shot, but if you keep thumbing through, you'll see each man clearly. The leader's at the end. I took his M4 from him and finished off his playmates in a stairwell. It's pockmarked with bullet holes but I got rid of most of the blood, not that any of the club patrons will notice or care."

Hicks swiped through the pictures, ignoring the gore. The others on the team might be surprised that Roger had been able to kill so efficiently, but not Hicks. Despite his flamboyant nature, he was one of the deadliest people Hicks had ever met.

And it wasn't as though Hicks hadn't been holding something back from Roger, too. "They took out our jet this afternoon. Over the Atlantic, off the coast of England."

It was Roger's turn to look surprised. "With what? How?"

"No idea, not that it matters. Probably with one of their drones. We filed a flight plan and full manifest to see if they'd strike, and they did. That's why we took one of the other jets and flew to Prague and drove from there."

"Which one? Not the new Gulfstream, I hope."

Hicks took his coffee from the table. "Yep. That's the one."

"That was my favorite. The bathroom was beautiful." Roger sat further back on the couch. "These bastards have some heavy ordinance, James. Are you sure hitting that building tomorrow is a good idea?"

Hicks looked down at the image of the hit team's leader. He didn't know how many of them were in Berlin, but they were already down five men. "Tomorrow, we'll find out for sure."

CHAPTER 18

SOMEWHERE

"THE PLANE WENT down off the coast of England in international waters," the German told him. "Just as I promised. The plane has been reported late. A preliminary search of the area has shown no survivors. We should consider this mission accomplished, comrade. The boil has been lanced."

But the Man did not share his colleague's optimism. "Yet I haven't seen any reports of a missing plane."

"Our sources are well placed and knowledgeable, my friend. Our enemy has suffered a great loss, much to our own advantage."

"We have lost men, too." The Man reminded himself to hold on to his temper. His friend had proven quite sensitive in their previous conversation. "I have learned of your efforts at the nightclub in Berlin."

The German paused for a moment. "Your resources are as

impressive as ever, comrade."

"I understand those men have gone missing as well. Perhaps it was unwise to expose us in such an obvious manner at such a critical time, especially without consulting me first. Perhaps you should have followed the man to see where he went rather than kill him."

"We don't care where he was going," the German said, "and we couldn't risk the possibility of losing him. We wanted to grab him and question him. We didn't anticipate losing an entire team in the process. Obviously, this man seems to be more skilled than we thought. Perhaps James Hicks was only the tip of the iceberg."

The Man had never underestimated James Hicks or any of the people in his organization, however big or small it might be. He knew Hicks had not been working for the Americans or the British or any other Western power. If he had, the Vanguard's sources would have been aware of his existence long ago. But he decided arguing with his comrade would serve no purpose other than to agitate him further, and there were other matters that required attention.

The Man asked, "Have your people detected threats in our other spheres of influence? What about a response from the Americans? Are they rattling their sabers behind closed doors?"

"Not yet." The Man could hear the smirk in his comrade's voice. "You know the Americans. They will hold years of hearings and investigations before they decide to act. By then, it will be too late."

Once again, his comrade underestimated his opponent while having too much faith in his own skill.

He chose his words very carefully. "I would appreciate

receiving reports on the American efforts twice a day. Their politicians may want to act deliberately, but their CIA and military will not. Just because we have neutralized the threat from Hicks is no reason for us to be imprudent. The forest has many wolves lurking within it."

The German said, "The man from the club is still on the loose. Perhaps we should lessen our imprint in Berlin."

"No. To do so would only risk exposure even more. Remain vigilant, and if this man from the club surfaces, contact me immediately, even if it is before your scheduled report."

The Man hung up the phone and sat back in his chair. He may have been curt with him, but men like him appreciated deliberate conversation.

The Man's son appeared at the entrance of his tent, bearing a tray with a pot of tea and two cups. "May I join you, Father?"

The Man motioned to the chair beside his table and his son entered. "Is everything okay, Father? You seem troubled."

He did not acknowledge this. It was not a son's place to question the actions of his father. But the slight was minor and unintended, so he allowed it to pass. Perhaps because he was, indeed, troubled. The Vanguard had launched an attack on a major city and the Americans were still carrying on with the ridiculous story about a gas explosion. The German may have believed the Americans to be fools, but the Man did not have the luxury of such beliefs.

The Americans were planning something. The question was what and when. The Vanguard had successfully eluded them for decades, using their own willful complacency in the years following the Cold War to advance his own beliefs. Beliefs out of fashion, but not without purpose. A battle fought on many fronts, not all of them seen.

No, the Americans may strike out rashly and blindly when they did, but they would strike, possibly against Iran or Syria. They were always safe targets for American ire.

The Man had no doubt they would strike, and when they did, he would be ready.

He remembered his son was there when he felt the young man looking at him. Concerned. He had too much of his mother about him and not enough of his father. Thankfully, he had many other sons. But this was a concern for another day. "Pour the tea."

CHAPTER 19

Berlin

"I THOUGHT YOU WERE dead," Demerest said.

Hicks had reassembled the phone and was on his way to the rally point Scott had picked out. "Good. If you think so, then our playmates think so, too."

"Sarah was worried sick when she heard about the plane. Jason told her your plan, but she didn't believe it. I think sacrificing the flight crew was a damned selfish thing to do."

"I didn't sacrifice anyone." Hicks kept his voice low as he threaded his way through the crowded street. He knew it was an encrypted line and he was speaking in English on a Berlin street, but he still didn't like giving details over a non-OMNI line. "The plane was programmed to take off and land on its own. No one was on board."

"You've got an answer for everything, don't you, son?"

"If I did, I wouldn't be here."

"And how's that working out for you?"

"Pretty well. Do you want to know details or do you still want plausible deniability?"

"I never used those words."

"You didn't have to."

Demerest didn't argue. "Will whatever you're planning help us get that proof we discussed?"

"I don't know for sure," Hicks admitted, "but there's a good chance it will. I may need your help to pull it off."

"What kind of help?"

Hicks was glad he was still on board with the program. "What kind of pull do you have with the German authorities?"

"All the pull I need within reason and with enough notice. Why?"

"Because things are liable to get dicey over the next couple of hours, and I might need some cover from some people in high places."

"Are you speaking metaphorically or literally?"

"Maybe both," Hicks allowed, "but metaphorically for now. We've got a solid lock on where some of our friends are located. I take it you can track this phone you gave me?"

"My assistant and I are the only ones who can, but we haven't yet. Do you want me to track it now?"

Hicks wasn't sure he believed him, but said, "I'll keep it on so you'll know where I am. I need you to make sure I have a wide berth in case things get out of hand. After all I've been through, I don't want to get shot by some cop thinking he's doing the right thing."

"I'll make some calls."

"Not now," Hicks warned. "Only if I call you. I don't want to risk these bastards getting wind of this before the show starts."

"I know, son. This isn't my first rodeo."

Hicks laughed. "Mine either. I'll call you when I know more."

He killed the connection and had to remember to not turn the phone off before he tucked it into his pocket. The feel of the Ruger under his left arm made him feel secure.

The M4 Scott had in his bag would make him feel even better.

H E FOUND SCOTT at a Starbucks located around the corner from where they'd go in. He was sitting alone at a table in the center of the store. The place was crowded, mostly by tourists looking for a taste of home and young people at tables lost in whatever they were looking at on their laptop screens.

A few customers kept eyeing the rare real estate of an empty chair at Scott's table, but no one dared asked if they could borrow it, much less join him. He didn't look like the kind of man who enjoyed company.

Hicks sat across from him and Scott pushed a large coffee his way. "Hope you take it black because that's what I got you. You don't strike me as the chai soy latte type."

He remembered that was Jason's choice, with a dash of vanilla. He used to have to bring it to him whenever they had one of their unavoidable briefings back when Hicks was the head of the University's New York Office and Jason his link to the Dean. Now, the roles were reversed and it was Hicks who gave Jason orders.

Any other time, he might have taken comfort in that and in

the memory, but he had other things on his mind. "Everyone in position?"

"No. I told them to go to the zoo. Figured they could blow off some steam before the show starts."

Hicks took the lid off the coffee and blew away steam of a different nature. Scott was in charge of the mission, so he had given him more latitude than normal. "Serves me right for asking an obvious question."

"They'll join us at the place right before we're set to go in," Scott said. "I staggered the times so we don't go in as a group and raise suspicion. Tali doesn't like the idea of sitting this one out in the van, but I told her she doesn't have a choice." He looked at Hicks over his cup before he drank. "Your girl's a feisty one."

"Yeah." Hicks drank his coffee. "She's only a contingency anyway. We might not need to use her, but she knows the city better than any of us so she's the best choice behind the wheel."

"I was stationed here for six years, remember?"

"But you'll be busy with other things, remember?"

"Amen to that. Anything will be better than all this talking and waiting. Mike said he's working on putting the street cameras on a continuous loop. It won't fool anyone after the fact, but it'll keep the cops from identifying us."

"Assuming we're still around to care about being identified."

"We will," Scott said. "We know what's coming. Those assholes in there don't. That will make all the difference. Besides, I've seen you in action and you're not too bad."

Hicks knew that was as close to a compliment as he was likely to get from Scott. He didn't particularly like Scott, but he never doubted the man's ability to plan a raid. In all his years with the Varsity Squad in New York, none of his ops had ever gone sideways. Hicks hoped today wouldn't be an exception.

He knew Scott had done his homework. He had spent the entire previous night and that morning working out every detail he could imagine, given the tight time frame. He had devised a sound plan of attack. The rest of the team had agreed with it. To question his confidence wouldn't accomplish anything.

Scott checked his watch and stood up. "Time to go. Bring your coffee with you. It'll help us blend in on our way there."

Hicks stood up and followed him out the door, taking a healthy gulp of coffee as he did so. It might be the last taste of home he'd have for a while. Maybe forever.

CHAPTER
20

THE SETUP OF the Vanguard facility wasn't similar to the Annex back in New York. It was exactly like it. If Hicks didn't know any better, he would have thought the Vanguard had copied his plans. But Hicks knew better. If they had been aware of the Annex, they would've hit that, too.

The building behind the Vanguard facility was a garage. From half a block away Hicks saw several cars going in and out, mindful of traffic, and not in any particular hurry.

"It's a nice setup they've got there," Scott said as they approached the place. "Smart, too. Cars going in and out all hours of the day and night. Perfect cover. The entrance we're looking for is on the top level. It's a common stairway anyone can use to get back down to the street. There's a door off to the left that looks like it accesses the roof, which it does. But there's another that looks like a utility closet. Even reads that way on the plans. Except that's our way in to the Holy of Holies."

"Maybe it really is just a utility closet."

"Pretty solid door for a utility closet, especially for a garage. It lines up perfectly with our building behind it. I scanned the rest of the place for an entry point and that door is the only one that makes sense."

"And if it turns out to be a closet?"

"Then I'll go to bed without supper. But trust me, that's the way in."

Hicks let it go. "Cameras?"

"Standard stuff. An attendant on the ground level who doesn't seem to be in on the joke. We ran him through OMNI and he came up clean. Born in Bermuda, believe it or not. Don't know how the hell he wound up here, but here he is. Has a wife and a couple of kids. Been here seven years and doesn't seem to care about anything except soccer. He's harmless. The night guy is a pimple-faced kid from the sticks. He came up clean, too."

Hicks wrote off the details to pre-game nervous talk on Scott's account. He took some comfort knowing even a man like Scott could get nervous before the ball went up.

Hicks ditched his coffee in a trash barrel on the corner before they crossed the street and entered the garage. He pulled his wireless earpiece from his pocket and slipped it into his ear.

"Home base, do you copy?"

Mike's voice came in loud and clear. "I've got you. You were the last one to sync up, so now I've got all four of you. Since I can't read what's in the building, we may lose contact once you breach. But your handhelds should remain connected locally so you should be able to communicate with each other at least."

It wasn't an ideal situation, but there wasn't much he could do about it. "See you on the other side, Ace."

They walked down the ramp then meandered up the driveway to the higher floors of the structure. They looked like two men looking for their car.

When they reached the top level, Hicks eyed all the cars, looking for anyone who might be serving as a lookout for the people in the facility. He didn't spot anything out of the ordinary until he saw the trunk of a Volkswagen Passat pop open next to the stairway entrance.

Roger stepped out from behind the wheel. Patel came out from the passenger side. Both had Beretta ARX100 semi-automatic rifles at their sides. Without breaking stride Scott reached into the trunk, removed a Mossberg 590A1 tactical shotgun, and held it against his leg as he approached the stairway door. Patel fell in behind him, with Roger covering the rear.

Hicks took the only remaining gun in the trunk and shut the lid. The Colt M4 might not have been the most powerful rifle on the market, but it was what he was used to. And in the moments ahead, familiarity and comfort might be all the edge he needed.

Scott went through the stairway door first, Patel second, followed by Hicks. Roger delayed a second before coming inside and shutting the door behind him. They followed Scott up the stairs and Hicks saw the doorway leading to the roof. Scott grabbed the knob of the door to his left and turned it.

Locked.

On cue, Roger stepped around them and wedged a small crowbar between the door and the jamb. The frame buckled as it bent in, separating it from the lock assembly. Hicks tensed for the sound of an alarm, but nothing happened.

Roger pulled the door open and stayed there while Scott ducked inside. Rahul went behind him. Hicks followed and Roger brought up the rear.

It wasn't a closet.

They found themselves in a narrow brick hallway, a single dim bulb in the ceiling their only light. Scott quickened his pace now, pausing only at the corner. He threw up his left fist, signaling the others to stop.

He ducked his head around the corner and quickly pulled it back. He whispered, "Same kind of door. Opens toward us. Key card entry. Definitely alarmed. Cover your ears, ladies. It's about to get awfully loud in here."

Scott rounded the corner and fired one shot at the lock, the sound booming in the narrow hallway. He fired two more shots, one at each of the door's hinges, before moving toward the door. The door fell forward into the hallway. Scott stepped on it as he moved inside. Patel followed, then Hicks, with Roger covering their backs.

Hicks knew they were in the main building now.

His stomach ran cold.

The entire top floor of the building was completely empty. No walls, no desks, no chairs, nothing to block their line of sight. Rows of harsh florescent light almost hurt the eyes, especially because the windows had been painted over.

But at least there was no place for anyone to hide. Not even ductwork in the ceiling. No cameras or sensors Hicks could see, either.

The team used the empty space to their advantage, fanning out into a staggered formation. Four individual targets were harder to hit than one group. As they moved, Hicks listened for sounds of an alarm. Flashing lights alerting the occupants to their presence. But all he heard was the hum of the lights from above as the four of them moved toward a door in the far left-hand corner.

One floor down, two more to go.

They all stopped when Scott stopped several feet to the side of the door, then knelt when Scott knelt. He was well in front of the rest of the team, too far away and too quiet for them to hear what he was saying without their earpieces.

"Steel door," Scott said. "Reinforced and key card lock. Small window and thick glass center high."

Hicks gripped his M4 tighter, waiting for whatever might happen next.

A face appeared in the door window. A pale, unfamiliar face that appeared for about a second. Just long enough to see them.

And long enough for Scott to fire at it.

"THEY'RE INSIDE THE building," Mike said through Tali's earpiece. "I've lost contact."

"That was to be expected," Tali said from the doorway of a building across the street from the van. "All is quiet in front of the building. No signs of activity yet."

"I've got eyes on you from the satellite," he said. "I'll be able to watch for another thirty minutes, maximum, before I have to hack another. And I still don't understand why you're not in the van."

"Street cops have a wise saying," she told him. "The car is a coffin. When the shooting starts, the first thing they do is get out of the vehicle. Same logic applies here."

"It's armored," he reminded her.

"It limits my range of motion," she said, "and the only spot I could find was past the building. I would've had to check my mirrors all the time. This way, I can see what's going on before it happens."

She remained perfectly still when she saw the front door of the building open, then close again.

She was careful not to move, looking down at her handheld like any other young woman checking her phone. The .45 was on her right hip if she needed it.

"Did the door just open?" Rivas said in her ear.

"Yes," she said, looking down at her blank screen. "Something is wrong."

THE GLASS IN the door window webbed, but didn't shatter. Scott racked another round and fired again, this time shattering the glass inward.

So much for the element of surprise.

"On my left, now!" Scott said as he bolted for the wall.

The three men hit the wall also. Hicks knew this would cut down on the firing angle from the shattered window. A gunman would have to stick his weapon all the way outside to hit them, rendering a steel door useless.

Scott shot at both hinges, denting them but not obliterating them.

"Patel, Primasheet. On me."

Hicks brought up his M4 to cover the two men as they raced toward the door. Scott pulled a grenade from inside his jacket and dunked it through the shattered window in the door. Two seconds later, a blast sent a shudder through the building. The door rattled but held.

Patel placed a long, thin strip that looked like contact paper just above the doorknob. But Hicks knew it wasn't contact paper. It was a breaching explosive as powerful as C4. A thin wire ran from the bottom of it, trailing behind them as he and Scott quickly backed away along the wall.

"Down, down, down," Scott said.

Hicks and Roger looked away, just as a powerful blast ripped through the loft from the door.

Scott moved through the smoke and kicked the buckled door further open. Patel moved right behind him. Hicks and Roger followed.

Scott moved past the dead man at the bottom of the top landing. Patel paused to check the man as Hicks and Roger continued downward.

Scott stopped at the second landing where there was another steel door like the one they'd just destroyed.

Hicks covered the stairs leading up from the lower floors. "Hope you brought a lot of Primasheet."

"Not necessary," Patel said as he came down the stairs. "Our friend up there had a key card."

He took up position next to the card reader at the left of the door. He looked at Scott. "You ready?"

Scott pulled another grenade from his vest. "Go."

Patel tapped the card. The door opened. And Scott threw the grenade inside.

Hicks heard yelling in the two seconds before the grenade exploded.

Scott shouldered the door all the way open and moved

inside. Patel moved in behind him and went left, rifle ready. Hicks moved in and cut right. Roger backed in, covering the stairway.

Hicks saw this floor, too, was a loft. Quick glance: folding tables, chairs, laptops. No walls, no office.

Scott's grenade had landed in the middle of the room, where three people were on their stomachs. Two women and a man, bloodied from the blast.

The women didn't move, but the man started crawling away. His hands were empty. Hicks fired a low burst and took out the man's legs.

Hicks scrambled toward the man, keeping an eye out for other targets. Scott was ranging ahead of him, sweeping the room with the Mossberg.

Hicks reached the wounded man and quickly ran a hand over his torso. No weapon, but an empty holster under his left arm. Hicks saw what the man had been crawling toward, a nine millimeter five feet away that had been blown free in the explosion. Hicks kicked the gun as hard as he could, sending it skidding yards away.

He pressed the M4's muzzle into the wounded man's neck. "Who else is here?" he said in German.

"Nobody!" screamed the man. "Just us. We're only accountants!"

In his earpiece, Hicks heard Roger say, "We've got company!"

And then the gunfire started.

TALI AND THE rest of the people on the street flinched when they heard the muffled explosion from within the building.

"Even I heard that," Mike said in her ear.

"Breaching explosive." Tali moved calmly but quickly toward the van. Rivas was right, it was armor-plated and would offer her the best cover if people came out of the building. She slid open the panel door and removed the AK-47 from the bay floor. An old weapon, but reliable. One she had grown up using.

She reached into her shirt and pulled out a fake Berlin police badge on a chain around her neck. Pedestrians backed away as she slid the door closed. "Polizei!" she yelled in German. "Move away, now."

She took up a position at the back of the van. She saw the front door of the building open and two men scramble into the street.

She raised her weapon and opened fire, strafing both men in the chest. They hit the wall, then slumped to the sidewalk. No blood. Kevlar. *Fuck.*

She saw movement from the doorway and ducked back behind the van just as bullets began to pepper the vehicle. "Call Jason," she told Rivas. "The shit has hit the fan."

ROGER HIT THE wall to the left of the door as he paused to reload.

Patel moved around him, firing blind into the stairwell.

"Fire in the hole!" Scott yelled as he tossed a grenade through the doorway.

Roger and Patel dropped back just before the explosion ripped through the stairwell.

Hicks brought the butt of his rifle down on the back of the wounded man's head. "Yeah. Just the three of you."

He ran toward the door as Scott fired two more blasts into the stairway. "Hicks, you lead."

Hicks burst through the doorway and went down the stairs. Roger had slapped in a new magazine and fell in behind him. Patel followed. Scott fed more shells into the Mossberg and brought up the rear.

Hicks found what was left of the four men in the stairwell. He had to step on them in order to make it down the stairs. He swung his rifle to the left.

Ground floor. No stairs to a basement. Another steel door ajar.

Hicks took up position to the right of the door. Gunfire erupted, but not aimed at him. Someone was shooting outside from the front door.

Someone was shooting at Tali.

Hicks didn't check the room. He didn't wait for cover. He put a shoulder into the door and burst through.

TALI WAITED FOR the doorway gunman to reload before she dropped to the sidewalk, rifle butt to her shoulder, landing in a perfect firing position. Just as she'd been trained. The gunman had been aiming high. She'd be shooting low.

One of the men on the street had begun moving back toward the safety of the building. He fired blindly in her direction. Another nine millimeter. The bullets sailed wide over the van.

Tali fired once. The round pierced the man's temple. This time there was blood. No Kevlar there.

Tali smiled. One down. Two left.

Another burst of automatic fire erupted from the doorway.

Again, the gunman fired high, hitting the van well above the wheel well.

Tali fired from the sidewalk, striking the door and doorframe. The glass scarred, but didn't break. Bulletproof glass. But it was enough to send the gunman back inside.

Then she heard shouting. Another blast from the gunman, this time firing at something inside the building. *James.*

She thought about moving for a fraction of a second, but no longer. She had a good field of fire. The second man she wounded was still on the street in front of the building, somewhere behind a parked car. Wounded, hurt, but still very much alive and probably armed.

James could take care of himself. He always had.

More shouts and more shots fired within the building.

Then nothing.

Just the sounds of people on the sidewalk, scrambling away from the scene; a few intrepid souls had stayed to film it all on their cell phones. She didn't worry about them. OMNI would scrub the images from the internet later.

She kept her aim on the building.

And in her ear, she heard a familiar voice.

"First floor clear," Hicks said. They could communicate now that he was near the open door. "Tali, what about the street?"

"One down, one wounded. Target is off to your left by maybe twenty feet. Kevlar. Probably armed."

"You got eyes on him?"

"Negative. Car's blocking my view."

"Move around to see if you can get eyes on him."

Tali hadn't been expecting that. She thought he'd try to handle it himself, given her condition. Maybe there was more to the man she loved after all?

She got to her feet and moved back along the sidewalk to the front of the van then made her way across the street, AK aimed at the spot where she believed the man had fallen.

She popped out between two parked cars. A tough shot for a wounded man with a handgun to make at this distance, but not for her Kalashnikov.

But the sidewalk was empty. The man had gotten away.

She lowered her rifle. "Target's gone. James. He must've crawled away during the battle."

Hicks didn't miss a beat. "Rivas, you got him on camera?"

It took a few seconds for him to respond. "Got him. White male, approximately six feet tall in a black suit, limping due east from your location. About a block away."

"Let me go," Tali said as she moved toward the building. "I know what he looks like."

"And he knows what you look like. No way. Mike, send the feed to Patel's phone. He'll track him down on foot. Tali, get in here. We've got a lot of work to do."

Patel ran past her as she stepped inside, smoothing down his hair and zipping up his jacket as he ran. He looked like any other of the city's young men dashing for a bus or to make his U-Bahn train. If she hadn't seen him exit the building, she never would have guessed he'd just been in a firefight.

But then again, that was what made him good at what he did.

Tali stepped inside and Hicks pulled the door closed behind her.

CHAPTER
21

Washington, D.C.

DEMEREST HAD JUST gotten an alert from the Agency's Germany desk when his phone began to buzz. He recognized the number. It was Hicks.

He toggled to his computer's tracking program on the phone he'd given Hicks. "Talk to me, son."

"We hit a Vanguard building here on Mohrenstrasse," Hicks said. "Things got public. I'm going to need someone to keep people away until we have a chance to see what we've got here. Trace my location, but don't come to this address. I'm calling you from the garage behind the building we hit. They've got some kind of jamming frequency in the building, so I had to step outside to call you."

Shit. "Any civilians killed?"

"No, but one target got away. One of my men is after him on foot."

"Okay," Demerest said. "Okay, that's good. That's very good. That makes it clean."

"Thanks. I'm glad you approve."

Demerest didn't appreciate the sarcasm. "It makes it easier to keep it quiet, goddamn it. I've already alerted my contacts at the Federal Intelligence Service that something was going down. They'll keep a lid on things and the cops at bay. One second."

Demerest lowered the phone and looked at Williamson. "Call Ernst. Tell him I need that favor over on Mohrenstrasse." He showed him the map on his desktop, which had the exact address. "He'll know what to do. Tell him I'll be in touch as soon as I can with more details."

Williamson went back to his desk and Demerest got back on the phone. "It's being taken care of as we speak. Are your people okay? Did you find the evidence we need?"

"Everyone made it through. They're checking the place now. Looks like we've got some satellite office here. Lots of computer equipment upstairs. We came in the back way, so I think we stopped them before they could crash the hard drives, but I'm not sure. There's some kind of device rigged to the front door. Looks like it runs upstairs. Might be some kind of crash alarm if the front door was breached."

"Then I'm glad you boys went in the back way," Demerest said. He had dozens of questions about what they had found, what they were seeing, and who had been inside the place. He'd been a field man too long to not be excited about finding a cache of enemy information. But he kept his enthusiasm in check. "Any of them left alive other than the runner?"

"One, I think. I'm on my way up there now to check. We'll take a look at the hard drives, too, and let you know what we find."

"How long will you need the place for?"

"Three hours," Hicks said. "Maybe less. I'll call back when I know more."

"Good. That's doable. Won't raise too much suspicion with the locals. Get as much as you can and fry the rest. I want to know what we're looking at before our German colleagues do. Safer all around that way."

"You read my mind."

"I can help your man with the runner," Demerest said. "Give me his position and—"

"No way," Hicks said. "My man can handle it. If we need you, we'll be in touch. I'll keep you posted."

Demerest couldn't blame him for being cautious. He'd been the same way in the field. In many ways, he still was. "Still don't trust me, do you, son?"

"No more than you really trust me. I'll be in touch. Hicks out."

The connection died, leaving Demerest staring at his phone. He couldn't remember the last time someone had hung up on him. No one had ever dared.

He looked up when Williamson reappeared in his doorway. "Sir, I've got the chief of staff's office on line one for you. I think this might be the call we've been waiting for."

Demerest smiled. His assistant had a creative grasp of the word *we*. "Put him through. And tell Ernst I might be a little longer than expected."

CHAPTER 22

Berlin

Patel ignored the questions people asked him at the corner as he ran past them. They'd all seen him come out of the building. He didn't blame them for being curious. Gunfire. Explosions. A brown-skinned man emerging from the chaos at a run. Was he a terrorist? Was this more Islamic trouble?

As curious as they may have been, no one tried to stop him. And when he was a block away, no one even noticed him. He blended back into the bustling human traffic moving to and fro along the busy streets of Berlin.

He checked his handheld constantly for the runner's location on his map. Mike spoke into his ear. "Hicks and the others are back inside, so their comms are blocked until they leave. It's just you and me now."

"How comforting," Patel said as he reached the corner and moved left, following the trail of the wounded man. "How accurate is this map?"

"As accurate as the cameras I can hack," Mike responded. "He's half a block away from you now. Standing still in front of a stationery store on your side of the street. Looks like he's cradling his ribs, maybe trying to get his wind back."

"Duly noted." He was less than half a block away from the man's position on the map. He looked for him through the crowds of people, but no joy. He spotted a sign jutting out above the crowd. Paper-La-Papp. "He still alone?"

"Yes, but he's got something in his hand. No one around him is reacting, so I don't think it's a gun." A few more clicks in his earpiece, then, "I zoomed in. It's definitely not a gun. It's a phone. If you get close enough with your handheld, OMNI can back-trace the call."

If he got close enough, Patel intended to do more than that.

Rivas seemed to read his mind. "Just don't kill him. I know Hicks will want Roger to question him."

"That's up to him, now, isn't it?"

Patel cut to the right side of the sidewalk and spotted his mark. He was just inside the doorway of the stationery store. It was a cool spring day, but his bald head was thick was sweat. The back of his black suit was even darker than the rest of it. He was on the phone and hunched over slightly, probably more from damaged ribs than out of a sense of privacy on a busy street.

Patel walked past him as if he was on his way elsewhere. All it took was a glance for him to verify the man was on the phone, but not armed. And only a trained eye such as his would have spotted the bulge under his left arm. At least it was holstered.

The target didn't spot Patel as he passed, too caught up in

his conversation to pay any mind to a passerby. He was speaking in German, quickly at that, far too quickly for Patel's minimal knowledge of the language to grasp.

He doubled back and tried to get the man's attention. "Excuse me, boss," he said in English. "Excuse me. Do you speak English?"

The man looked at him and tried to move away, but Patel blocked his path. "May I borrow your phone?" He even showed him his handheld. "Mine's just died and I need to make a call. I'll pay you. Hello? Speak English?"

The man flipped him off and tried again to go around him, but stopped when Patel pressed the muzzle of his Glock into his groin.

"Why so unfriendly, boss? Going somewhere?" He pocketed his handheld and plucked the phone from the man's hand. "Hands up right where you have them, just like you're still on the phone. Move for that gun and you're a dead man."

Patel brought the man's phone to his left ear. "I'll bet you speak English, don't you?"

The voice on the other end said, "Yes. Yes, I do, but not as often as I'd like. Why don't you stay right where you are so we can have a talk?"

"No, thank you," Patel said. "I've got a new friend I'd like to get to know. But we'll meet soon, don't worry."

He thumbed the phone off. "Mike, did you get that?"

"Got it. Now lose that phone and get out of there."

"I'm on my way back. Do what you can to alter the street cameras accordingly."

"I will," Mike said. "Now get the hell out of there."

Patel dropped the phone on the sidewalk and crunched it

under his heel. He smiled at the wounded German. "Now, let's all behave ourselves and get moving nice and slowly. No reason for you to die, too. Not yet, anyway."

WHILE SCOTT, TALI, and Roger finished searching the building, Hicks had spent the last ten minutes looking at a silver box installed above the front door.

He knew it wasn't a doorbell. It was too new to be a relic from another business that had been in that space before. It was fifteen feet off the ground, making it impossible for him to see it up close. No one had been able to find a ladder in the entire building.

It was too high to be a fuse box. It had been placed high for a reason. Someone didn't want it tampered with.

He could see an electrical line came out of it and ran upstairs, disappearing into the ceiling.

There was no obvious reason for it to be there, but it *was* there for a reason.

Hicks walked upstairs to the room where the laptops had been set up. He looked at the front wall and saw the wire didn't continue up to the third level. He wondered if the wire ran under the floorboards. He eyeballed it and saw it led to a port in the floor beneath the tables where the laptops were set up. Several sets of wires ran from the port, directly into the docking station of each of the three laptops. Hicks walked over to take a closer look.

Three of the plugs were clearly power cords. A second set looked like standard fiber optic cables that probably gave the laptops access to the internet.

But the third set of cables didn't make sense.

He took a closer look at the laptops. All the USB ports on each device had been removed. Disk drives, too. Someone had gone to a lot of trouble to make sure no one could download information on a memory stick or a disk.

What's that extra wire for?

Scott interrupted his thoughts. "We're ready to go, Hicks."

Hicks kept looking at the wires. "Not yet."

Scott didn't look happy. "Look, we've been over this goddamned place twice already, and the only thing we found was a half-assed torture area up on the third floor. A chair and a couple of jumper cables attached to a car battery. Crude but effective. Looks like it got plenty of use, too."

"Was Roger impressed?"

"Disgusted, more like it. Said it looked amateurish and 'lacked panache,' the sick fuck."

That sounded like Roger. "What about the rest of the place? Any papers?"

"No files, no paper, and no cash," Scott said. "They have a safe in the corner over there, but it's empty."

Hicks was still puzzling over the purpose of the last set of wires. "You take photos and prints from the dead?"

"Done, even on the guys in the stairwell. The grenade didn't leave much but we got what we could. Everything will upload to OMNI as soon as we're outside and get a clear signal. Look, I'm not trying to be a hard ass here, but we've been here two hours already. Tali and Roger are loading the weapons into the car, and the street out front is full of cops with more on the way. If they set up a perimeter around this place and search the trunk, we're fucked. I say we plug the survivor, pull these laptops, and get the hell out of here. Maybe Rivas can get something off the computers back at the Penthouse. If he can't, your new friends at Langley can probably do it."

Hicks didn't budge. "We've still got an hour before the cops come in. Besides, Mike's not a tech. He's here to provide tactical support while we kick in doors. I'm working on something."

Those wires.

The Vanguard had gone through a lot of trouble to secure this building. They hadn't done it to protect money in the safe or the torture area upstairs. There was nothing else in the building to take.

It had to be about the laptops, what was on them or the information they could access. They were using laptops, not desktops, so they wanted mobility, but there was something about the extra wire to each device that didn't make sense.

The building had been shielded to prevent cell phones and their handhelds from working. The Vanguard was obviously technically savvy. The third set of cables served a purpose. Just like the steel doors and the removed USB ports served a purpose.

Security.

He looked over at the wounded man. Scott had bound his hands and ankles with plastic strips. "He still alive?"

"Barely. Why?"

Hicks held out his hand. "Let me borrow your knife."

Scott produced his combat knife from his vest. "You already shot the poor bastard. Are you going to stab him, too?"

"Only if I have to." He stood over the man and said in German, "Tell me how to access the laptops."

"Please," he replied. "I'm dying. I didn't do anything to you.

192

I'm just an accountant. Get me to a hospital."

"I don't know too many accounts who have nine millimeters in their desks, and all three of you were armed." He moved the knife from one hand to the other. "Tell me how to disable the security features on the laptops."

"I know nothing of any such features."

Hicks dropped to a knee right next to the man's face, causing him to flinch. "Three sets of wires, asshole. One for power. One for the internet. The third one fries the hard drive if the laptop's undocked without the proper password." He laid the blade on the man's cheek, just below his eye. "Tell me I'm wrong."

The wounded man swallowed hard. "The wire is connected to the keypad at the door. If the door is kicked in or someone does not enter the right code, it triggers a bleaching program that wipes the hard drives."

Hicks patted his cheek with the blade. "Good boy. And you're going to disable them for us."

"No. I mean, I only know mine, I swear it!" His face was thick with sweat from pain and fear. "They wanted it that way, so no one could ever access the network from more than one laptop at once. Mine is the last one on the left."

Hicks didn't want to believe it, but it made sense. If the Vanguard had been this intent on security, they had probably compartmentalized access. "Give me your user name and password."

"If I tell you, you'll take me to the hospital?"

"If you don't tell me, you won't be going anywhere."

Scott brought his boot down an inch from the man's ruined legs.

The man screamed out his user name and password.

193

Hicks went to the laptop and was about to begin typing when he realized the keyboard didn't look right. It took him a second to realize why, but only a second.

There was a black pad above the number keys on the far left of the keyboard. A pad just big enough for a thumbprint. It would have been easy enough for someone to miss it if they were in a hurry. Fortunately, Hicks had all the time in the world.

He looked back when he heard the man on the floor sobbing.

Hicks admired his dedication. "Nice try, Fritz. Come here."

He wheeled over a chair and cut the plastic strip binding his wrists. The man screamed as Scott helped Hicks dump him in the chair and push him over to the laptop, his legs dragging the entire way.

Hicks leaned over him, knife pressed against his throat. "Open it up. Any mistakes, you die in this chair."

With a trembling hand the man tapped the spacebar, and the screen came alive. The camera on the laptop activated, scanned the man's face, and prompted him to use his thumbprint to proceed.

The screen opened to a spreadsheet filled with more data and tabs than Hicks could count.

"Now disable the security measures so we can undock the computer. Turn off the screensaver and enable the Wi-Fi so I can still use it afterward." He pressed the knife harder against his throat. "And don't forget I read German."

The man's hands were shaking so much it took him several tries, but he was finally able to type the right commands to allow the laptop to be safely undocked.

When the man sagged and began to weep, Hicks knew he'd entered the right code. He removed the laptop from the docking station and saw it was still operating.

Scott went for his side arm to finish the man off.

Hicks stopped him. "Give him a dose of morphine and a shot of XStat for his wounds. We'll leave him here for the cops."

Scott's hand stayed near his sidearm. "Are you fucking kidding me? He saw us. He heard our names. He can identify us."

The man flinched as Hicks dug his hand into the man's pocket and took out his wallet. In German, he said, "You can identify us, but now we can identify you, too. We'll find you and you won't be happy when we do. Tell me you understand."

The man nodded as quickly as he wept.

Hicks released him with a shove and handed the knife back to Scott. "Give him the morphine and XStat and let's get the hell out of here."

Scott swore as he opened a Velcro patch on his vest. "I don't like this."

Hicks closed the laptop and went to find Tali. "Join the club, Ace."

CHAPTER 23

The Penthouse, Berlin

WHILE TALI AND Mike analyzed the Vanguard laptop off-site, Hicks, Patel and Scott were in the Penthouse living room, watching the camera feed of Roger preparing their prisoner for interrogation.

After injecting him with a mild sedative that kept him still but conscious, Roger had cut away the man's clothes before tying him to a straight-back chair in one of the back rooms of the Penthouse.

They could hear Roger humming a section from *Die Walkure* as he finished applying the last node to the prisoner's naked body. He was still humming as he left the room.

A vein in Scott's neck was beginning to turn red. "I thought Hicks was crazy for letting that other Kraut live. Then I find out you brought one of the sons of bitches back here. Congratulations, pal. You win the Dumbest Move of the Day award."

Patel shrugged. "What else was I supposed to do? He was calling his mates to come pick him up and I couldn't very well follow him on foot, now could I? The laptop you nicked might have data, but this man?" He pointed at the screen. "This man's got live intelligence. He can tell us a hell of a lot more about what we're up against than any laptop could."

"He's right," Hicks said. "Bringing him here was the right call."

Scott's vein turned purple. "You wouldn't bring the laptop up here, but you're okay with a prisoner being on the premises."

"The laptop's probably got a tracker on it," Hicks said, "or will as soon as it hits a Wi-Fi signal. That's why I've got Rivas and Tali uploading the hard drive to OMNI off-site. They'll hand off the laptop to one of the Barnyard's Farmhands after they're done."

"At least you're keeping the same terminology," Scott said, "if not the same methodology. I still don't trust those Agency bastards."

"Neither do I. That's why we're copying everything to OMNI before we even let the Barnyard know we have it."

"And if the Vanguard tracks Tali and Rivas to wherever they're uploading the information?" Scott asked. "What then?"

Hicks had thought of that. He'd thought of the danger he'd put Tali and the baby in. He remembered the danger she had been in on the street. She'd handled herself well enough then. He hoped a simple upload and handoff would be a minimal risk. *But still.* "We've got a contingency in place if something goes wrong. Don't let the wheelchair fool you. Rivas used to be a hell of a field man in his day. Saved your ass once or twice as

I remember."

"I remember he had two good legs when he did it."

Hicks couldn't argue with him there. He couldn't entertain his concerns either. Not for Tali's sake. Or his own. "His legs might be gone, but he's still Mike Rivas."

Scott folded his arms and kept his mouth shut.

Patel sat forward and squinted at the television. "Where the hell did Roger go, anyway? What's he up to?"

Hicks knew better than to try to guess what Roger was doing.

Roger appeared back in frame, still humming, wheeling a large black and silver equipment case into the room.

They watched him pull over a chair and sit down only about a foot away from the prisoner. Hicks knew Roger preferred his interrogations to be intimate affairs.

Roger smiled with all the warmth of a country doctor consulting an old patient about their arthritis. "I know you're a professional soldier, my friend. A ruffian. A mercenary. The amount of scarring on your body tells me you've seen your fair share of action, so there's no sense in being coy about how this is going to end. You have seen where we are. You know where this building is located. You have also seen all our faces and probably heard one or two of us call each other by name, haven't you?"

The prisoner's head lolled a bit as the effects of the sedative began to wear off, but he kept his silence.

Roger went on. "So you know there is absolutely no way this ends with you walking out of here. Nothing you tell me will win you your freedom. Your journey ends here, in this room. When I'm done questioning you, I'm going to put your body in that box I just brought in here. Then, I'll wheel you downstairs and dispose of you with the rest of the hotel's garbage. No one will ever be the wiser."

He leaned further forward so the man couldn't help but look at him. "Nothing will change how this ends. We've already scanned you for tracking devices and we know you don't have any. Your friends have no idea where you are and no one is coming to rescue you. And since you tried killing us today, no one here will take mercy on you." He pointed at the case. "That box is your destiny."

The prisoner looked over at the box, then back at Roger. His Adam's apple bobbed as he swallowed.

Roger continued. "I know how helpless you feel right now, but you've got more power over your situation than you think. You see, you control how much pain you feel between now and the time I put you in that box. I've hooked you up to two different sets of equipment. The first is a lie detector. It's a bit old, I'll admit, but accurate enough for our purposes here today."

He picked up a small box from the floor. "You'll find the second machine familiar. The nodes I just finished applying to your chest and thighs are attached to a car battery capable of giving you quite a shock. It's the same setup I noticed back in your facility, so you know how it works." Roger's smile broadened. "Karma can be a real bitch sometimes, can't it, my friend?"

Roger jiggled the box.

The prisoner flinched.

Roger set the box on the table, at his elbow. "The rest of it is really straightforward. I'm going to ask you several questions. I already know the answers to many of them, but obviously there are some bits of information I'm going to need you to tell me. If I didn't need answers, you'd be dead by now. If you tell the truth, we keep talking like two professionals should. But if you decide to lie to me, either the machine or I will know it and I'll give you a jolt. Then we go all the way back to the first question and try again. If your previous answers don't match up, another jolt and we start again. Each jolt will be longer in duration and exponentially more painful. I won't stop, no matter how much you beg me to. Is that clear?"

The man's Adam's apple bobbed again. Hicks was surprised to hear him ask in Russian, "And if I tell the truth?"

Roger brightened. "That's the spirit," he responded in Russian. "As long as you're truthful, the jolt box stays on the table and your reward will be this." He picked up a syringe from the table. "Remember how you felt when we first tied you to the chair?"

"Yes," the man croaked. "I felt very…peaceful."

Roger jiggled the syringe. "That was this. Heroin. Rather high quality, if I do say so myself. I gave you just enough to calm your nerves and make you pliable. Tell me the truth, and when you've answered all of my questions truthfully, I inject enough of this in your system to make you go to sleep and never wake up."

The man's eyes narrowed. "And if I refuse to tell you anything?"

Roger set the needle aside. "Oh, you'll tell me plenty of things before we're through. And eventually you'll get around to telling me the truth. I think that'll happen sooner rather than later. You're not the hero type. If you were, you wouldn't have cut and run once the going got tough back there."

Roger sat back and looked the man over. "You strike me as a reasonable young man, so I think you're smart enough to know when a situation is hopeless. Tell me the truth and you'll die with dignity. Your life will end in state of pure, blissful euphoria."

He suddenly rocked forward and grabbed the arms of the prisoner's chair. Their faces were less than an inch apart. "But if you lie to me, I'll bake you like *zharkoye*. Either way, the box in the corner awaits. How quickly you end up there, and how much you suffer before then, is entirely up to you."

Roger gave the prisoner's legs a goodhearted shake as he stood. "I know this is a lot to absorb all at once, so I'm going to give you a couple of minutes to process it all, and when I come back, we'll begin."

He hummed *Die Walkure* once more as he stepped out of the room, and was still humming it when he joined the others in the living room. He poured himself a cup of coffee from the silver pot on the table. He sat in a chair and took a deep swallow, as if he'd just sat down after a long trip home from work.

"How did I do?" He sipped again. "I think we're off to a pretty good start, if I do say so myself. Shame to kill him, though. Nice body. And he's hung like a horse, especially for a Russian."

Scott cursed and walked out of the room.

Patel poured himself some coffee, too. "Okay. I'll ask. What the hell is *zharkoye*?"

"It's Russian," Hicks said, "for pot roast."

Patel set the pot back down and brought a hand to his mouth.

Roger wrinkled his nose at him. "It'll be fine. Don't be such a pansy."

Hicks handed Roger a notepad. "Here are some of the

questions we want you to ask him. It starts off with basic stuff. Names of the other people in the facility. The nature of what they did there. His boss. Who they interrogated there and why. Then it goes deeper into their operations. Ask him about Tessmer."

"I'll do that." Roger sipped his coffee as he read over the list. "You've always had such excellent handwriting for someone who spends his days on a computer. I'll bet you got an A in penmanship."

"Just make sure you get an A in interrogation." Hicks got up to leave. To Patel he said, "You're sure Rivas was able to ghost this guy's phone before you smashed it?"

Patel winced as he swallowed whatever had risen in his throat. "That's why I crushed it in the first place."

"Good. We need this asshole to give us something I can use when I call his friends."

Scott came out of the kitchen area. "After what we did to the Vanguard today? No way he talks to you. I'll bet he's on a plane halfway around the world by now."

"It's worth a shot, isn't it?" Hicks took his jacket from the back of his chair. "I'm going out for a bit. Text me if you get anything out of the prisoner." He pointed at Roger. "And don't kill him until you have to."

"My interrogation will be the model of decorum." Roger drained his cup and poured himself another. To Scott and Patel he said, "You boys ought to make some popcorn or nachos. I promise it'll be a hell of a show."

Hicks shrugged on his jacket as he stepped into the elevator and keyed it closed. *Fucking Roger.*

DEMEREST HAD PROMISED to not track the phone he had given him, but Hicks still took precautions. He had removed the battery from the phone, sealed the phone and battery in tin foil, placed each piece in a separate plastic bag, and stowed them in the toilet tanks in the lobby bathrooms of two separate hotels blocks away from the Penthouse. He'd picked lobby bathrooms because it would make him easier to blend in with guests and visitors and tourists looking to use the restroom while they toured the old city.

It may have been overkill, but overkill had kept him alive long enough to know precautions made sense. He could have had Jason ghost the phone remotely, the way Rivas had ghosted the phone from the prisoner. But this was different. He didn't necessarily want Jason or OMNI tracking what he said to Demerest or vice versa. He still wasn't sure if OMNI had been compromised by the Vanguard, so best to keep things separate for now. The foil and the water in the toilet tanks should be enough to scramble any tracking devices either component might have. Langley was nothing if not resourceful.

Hicks called Jason on his University handheld as he began retrieving the various components of Demerest's phone. "I want a report on your diagnostics of OMNI."

"I've run several hundred tests since the attack, of every type you can imagine. I haven't found anything. No one has even come close to testing the network, much less hack it. We are as secure as we've always been. I don't know how they found out about 23rd Street, but it wasn't through OMNI."

It may not have given Hicks answers, but knowing the backbone of the University's operations was safe gave him peace of mind. He had shut down all University operations right after the attack, meaning all Faculty Members and Assets were idle. No information was going out and none was coming in. It was time to change all that. "Send out the all clear and get everyone back to work. Tell them to report anything suspicious."

"In our world, sir, everything is suspicious."

Hicks looked at the phone. Everyone was a comedian. The last Dean hadn't been treated like this. People spoke to him with a reverence usually reserved for a pope. He decided to ignore it for now. "Have them focus on new threats that don't fit their current operational outline. New sources that pop up out of the blue. Uncooperative sources that suddenly want to meet. People following them. Things like that. We still don't know how far the Vanguard can reach, so I want everyone to stay vigilant. And no mention of the Vanguard to anyone, understand? I don't want our people worried about bogeymen, just their jobs."

"Consider it done," Jason said. "In the meantime, Tali and Mike are uploading a hell of a lot of information to OMNI from that laptop they captured. Some of it had tracking software we were able to sponge out before we got it, but it's a gold mine. Account numbers, amounts, company names, assets. I'm sure the Vanguard has already begun changing a lot of the information, but Langley should still be able to trace some of it."

Hicks was glad he didn't just dislocate those cords. "Are you seeing anything about Vanguard leadership? Names and addresses?"

"Maybe," Jason said, "but the amount of data they're uploading is giving OMNI a run for her money. She's only begun processing one percent of it and there's a lot more of it on the way. Every byte of it has been encrypted. It's a massive amount of information and the encryption doesn't make it any easier. She's a powerful system, but even the most powerful system has limits."

Hicks didn't know when Jason had begun referring to OMNI as a female. He had also never thought of the system having limits, but he supposed it did. He hadn't thought of a lot of things until a few days ago. "Of the one percent she's analyzing, what is she looking at?"

"Vanguard money flowing out of Asia to all parts of the world, including your bank in Berlin. Hong Kong seems to be a hub for deposits and disbursements. Analysis of the few emails she's analyzed shows the Vanguard has two equal arms. The Chinese run the financial aspects while the Russians do the grunt work. Selling weapons, moving the cash, kicking in doors when necessary."

Hicks knew that fit with their Communist ethos. "From each according to their abilities, right? What about that phone Rivas was able to ghost from the prisoner Patel grabbed on the street? Is that still active?"

After a few clicks, Jason said, "It looks like a burner phone, but it's still active. I'll send it over to you now. It'll appear as a 'V' icon on your device. You're not thinking of calling him, are you?"

"I've got to update our friend at the Barnyard first. After that, I'll call the Vanguard number through one of our Operators. I'll feel better talking to him knowing our people are bouncing the signal around the world."

"I'll make sure they're ready for your call," Jason said. "Bouncing the signal effectively will take some minor setting up. Wait." He paused for a few seconds, then said, "I just got a text from Tali. She said she and Rivas should be done with the upload within the hour. You can tell Demerest he can have the laptop by late afternoon if he wants it."

"I'll mention it to him. Anything else?"

"I see Roger has begun his interrogation of the prisoner."

Hicks had forgotten Jason could watch the feed from the Penthouse via OMNI. "I left before he got started. Is he having any luck?"

"That would depend on your definition of luck. He seems to have made use of the battery. Let's just say I'm not going to be having steak for a while."

That wasn't good news. The odds of him extracting anything useful from the man before he called Tessmer dropped with every charge. "Thanks for the visual. I'll call back after I talk with Demerest."

H ICKS RETRIEVED THE phone's components from both restrooms. He had been looking for people eyeing the lobby of each hotel. Errant glances that lasted a split-second too long. People working too hard to be casual. Demerest already knew what he looked like, and if he had been tracing the phone components, whoever was watching them knew it, too.

He spotted a few likely suspects, but no obvious Farmhands.

He took his time as he walked to Waldeck Park on Jakobstrasse, checking his flanks and his rear for anyone who might be following on foot or in a car. Technology had reduced the need for old-school tail jobs, but it still paid to be vigilant.

He found a bench deep within the park, one that gave him good views of anyone approaching the area. He waited for a few moments to see if anyone was paying particular attention to him. No one was, so he re-assembled the phone.

Forty-eight hours of the seventy-two-hour head start Demerest had given him were already gone. He didn't like the idea of calling in like a goddamned rookie, but Demerest was too important an ally to blow off.

He wasn't surprised when Demerest picked up right away. "You've been busy, son."

"I told you I would be. Thanks for pulling strings to give us time to look through the place. We got some information I think you'll find useful."

"I sure as hell hope so," Demerest said. "Things are becoming more complicated as we speak. Your stunt today raised a lot of eyebrows around here. My German counterparts are asking me a lot of questions I don't want to answer."

"Or could, even if you wanted to."

"I'm trying not to dwell on that part. The man you left behind raised a lot of curiosity. Why the hell didn't you just kill him?"

"Because the laptops were rigged to be wiped clean if they weren't undocked properly. I promised I'd let him live if he helped us. He lived up to his end of the bargain, so I lived up to mine."

"How noble," Demerest said. "We don't have the luxury of being noble."

"And we don't want to run the risk of being like the Vanguard," Hicks answered. "Their way of doing things has put them on the defensive. When word gets out we let one of their people live, it'll create doubt in their ranks. Might save one of my people down the line. I decided it was worth the risk. Is he talking to the German cops?"

"No. He said they're just accountants and doesn't know who or why someone would rob the place. He claims he was unconscious the whole time. Said there was an explosion, lots of gunfire, but he didn't see anything. The safe was empty so my contacts in the German security services are pushing the notion that it was a robbery, but the Berlin cops aren't stupid. They know someone administered first aid to the man and want to know why. The missing laptop didn't help, either. Fortunately, they pulled the laptops from the docking stations and wiped the hard drives clean."

"Good. That makes the third laptop that much more valuable. Give me a contact and I'll arrange to have it delivered to your people here in Berlin later tonight."

"After you've downloaded the information first, of course. What's the matter, son? Don't trust me to share?"

"I don't trust you any more than you really trust me, remember? That's why you have people looking for me, isn't it?"

Demerest's silence told him everything.

"I thought you said you wouldn't be tracking the phone."

"Situational realities changed that arrangement," Demerest said. "Clever of you to hide the phone and the battery in separate places, but the tin foil was a bit much, don't you think?"

"I thought you'd live up to our agreement. Makes me wonder if I can trust anything you say."

"You can trust it, especially now," Demerest said. "The president has decided to push through my appointment to DNI."

"Congratulations," Hicks said.

"Not so fast," Demerest said. "It comes with a catch. I've been tasked with verifying Iran's involvement in the drone strike on New York before the post becomes official."

Hicks closed his eyes. "Shit."

"That's one way of putting it," Demerest said. "Things on the international front have gotten worse faster than I expected. Israel has caught wind of Iran's ownership of the drone that hit New York. Since Russia has close ties with Iran, they're openly wondering if both countries aren't making a move against the U.S. and Israel. Someone mentioned it to POTUS directly. I'd move up that seventy-two-hour deadline I gave you, but I don't think it would do any good."

"It's tight enough as it is," Hicks admitted.

"Tight or not, we're beyond the point of conjecture and speculation," Demerest said. "Everything is happening behind closed doors for the moment, but not for much longer. I need to put a face and a name to the Vanguard so I can prevent them from going after Iran for something they didn't do and triggering a war. The sooner I do that, the bigger help I can be to you. I need a name in the Vanguard, son. I need it now."

And there it was. The Ask. Hicks was surprised it had taken Demerest this long to get to it. "No."

"It doesn't even have to be viable. The name you gave to Tayeb will do. If it was good enough to get him killed, it'll be good enough to show everyone we're close to finding the people who really hit us. The longer we wait, the harder it'll be to avert war with Iran and whatever repercussions that causes."

"Calm down. Desperation doesn't look good on you, Carl."

"No reason for this to get nasty, but it can get nasty real fast. A lot of people are asking what's at the bottom of the pile on 23rd Street. I've been able to quell their curiosity for now…but if I stop quelling, some people will start looking. Who knows?

Maybe your name will come up. Like I said, one name's as good as any. And you check off a lot of boxes. That gas explosion could just as easily be spun as a homegrown terrorist building a bomb that went bad."

Hicks sat back on the bench and looked up at the sky. The first stab of a desperate man was always the most dangerous. He had been wondering how long it would take Demerest to threaten him. Now, he knew.

It was time to remind the company man who he was dealing with. "Schneider was the last person to threaten me, Carl. Ask the Mossad how that worked out for him."

"I'm not Schneider. And I'm also not the one who's stuck in the middle of Berlin with a bull's-eye on his back. So I'm changing our arrangement. I promised you seventy-two hours and I'm going to keep it. I'm going to text you the name and number of a contact who will pick up the laptop within the hour. And if my people don't have that device in their possession by then, or if I don't get a name from you by tomorrow, your name starts appearing in reports. Understood?"

Hicks gripped the phone tighter. OMNI had already recorded the full conversation of their deal, but that was a gun he could only fire once. It was too early to use that now. Later, maybe, but not now. He was going to give Demerest the laptop anyway, so he decided to give in. "My people will be in touch with your contact to arrange a drop site within the hour."

"I'm glad you listened to reason, son."

"My pleasure. Just remember that if you ever threaten me again, I'll kill you."

Hicks killed the connection and pulled the battery from the phone. He tossed the battery in a puddle of rainwater off the path. The resulting pop and hiss was music to his ears. The son of a bitch had a tracker in the battery after all. Sometimes, he hated being right. This wasn't one of those times.

He stood and walked through the park for a bit, casually dumping the phone in the nearest trash bin. It was a nice afternoon and the darkening sky promised a beautiful sunset. He wished he could have enjoyed it, but he didn't have that luxury.

He kept walking to another area of the park and found another empty bench. He looked for cameras or people watching him, but didn't find either.

He dug his earpiece out of his pocket and slipped it into his right ear. He pulled out his handheld and saw the V icon on the home screen. He called the University switchboard.

"How may I help you?" This time the voice belonged to a female University Operator.

"This is Professor Warren," Hicks said, giving her the all-clear sign. "I was told you'd be expecting my call."

"Yes, sir. Would you like me to place the call using the new icon on your screen?"

"I would. I'd also like you to stay on the line and speak to me in my earpiece. I want you to try to trace the call. If you get a hit, I need you to tell me about it. If you could get me a location on their phone, even better."

More clicks on her end. "Yes, sir. Placing the call now."

He brought the handheld up to his left ear. The call went through. He thought he might get voicemail, but it was picked up at the last moment.

"I take it this is not Henrik," a man's voice said in English.

"You take it correctly."

"Ah, then this must be the man who has been causing me so much trouble."

Hicks grinned. "The one and only. And who are you?"

"To paraphrase a line from an appropriate piece of great American literature," the voice said, "call me Tessmer. After all, it's the name that got us started on this journey, isn't it?"

Hicks expected to feel some excitement, some relief, at finding the man he had been hunting. His first real link to the Vanguard.

But he felt nothing. Not disappointment. Not joy. Nothing except a chilly wind on his face as he sat alone on a park bench in Berlin. "Tessmer your real name?"

"No more than James Hicks is yours," Tessmer said, "but it's a good enough place to start. You've been quite busy for a man who's supposed to be dead. You seem to be immune to missile strikes and airplane disasters."

"Don't forget my affinity for breaking and entering."

"And taking that which does not belong to you," Tessmer said. His English was nearly flawless, with only a hint of an accent that sounded closer to Dutch than German or even Russian. "No, I haven't forgotten that. I have no intention of wasting time by fencing with you, so let us get to the heart of the matter. Why don't we meet face-to-face and talk this out like civilized gentlemen?"

"Why? So you can hit me with an RPG like you did with Tayeb's crew in Moscow?"

Tessmer surprised him by laughing. "That was a bit theatrical, wasn't it? Wasting that kind of ordinance on a room full of Jews. A regular grenade would have been much cheaper."

Hicks's hand balled into a fist. "Tayeb was my friend, you

son of a bitch."

"I gathered that," Tessmer said. "Poor Ronen. His field skills were a bit rusty. He'd begun to contact old sources of his to ask them about a mysterious man named Tessmer. He had been sitting behind a desk so long he had no idea his old contacts had become my employees. Had he been more careful, he may very well still be alive today. But if he had, you and I wouldn't be having this lovely chat right now, would we? Isn't it fascinating how one slight misstep can change the entire course of one's life? So many people would still be alive if he had been just a bit more discreet. Or if he had still been behind that desk in Tel Aviv where he belonged. But since you were undoubtedly the one who got him back in the field, perhaps you're to blame for his death and the deaths of his comrades."

The more Tessmer talked, the more Hicks learned about his background. Tessmer wasn't just some common criminal. He wasn't just an arms dealer or a mercenary. He was running a psychological operation on him right now. He was working him, trying to get him to blame himself for all that had happened. He knew what he was doing. He had been trained.

So had James Hicks. "You lost a few men yourself, Ace. Thanks to me."

"Yes, I have. There have been losses on both sides, and this will continue to be the case unless we reach some kind of understanding."

"The only understanding we're going to reach ends with a bullet."

"All the more reason that we should meet each other," Tessmer said. "Just the two of us. Not like a couple of gunslingers in the middle of the street like one of your tawdry western movies, but in a setting and manner befitting the professionals we are. We can discuss the return of the man you captured and the laptop you took from me, among other things."

Hicks hadn't expected him to ask for a meeting so soon. He also hadn't expected him to answer the phone. Tessmer was proving to be an unpredictable man. "Where and when?"

"Say Istanbul? Tomorrow at three o'clock? That should give you plenty of time to get there."

The Operator spoke in Hicks's earpiece. "He's actively tracing the call. He's bouncing his own signal all over the world, so I can't get a fix on him. But OMNI is picking up ambient noises on his side of the line. Horns and police sirens and traffic noises in the background that match similar patterns of Berlin. He's close, sir."

"Why Istanbul? You're in Berlin and so am I. Let's meet tomorrow at eight in the morning."

"My compliments. You've succeeded in impressing me."

"And I don't give a shit. Where do you want to meet?"

"I will send you a text with the time and location. I'd say come alone, but why waste time with requests neither of us has any intention of honoring?" Hicks heard another voice in the background. "One moment, please."

In Hicks's ear, the Operator said, "He's talking in Russian, but has his thumb over the mouthpiece. I can't hear what he's saying."

Tessmer came back on the line. "Good news. We can cross one item off the agenda for tomorrow's meeting. The missing laptop has turned up after all. We'll be in touch."

The line went dead.

The Operator said, "The call has been disconnected, sir.

Absolutely no idea on their location, but OMNI is already running a search on ambient noise, so…"

But Hicks didn't care about ambient noise. Tessmer had somehow located the laptop. The same laptop Rivas and Tali were uploading to OMNI.

He killed the connection and dialed Tali's handheld. She didn't pick up.

He called Rivas's handheld. He didn't pick up, either.

He fought the panic rising in his gut and called Jason. "I'm already trying to get a fix on Tali and Rivas's location."

"They didn't pick up." His breath caught and he tried not to hyperventilate. *Not Tali. Not now. Not today. Not the baby.*

"OMNI's reach is weak in this part of Europe," Jason reminded him. "They're probably in an area with a high volume of wireless traffic that's making it harder for us to pinpoint. They may be using their handhelds to boost OMNI's signal for the upload. I know they're roughly two miles away from the Penthouse, but it takes a few seconds to pinpoint their exact location."

Hicks heard a ping on Jason's end of the line, then, "They're in a coffee shop in central Berlin, three miles away from your current position, two miles away from the Penthouse. I don't know why they're not picking up."

Hicks was up and running for the street. "Text them to kill the upload and get the hell out of there now. They need to split up. Assign them separate fallback positions close to their current locations. I want Patel and Roger to stay with the prisoner, but have Scott get the van and pick them up immediately. Then contact Demerest and have him get his people to the coffee shop ASAP. We'll have to make do with the information we've already uploaded to OMNI. Send me their exact location now. I'm on my way."

CHAPTER 24

As Rivas clicked through windows on the laptop, Tali eyed the other patrons in the coffee shop. Most of them were tourists babbling about the sights they had seen that day. The rest were office workers, cubicle drones looking for an extra dose of caffeine to get them through the rest of the workday. Tali had been passively listening to the plethora of languages around her. German, French, English, and Japanese.

That was why she decided to speak to Rivas in Spanish. "How much longer is this supposed to take?"

"I don't know," he replied in Spanish. "I didn't know when you asked five minutes ago, and nothing in the past five minutes has changed that. I'm not tech support. Jason can make these damned things jump through hoops, but not me. All I can do is watch the files upload to OMNI."

"Fine. So tell me how many have uploaded so far."

Rivas toggled back to one of the screens. "Thirty percent."

Tali tried not to show her disappointment. She tapped her paper coffee cup instead. "Why is it taking so damned long?"

"Because we're uploading massive encrypted files, and our connection to OMNI isn't as fast as it would be back home. The security measure isn't helping it go any faster. The further east you go..."

"The weaker OMNI gets," Tali finished the sentence for him. "I know." She checked her phone again, but no word from Hicks or from Jason about handing off the laptop to the CIA. Since they had only uploaded a third of the files, she wasn't complaining. But she didn't like being out in the open like this, either.

"Maybe if you closed some of those windows, the information would upload faster."

Rivas clenched his jaw. "And maybe you should remember I'm not a rookie on his first assignment. Hell, you wouldn't even be here if I wasn't in this fucking chair."

"But you are, so here I am." She didn't like the way she'd sounded when she said it. "Sorry. I just hate being exposed like this."

"I'm not exactly having the time of my life either." Rivas looked at the screen. "Thirty-five percent now."

Tali realized her foot was beginning to tap and she stopped it. It was the only nervous habit they had not been able to break her of in training. She only did it when she got nervous, so she didn't do it often, but she was nervous as hell now. Being out in the open like this with a laptop that may be pinging their location to the Vanguard was a pretty good reason to worry. They had taken out Tayeb's people with an RPG. Launching one into a crowded coffee shop would be a piece of cake.

She had always prided herself on avoiding risky situations whenever possible. She never operated in the open like this, and a coffee shop in the middle of Berlin was about as open as it got. Too many faces to watch, expressions to read. Too many ways someone from the Vanguard could blend in. Too many ways to be spotted without knowing it.

She fought to keep her feet flat on the floor as she continued observing the customers. Those who came in and those who'd been there for a while and those who ordered their coffee and left.

The line for coffee was long and growing longer by the second as the overwhelmed baristas struggled to keep up with orders for lattes and Frappuccino. Many of the people in line looked around absently at the other customers in the shop before they defaulted to checking their phones. Almost all of them looked over at her or Rivas. Mike's wheelchair drew glances and a brief flash of sympathy before turning away. Women looked at her green jacket over her black sweater and jeans. They checked out her boots and her dark hair pulled back into a ponytail, making their own mental critique of her fashion sense. Men stole glances, too, though more for how she filled out what she was wearing rather than the outfit itself. She even drew a fair number of smiles. She ignored them all.

She didn't mind the looks she received.

She paid more attention to the looks she didn't get. Not because it offended her ego, but because they might already know who she was.

One man stood out. Tall. Bald. Lean. Late thirties. Leather jacket. He had just entered the shop and stood at the end of the line. He didn't look like the type who'd come in for a latte or a hot cocoa. And he looked everywhere except at them.

In fact, he made a point of not looking their way.

She mentally tagged him Baldy.

She watched him as she sipped her coffee, even though more caffeine was the last thing she needed. "Possible contact. Twelve o'clock. Bald man. End of the line."

Rivas kept his eyes on the screen. "Keep an eye on him and..."

He stopped when Tali's phone began to buzz on the table. She picked it up and saw it was a text message from Jason.

KILL UPLOAD AND EVACUATE NOW. DEPART SEPARATELY. FALLBACK POSITIONS TO FOLLOW. EXTRACTION SOON AFTER.

"We're blown." Tali slipped the handheld into her pocket and stood. "Kill the connection and get out of here. I'll head west, you head east. Jason will text us fallback positions when we're clear."

"Forty fucking percent. Damn it."

He closed the laptop and Tali slipped it into her bag. "I'll take it and try to lead them away if they're watching. Wait fifteen minutes, finish your coffee, and move on to your designated location. Are you armed?"

Rivas's hand was steady as he reached for his coffee. "Been armed every day of my life since I was twenty years old."

Tali slung the bag onto her shoulder. "Good. I'll see you back at the Penthouse."

She threaded her way through the tight confines of the coffee shop. She didn't run and she didn't shove anyone out of the way. She simply moved with purpose, like most of the people in that part of the city. She stole a quick glance at Baldy. He was still the last one in line, only now he was on the phone.

Shit.

She pushed through the revolving doors and broke to the right. She had no idea how far away the Vanguard men might be. She didn't know if Baldy was with them but was pretty sure he was. They could be half a block away or already on-site. She didn't know if Hicks or Scott or Patel were on their way to the coffee shop, but that didn't matter anymore. For the moment, she was entirely on her own. Jason would send her the fallback position when he saw she was clear. At least someone was watching her.

She blended in with the street crowd, moving with purpose, resisting the urge to break into a flat-out run. She was just another busy person on the streets of one of Europe's great cities.

As she reached the corner, she began to breathe a bit easier. Being on the street was better than being in the coffee shop. The street gave her maneuverability and options. The street also made her a moving target, though still a target nonetheless.

She edged her way through the crowd at the corner and was about to hail a cab when she spotted two men jaywalking in her direction. They were both broad and bulky and looked a bit winded. The thin sheen of sweat on their foreheads confirmed they had been in a hell of a hurry to get there.

And each man looked at her a second too long for it to be a coincidence.

Vanguard men.

She looked behind her and saw Baldy come out of the coffee shop and head in her direction.

A three-man goon squad. At least she knew what she was

up against.

She forgot about waiting for a cab and decided to take another right at the corner. The coffee shop was already half a block away, so Rivas would have to take care of himself.

She quickened her pace, but did not run. Not yet. People scattered when someone ran at them. Right now, she needed as many people around her as she could get. Too many targets presented a problem, even to the butchers of the Vanguard.

She scanned the faces of people coming her way as she moved through them. Men and women. Young and old. The well-dressed professionals and aging hipsters who had spent a lot of money on clothes that looked cheap, and bored teenagers trudging home from school wishing they were anywhere but there.

She observed them all as she moved because any one of them could be with the Vanguard. They would certainly send more than three people after her. Probably two more at least, especially if it was a kidnapping. If they wanted her dead, the men she had already seen would have shot her on sight. They had decided to follow her instead. They probably didn't want to risk hitting the laptop in a gunfight. They probably wanted to kidnap her instead, get the laptop and a hostage as leverage over Hicks for the Vanguard man they'd caught.

They had to be delicate.

Fortunately, Tali did not.

She moved through the thickening foot traffic, knowing the large crowd might prevent the Vanguard from shooting her but not from grabbing her. If anything, they would use the crowd to their advantage. Grab her and the laptop, tuck them both away into a waiting vehicle, and be on their way.

She had never been any man's pawn and she wouldn't be one now. And neither would the little miracle she knew was growing inside her.

Tali walked another block, moving faster through spaces in the foot traffic as she sensed the three men behind her were losing ground in the thickening crowd. If she could just make it to the corner, make it to a taxi or a hotel lobby or even another crowded bar, maybe she could find a way to escape, maybe—

All thoughts of possibilities died away as she watched a man speed-walk toward her from her right. She heard a vehicle, a van that did not sound like Scott's van, pull over to the curb on her left.

A classic kidnapping setup, just like Stephens had used to try to grab Hicks back in New York.

Her training kicked in. She felt the Glock in her hand before she had decided to grab for it.

She aimed it at the speed-walker and fired a single round at nearly point-blank range into his forehead.

Instinct made the people around her scream and run away, clearing a widening circle on the sidewalk, leaving her completely exposed.

Tali was not afraid, but put fear into her voice as she shouted in German, "Please, help me! My husband. He's trying to kill me and my daughter! Please!"

But the people kept moving away from her as she spotted the two men from the corner struggling against the crowd, both grabbing for something beneath their long coats. They may have even yelled *Polizei* as they pushed people aside. Baldy was right behind them.

Tali brought up the Glock again as she backed away. The

panicked civilians had parted just enough to give her a clear target.

She aimed at the closest man and squeezed off another round, striking him in the face. She shifted her aim to the second man, who'd begun charging toward her, and fired. The bullet hit him on the top of the head and he fell backward.

The crowd screamed and began to bolt in all directions, blocking Baldy from her. Her mind worked fast as she backed away from the men, continuing on her path. She had fired three times, leaving five rounds in the clip. She shifted her aim to the van as she continued to back up. The driver was looking at her, but...

She stopped thinking when she felt a knife slip through her jacket and skin, between her ribs and puncture her heart. Or maybe it was her lungs? It had all happened so quickly that she wasn't sure what had happened, only that something was in her body that didn't belong there. Something had been done that could not be undone. Final.

A flame had blown out that could never be relit.

She thought of all these things as the blade was withdrawn as quickly as it had been inserted. She heard her Glock rattle on the sidewalk as it fell from her hand. She felt the computer bag slip from her shoulder as she fell to the sidewalk.

She dropped to her knees, surprised that the impact didn't hurt, before falling face-first onto the pavement. She didn't see anyone rushing toward her. She couldn't hear their screams anymore. She could only hear the beat of her own heart as her blood rushed in her ears. She felt the warmth of her own blood begin to cover her back, making her sleepy. So sleepy.

She may have heard a siren approaching, but wondered if

she only wished it so.

She only hoped they got to her in time to save the baby she and James had made. Their impossible miracle was better than either of them could ever hope to be.

The pavement was cold, but she was warm. And sleepy. So very sleepy.

CHAPTER 25

RIVAS CRUSHED HIS paper cup when he heard the first gunshot. He ignored the pain from the hot coffee that ran over his hands. He didn't feel the hot coffee that had poured onto his deadened legs.

Everyone else in the café reacted to the shot, too, interrupting their conversations as they turned in the direction it had come from. The same direction he'd watched Tali go. His stomach clenched when he heard the two additional shots, one right after the other.

Screams from the sidewalk echoed through the coffee shop. Patrons began to crowd the windows while others backed away, leaving Rivas as one of the few by the windows. If anyone was concerned about the solitary man in the wheelchair amidst the chaos of a street shooting, they hid it well.

The chaotic scene he watched through the window told him

something had happened. People had been killed. Knowing Tali as well as he did, he estimated the number to be at least three because he had heard only three shots. "One Shot, One Kill" had always been her motto.

He hoped she'd gotten away. He wished he'd been there to back her up. He wished he could go to her now and report back to Jason what had happened, but he couldn't do that.

He watched the chaos unfold on the street. People dashing back and forth away from the scene. His wheelchair would either knock people over or, worse, the panicked crowd would knock over his chair and trample him to death. All the training in the world couldn't help him survive a stampede.

He'd seen it happen enough times in various places around the world. Major cities, small towns, capitals of the world, and third-world villages. People always responded the same way to danger. Run. Flee. Worry about where you were running to and what you were running from later.

The wheelchair had taken that instinct away from Rivas. He had no choice but to stick where he was. The Beretta in the side pocket of his wheelchair and M4 tucked in the pouch under his chair offered cold comfort. The street was too chaotic for him to leave.

He was trapped.

He reached for his handheld when it began to buzz. He looked at the screen and saw it was Jason. He tapped the screen and gave his all-clear cover name. "This is Professor Narvaez."

"Tali is a block away and not moving," Jason told him.

Rivas looked around to see if anyone might be listening, but the other patrons were too busy deciding to panic to pay attention to the cripple by the window. He didn't know if Jason spoke Spanish, but replied in Spanish. "Three shots fired. Lots of people running back and forth. Sirens inbound."

Jason seemed to understand, but responded in English. "Any idea about Tali?"

"Not from here."

Jason swore. "She's not moving and I can't get a live satellite image of the scene."

Rivas leaned forward in his wheelchair. "Does she still have the laptop on her?"

"I don't know yet. OMNI's reach in Europe is weak."

"Damn it!" Rivas slammed his fist down onto the table. None of the other patrons seemed to notice. "We need to know if they took the bait or not."

"The upload to OMNI is continuing," Jason said. "Past fifty percent. That's all I know. If they took the laptop from her, they haven't stopped the upload."

He ignored his aching left hand. "Christ, Jason. If she died for nothing…"

"We don't know if she's dead, and there's nothing we can do about it anyway," Jason said. "Besides, there's been a change of plans. Demerest has people in the immediate area. They're ready to pick up the Vanguard laptop from you right now. I suggest you tell them where it is. It's already cost us so much. It's their problem now."

Rivas looked up when a woman with long reddish hair and pale skin stood in front of him on the other side of the window. She was bright-eyed and pleasant, looking more like a flight attendant than someone who might be working for Charles Demerest at the CIA. She pointed at his phone, then at her face. She even managed a smile.

"I think one of them is here," Rivas said. "She's telling me to scan her face. Hold on."

He took the woman's photo with his handheld and watched OMNI run it through every database in its considerable reach. The response would have been nearly immediate in the United States, but they were in Berlin. It took about thirty seconds before the match came back with three positive identities on one Patricia Levin. Her driver's license said she lived in Chevy Chase, Maryland. The other window showed her State Department identification file. The third showed her true employer—the Central Intelligence Agency.

"She checks out," Jason told him. "That's the same person Demerest said would come for the laptop. Give it to her, then get the hell out of there. I'll send you a fallback position when you're far enough away."

He beckoned her to come in as he pocketed the handheld. As she made her way in, he dropped his hand into the side pouch of the wheelchair. He wrapped his hand around the .45 and aimed it at her through the pouch. She sat in the same seat Tali had occupied before she'd left.

She looked down at the pouch of his wheelchair before she sat. "Is that a gun in your wheelchair or are you just happy to see me?"

Rivas wasn't in the mood for games. "What happened to my partner?"

"I haven't the slightest idea," she said. "I just got here, so your guess is as good as mine. All I care about is the laptop."

"Glad to see they still teach compassion at the Barnyard."

Her bland expression didn't change. "The laptop, please."

Rivas felt himself redden. He hated giving up like this,

especially after the price they had paid to get it, but he had no choice.

He pulled the Vanguard laptop from the pocket on the left side of his wheelchair and handed it to her. "I'd watch my ass if I were you. One look at the laptop my partner had and they'll know we were using it to upload information from the real device. They'll lock on to your location pretty quick."

"I wouldn't worry about that." He watched her slip the laptop into her knapsack. It wasn't just a knapsack. It was a lead-lined sleeve within a lead-lined case. It would be enough to block any tracking signal from the laptop. Enough to block the upload to OMNI, too. Rivas knew OMNI had access to Langley's systems, but that had been before they knew about the University. Now that they were aware, they would probably be vigilant.

Levin zipped up the knapsack. "If you had simply brought this to us when you got it, none of this would've happened."

"Yeah," Rivas said, "because you people have such a stellar history of being able to keep secrets."

Levin looked disappointed, the way a soccer mom might look if her kid told her he'd just failed algebra. "I hope your friend is alright. I really do. But if she's not, just remember we're not the ones who played games on this one. That's on you."

Rivas looked in her eyes. "Fuck. You."

He watched her stand and walk out of the café. The street had become more crowded now as people's fear gave way to curiosity. He lost sight of her as soon as she stepped outside.

He decided maybe that was for the best.

He watched the crowd on the street grow thicker as he heard himself beginning to pray for Tali.

CHAPTER
26

HICKS PUNCHED THE elevator door to The Penthouse as he waited for it to come back down. He didn't know if any of the hotel workers had heard him. He didn't care either. He'd spent the better part of the past three hours trying to get answers about what had happened to Tali and Rivas at the coffee shop. Was Tali safe? Was their baby safe? Had Rivas gotten away? Had the Vanguard recaptured the laptop? Did Demerest have it now?

For a man accustomed to instant answers, the lack of information was frustrating. The lack of information about the woman he loved and the baby she carried made it unbearable.

Jason's reply had been frustratingly constant. "Return to the Penthouse immediately. We can coordinate better from there."

Rivas had left the coffee shop by the time Hicks had gotten there. The street was already thick with civilians craning their necks to see what happened. The police had done a poor job of securing the area and the scene was surrounded. None of the spectators would move and there was no way Hicks could force his way to the front of the group without causing a riot. He had asked ten different people what had happened and gotten ten different responses. The most common denominator in all their stories was that some people had gotten shot and some people had died. After that, their reports varied to the point of being useless.

He had tried reaching Tali on her handheld, but she didn't answer. He had tried tracking her handheld, but OMNI couldn't find it. He had asked Jason and Scott for updates. Both told him the situation was dangerous and fluid and he needed to get back to the Penthouse as soon as possible.

Neither of them knew what had happened to Tali.

Or so they had said.

He even tried to listen in on the Berlin first-responder chatter about the incident. All he heard was that shots had been fired and there were multiple injuries. Ambulances were inbound. The chatter was vague, meaning they didn't know what they were dealing with. The fact they were chattering at all meant the German Federal Security Services had not clamped down on the investigation yet. He hoped Tali was still alive. He hoped their baby had survived as well. But hoping had never been good enough for James Hicks. He had to *know*.

Unable to see anything from the street, Hicks had tried to access a satellite to get an overhead view. But OMNI had been unable to find any available satellites to hack. The rest were either too secure or didn't have powerful enough cameras.

He thought about trying to gain access to a rooftop so he could watch what was happening from above. But the helicopters circling overhead meant the police were looking for someone. Popping out on the rooftop in the middle of a manhunt might lead to a bullet in the brain.

He had decided maybe Jason and Scott were right. Maybe he should head back to the Penthouse.

But before he gave up entirely, he grabbed a cab and took it to the fallback position where Jason had told Tali to go. Zentraler Omnibusbahnhof was Berlin's central bus station, and an ideal place for someone to blend in while they waited to be picked up. Or, in Tali's case, extracted from a dangerous situation.

He'd walked through the bus station, looking for her. He'd seen many women who looked like her—slender, olive-skinned, jet-black hair—but none of them were her. He spent the better part of an hour waiting inside then outside to see if she had made it. To see if *they* had made it.

His eyes never stopped moving over the seemingly endless stream of people going into and coming from the bus station. Many of them resembled Tali, but none of them were her. None of them moved like her or gave him that same warmth he got whenever he saw her. He checked his handheld constantly. Still no sign of her on OMNI.

Reluctantly, he returned to the Penthouse.

When the elevator doors opened, Hicks stepped in and keyed the elevator to go back upstairs. He checked his handheld one last time in case maybe Tali had made it to the fallback position at the bus station. In case she had tried to reach him.

But the handheld offered no answers. Still no contact.

His knees almost buckled as he began to accept that something had gone horribly wrong. He shook it off and straightened himself out as the elevator reached the Penthouse.

There was no point in letting the others see him like this.

When the elevator doors opened, Hicks saw Roger rush at him with something in his right hand. Instinct kicked in and Hicks tried to knock Roger's hand away.

But Roger dodged the blow, thrust his left hand under Hicks's chin, and injected him in the neck with a pneumatic syringe.

The gentle hiss of the injection died away and Hicks felt himself falling, stopping in midair. He felt like he was floating, the way he'd felt all those years ago in jump school, in those precious seconds before his chute opened as he plummeted to earth, only to stop as he was jolted to a halt and glided down to the landing area.

Hicks's vision was blurred, his hearing muffled, and he couldn't feel any part of his body, not even his face. It was as though he was in a coffin, buried alive within his own body. He may have even panicked if he could have generated enough feeling to do so.

But he did not panic. His mind wouldn't let him. He felt a certain power in his powerlessness, a strength in his numbness. He had been forced to let go of all his troubles, all his worries. The Carousel of Concern that spun constantly in his mind had drifted away in the darkness and was nowhere to be seen. It hadn't been blown to bits as it had back in New York City. It had simply ceased to matter. He soon forgot how he'd come to feel this way, but for the first time in as long as he could remember, James Hicks felt nothing at all. And he had no complaints.

ICKS DIDN'T KNOW how long he had felt this way when he realized his vision was beginning to clear, and so was his mind. Time had been a burden he no longer carried or cared about. He felt too peaceful to care about seconds and minutes and hours and limits.

He realized he was sitting upright. With his peripheral vision, he saw his arms resting atop the plush arms of an easy chair. He eventually found the strength to move his head from left to right. A cord was tied around his chest, keeping him in the chair. He couldn't feel anything else of his body. The paralysis should have made him panic, but gave him a sense of calm instead. Maybe his troubles were finally over. The burdens he had carried for so long would belong to someone else. What those burdens had been were lost to him for now, but the impression they had left in his mind was still there.

His hearing began to return and he heard a familiar voice saying, "James." He recognized the word and the voice. Roger Cobb was saying his name.

Roger spoke again. "I know you can't speak yet, but I need you to look at me if you can hear me."

With more effort than he thought he could muster, Hicks lifted his head and saw Roger just at the edge of his field of vision.

Roger smiled. "That's good. That's very good. Now look around and try to remember where you are."

Hicks felt his vision begin to clear even more as he looked around. He realized the room seemed familiar to him. It was his bedroom. In the Penthouse. He *remembered.*

He realized Roger was sitting on the edge of a bed, his bed, while Hicks was sitting in the plush white chair in the corner.

He had never sat in that chair before, using it instead as a place to dump his clothes when he got undressed each night. He still couldn't feel enough of his body to know if it was comfortable. He couldn't feel anything other than his head. He still couldn't move a muscle or wiggle a toe. He didn't even want to try. He'd prefer not to be able to move his head, either, if he could manage it. The cocoon he'd been in had been warm and dull and perfect. He wanted to go back.

Roger shifted himself so he was in Hicks's view and Hicks remembered he was there. Roger tucked a finger beneath Hicks's chin and held his head upright. "I gave you something to make you calm. It's harmless, and the fact that you're regaining a range of motion in your neck shows the medicine is already beginning to wear off."

But he didn't want it to wear off. The term itself had meant something temporary, something with defined edges and boundaries. He had grown to enjoy the weightlessness of unimportance. The freedom of insignificance. Why was Roger pulling him away from all of that? They were friends, weren't they?

Then he remembered all the way back to when he had begun to feel like this. To a time when Roger had stabbed him in the neck with something. Why had he done that then? Why was he threatening to take away such a wonderful gift?

Hicks realized his head was beginning to feel heavier. He pulled his head away from Roger's finger. Shadows of questions began to form in his mind, but the link between his brain and his mouth had not been reestablished. A question would begin to form, only to evaporate in the ether of his bliss. But enough questions burned away to leave enough ash behind for him to understand what they all meant. He looked at the ash and read what he saw. His own voice echoed in the chambers of his mind as he heard himself ask, "Why?"

"Because I have some unpleasant things to tell you. Things I needed to tell you in a certain setting. I needed to make sure you couldn't hurt yourself or anyone else when I told you Tali Saddon is dead."

Tali Saddon. That was a name, too, just like Roger Cobb. A name that had meant something important to him at some point not too long ago. The mist in his mind drifted away as the full memory of who she was and the meaning of Roger's words hit home. The words struck him at the very core of his being. *Tali was dead. Their baby was dead.*

He still could not feel his arms or legs, but an ache somewhere deep within him began to spread throughout his entire body.

He felt a single tear run down his cheek. Only one word made sense to him. "No."

"She was killed a block away from the coffee shop, long before you got there. Thirty minutes at least, probably more based on how we tracked your location. She died well, James. She drew the Vanguard men away from Rivas with the laptop we were using to upload the information to OMNI. She was a hero."

Hicks heard what Roger was saying, every word dulling the numbness and bringing him out of the warm fog he had enjoyed for so long. He felt more tears on his cheeks as he struggled to form another word. "How?"

"She killed three of her attackers before a fourth one stabbed her from behind. He stabbed her in the heart. It was a clean wound, probably a dagger. I doubt she felt any pain. It was a good death."

Most of the feeling had returned to his face, allowing him to feel the coolness left on his skin by evaporating tears. Tears at the memory of who Tali Saddon was and what she had meant to him. Tears for what had been so special about her. "The baby?"

Roger looked away.

"No." Hicks shut his eyes, shut them hard until he saw bright sparks through the darkness. "No. Not that. Please."

Roger drew his thumbs across Hicks's cheeks, removing the tears. "That's the reason I gave you the injection, my old friend. I needed you to hear the truth and not what you wanted to believe. What she wanted you to believe. I needed you to understand that she lied to you, James. She wasn't pregnant. There was no baby because there never could have been a baby."

Hicks found enough strength to lurch forward in the chair, trying to launch himself at the man who was lying to him now. This man who was supposed to be his friend. Maybe it wasn't Roger Cobb after all. He remembered being drugged. Maybe this was all just an elaborate setup by Tessmer to break him of his will. To get him to talk. Maybe…

But Hicks didn't launch himself anywhere. He could only move his head. His arms and legs and the rest of his body were still dead.

Roger gently eased Hicks's head back in the chair. "I checked on her medical records when you told me she was expecting. Not just the records we had on her with the University or even those she had on file with the Mossad, but all the way back to when she was just another girl growing up in Tel Aviv. I found she had been in a serious car accident when she was eleven years old. Her reproductive organs were damaged and her uterus never developed properly, at least not to the point where she could bring a child to full term, if she could become pregnant at all. Her infertility was probably the reason the Mossad trained her to be a seducer of men."

Hicks lunged again, feeling more power in the thrust. His arms and legs were still dead, but now he could feel the blood flowing through his chest and shoulders. He knew he was tied to a chair, but this time put enough force behind it to make the chair creak from the effort.

He leaned as far forward as he could against his restraints and glared at the man who was lying to him now. The man who was supposed to be his closest friend. The man who had injected him with paradise only to ruin it with lies. The man who had just told him the woman he loved was not only dead, but a liar as well.

Hicks saw Scott appear in the doorway of the bedroom. "He's coming out of it. Give him another shot."

"No." Roger never took his eyes off his friend. "That will only delay the inevitable."

"Damn it, Roger. His strength is coming back. He'll kill you if he gets loose."

"Get out," Roger snapped. "Watch the prisoner. We'll be out in a minute."

Scott slammed the bedroom door behind him.

Hicks was still panting, feeling his strength returning gradually with each passing second. Scott. Roger. This room. All of it seemed real. All of it felt like it had when he'd left the Penthouse earlier that day, but nothing Roger was saying made sense.

Hicks felt his breathing become more rapid. His rage building.

Roger gently took Hicks's head in his hands and thumbed away more tears. "I kept you sedated while Jason and Demerest pulled some strings to have the coroner examine her remains. I have a copy of his initial report for you to review whenever you're ready. It confirms she wasn't pregnant and could never be pregnant. You told me she called your child a miracle baby. Maybe that was because she knew how unlikely the odds were. I don't know if she lied to you because she was afraid you were going to kill her over Jabbar, or if it was just wishful thinking on her part, but Tali Saddon was not carrying your child or anyone else's."

Hicks felt the blood begin to pound through his veins, sparks of feeling returning to his hands and feet, portions of his arms and legs. But it was his chest where most of the feeling had returned. And his mind, his damnable mind, was no longer numb. It absorbed every word Roger was saying.

And it was his mind that knew, deep within it, that every word Roger was saying was true.

And when that pain and that truth and that anger and that frustration crashed together in the center of his chest, James Hicks let out a bellow that lasted for as long and loud as he could manage. He raged against his paralysis. He raged against the cord around his chest. He raged into the face of Roger Cobb. He reddened and strained and roared until whatever was in his stomach came up. And as was Roger's way, he had a bucket ready.

When Hicks's stomach was empty, Roger took the bucket into the bathroom, dumped it in the toilet, and flushed. He returned with a towel and wiped the remnants of sickness from his friend's face.

"Everything I've told you is completely true and verifiable, James. What you do next is entirely up to you." He finished wiping his face clean and set the towel aside. "You and I have seen what news like this has done to some people. To people better than you or I will ever be. You've just lost someone you cared about very much. A woman, a lover. The mother of the child you wanted desperately to believe was real, but knew deep down was not. That was then. This is now, and what you decide from this moment forward will decide the course of the rest of your life."

Somewhere deep inside himself, Hicks knew he was right. He also knew that, at that moment, he was too sore to care. "Not now, Roger."

"Yes, now, because this is important. We've both seen what happens to men in your position. We've seen them become blind to reality. We've seen them set logic aside and indulge in vengeance. Rage. And we've both seen how it ultimately destroyed them, turning them into liabilities that need to be mitigated by men like you and me."

Hicks felt that all the feeling had returned to his head, to the point where he felt a dull ache settling in behind his eyes. The same dull headache he'd always gotten whenever things got tense. He wanted to rub his eyes, but still couldn't move his hands. "I can't do this right now. Tali's dead. At least let me—"

"Let you what?" Roger asked. "Mourn? Wallow in your loss? We don't have the luxury of time, James. We're on the verge of getting our first real grasp of who the Vanguard is and how they operate. We're too close and have lost too much to allow sentiment to get in the way. You have to make up your mind as to where you stand, and you need to make it up here and now before you even leave this room."

He paused long enough for Hicks to say something, but Hicks had nothing to say. Roger went on. "I've done a lot of things for this organization, James. I've done a lot of things for you, too. I owe you. You've saved my life more times than you will ever know. You're the closest thing to family that I have. I'm with you all the way no matter what you decide, even if I disagree with it. I just don't want you to throw your life away to avenge a lie."

Roger took the towel as he stood. "The injection I gave you is a sedative of my own devising. The feeling will return to your extremities in a few minutes. You should have full range of motion within the next thirty minutes or so. At that point, you'll be able to undo the rope I tied around your chest and sit up on your own. I'd wait a couple of minutes before you stand because you'll be pretty wobbly for a while. When you're ready, we'll be outside waiting. Your Ruger is still under your arm. You can shoot me in the head for doing this to you if you want. Or you can dust yourself off and hurt the people who have cost you so much."

When Hicks spoke, his voice was hoarse. "Did Rivas make it out okay?"

"He's fine and he's here, too. We'll give you a full briefing when you're ready."

Hicks watched Roger walk to the door. "One more thing."

Roger turned with a hand on the doorknob. "Yes?"

"If you ever do that to me again, I won't like it. And I won't forgive it, either."

"Then let's hope I never have to."

Roger quietly shut the bedroom door behind him, leaving Hicks alone with his thoughts. His damnable, miserable thoughts.

More tears came, and he was unable to stop them.

CHAPTER
27

AN HOUR LATER, Hicks opened the bedroom door and stepped into the hallway leading to the main living area of the suite. He didn't know what time it was, but judging by the view from the windows, dusk had already begun to fall over Berlin. He found Patel, Scott, and Roger huddled around Rivas as they looked at a laptop on the coffee table.

For a split-second, he wondered why Tali wasn't there…but only for a split-second. He felt dizzy and had to prop himself against the wall to keep from falling over.

The sound caused all the men to look at him. Roger got to his feet and approached his friend. "I told you the sedative took a while to wear off. Come, let me help you."

Hicks pushed himself off the wall and fired a straight right hand, connecting with Roger's jaw. Cobb stumbled backward, falling over the arm of an overstuffed chair.

Roger smiled as he rubbed his jaw. "I'll take that as a sign you're feeling better."

Hicks readjusted the holster under his left arm. The presence of the pistol made him feel closer to his old self. It gave him the clarity he needed.

He cleared his throat as he looked at Scott, Patel, and Rivas. "We took a pretty big loss today. Tali meant a lot to the University, to this team, and to me personally. But none of that really matters right now. The best way to honor her memory is to stop the same bastards she was fighting." To Rivas, Hicks said, "Glad you made it out okay."

Rivas looked down at the keyboard. "Wish I could've done something to help Tali."

"She killed three of the four men after her," Hicks said. "I'd say she didn't need your help."

He didn't want to talk about Tali anymore. He couldn't allow himself to dwell on what he had lost or what had happened. He had to focus on what was happening now and what would happen tomorrow. He had to be ready on the off chance that Tessmer kept their meeting.

"Were we able to track the bastard who killed Tali?"

"No," Patel answered. "We know they took the mirroring laptop from her, and we tracked the equipment for another two blocks north before the bleaching program kicked in. Since they didn't take her handheld, the program activated automatically. They'll get nothing off the device."

Rivas added, "Demerest's people have the laptop now. Probably going through it as we speak. Since there was no obvious connection to OMNI, the system is still secure. Jason's monitoring it for hacks, but coming up empty."

"How much of the Vanguard laptop were we able to upload to OMNI?"

"About sixty percent before the bleaching program activated on the ghost computer," Scott said. "We didn't get everything, but we still got some pretty impressive stuff."

Hicks pointed to the large television screen as he took a seat on the couch. "Show me."

Rivas tapped a few keys and the television screen showed the same view of his laptop. "The amount of information on the laptop was enormous. They've got a secure cloud set up that's not all that unlike OMNI, but doesn't appear to be as powerful. It's double encrypted and OMNI's having a hard time breaking the code. From what we can see, the Vanguard is made up of two completely different factions."

"Chinese and German," Hicks said. "Jason told me that already. Give me something else. What about Tessmer? Anything on him?"

"No," Rivas admitted. "I was searching for information on him even as I was uploading files to OMNI. Nothing came up."

Hicks wasn't surprised. Tessmer had admitted the name was an old identity. He doubted the Vanguard would have anything like an official organizational chart, but he had hoped the information could tell him something about their leadership.

"What about the Chinese faction of the Vanguard?"

"Just as foggy as the Russian side," Patel said. "Their financial files are by far the largest and therefore the hardest to search through at this point. We've asked OMNI to avoid the spreadsheets and financial files altogether and focus on the emails instead. Even then, OMNI has only been able to search roughly five percent of the financial data alone, but has come up with one common phrase."

Rahul pointed at the television and saw one name pop up from all the thousands of emails OMNI was currently scanning:
Laoban

"My Mandarin isn't what it used to be," Rahul admitted, "not that it was ever very good in the first place. However, this word, roughly translated, means 'the boss,' or even more roughly translated, 'the man.' It's not a term of reverence, like chairman, but more of a term of status, where one fits in the order of things."

Hicks blinked away a bout of dizziness. Probably the after-effects of Roger's injection. "Thanks for the sociology lesson. I don't give a shit why they call him whatever they call him. I want to know who he is and where he is."

Rivas said, "We're already looking for him, but that's going to take a little time. The Vanguard isn't big on leaving stray details in their files, so finding him is going to take some doing. I hate to say this, but we might need to rely on the Barnyard to help us with the remaining information."

Another delay. Hicks's headache began to spike. He asked Roger, "Did you get anything out of the prisoner?"

"A few useful items after some gentle coaxing," Roger said. "They had about fifty men here in Berlin in various capacities. All of them ex-Russian Army. Even a few old Stasi hands from those heady days of the Berlin Wall are still lurking about, though largely in a leadership capacity."

Hicks caught that. "Did he tell you the name of their boss?"

"He called him Sasha, though he's German-born. Around seventy years old or so, which means he's probably ex-Stasi, too. I asked him about Tessmer, of course. I even showed him the old mug shot from Bonn. He said he'd never heard the name before and never saw the man in the photo, either. I believed him and so did the polygraph."

"So what? Tessmer admitted he was using another name when I talked to him."

"Not only another name," Roger said, "but possibly a completely different face. He's probably had extensive plastic surgery since that photo was taken. He could look like anyone by now."

Hicks should've understood that before Roger laid it out for him. He wasn't thinking straight. He decided to blame it on Roger's injection rather than the grief over losing Tali.

"What else did you get from him? Names? Dates? Locations?"

"He worked mostly out of the facility we raided today, which is frequently visited by his boss, who we should refer to as Tessmer for lack of a more accurate name. He spends a couple of days a week there reviewing the financials before calling someone on the phone and speaking Russian, surprisingly good Russian for a German, to someone overseas. Our friend assumes it's overseas because they frequently have to shout to hear each other, probably due to a bad connection. Could be that our Tessmer is speaking to Rivas's *Laoban*."

"What about locations? Where his boss might be now? Anything like that?"

He checked his watch. "We're due to begin another session soon. I'll make sure I ask him then."

"Just make sure you keep him alive," Hicks said. "He's my bargaining chip with Tessmer." Hicks felt another bout of dizziness come over him, but shook it off. "Something came up right before everything happened with…Tali. While I was out, I used the Operators to reach out to Tessmer thanks to the phone Mike ghosted from the prisoner. He wants to meet tomorrow morning."

None of the men looked at each other, but all of them, even Scott, had the same mixed expression of surprise and eagerness. No fear or hesitation. Not even after what had happened to Tali. Hicks took that as a good sign.

Scott asked, "Do you think that's still on? Even after what happened outside the coffee shop today?"

"Let's proceed under the idea that the meeting is still taking place. I'll make a couple of phone calls and see what I can find. In the meantime, I want everyone to get something to eat and get some rest. Rivas and Patel, you can monitor OMNI's progress on the data via your tablets from your rooms. No sense in wasting time crouched over a laptop when you should be getting sleep. Trust me, I have a feeling we're going to need every second of rest we can manage."

"That goes for you, too," Roger said. "You've had a horrible day. I can give you something to…"

Hicks found his jacket across one of the chairs by the elevator and put it on. "It's seven o'clock now. I want all weapons cleaned, locked, and loaded with lights out by eight thirty. Pack extra heavy because we're going to see some action tomorrow. Set your alarms on your handhelds for five in the morning. If we need to make it earlier or later than that, I'll change them remotely."

Scott stepped forward as Hicks keyed the elevator open. "Where are you going?"

"To make a couple of phone calls."

"You need someone with you?"

Hicks ignored the question as the elevator doors slid shut. He'd said enough for one day.

CHAPTER 28

Although he was fairly certain OMNI's integrity hadn't been compromised, Hicks still walked three blocks away from the Penthouse before calling Jason. The Vanguard had proven to be incredibly technologically efficient. The bleaching software on the mirroring University laptop should have wiped out the hard drive, but the device had still been linked to OMNI. He didn't want to take any chances by putting the Penthouse at risk. He'd already lost enough people for one day.

It was a pleasant spring evening and the streets were full of people enjoying a gentle night. He overheard some of them talking about the shootings that had occurred earlier that day. Wasn't it horrible? Was it terrorists? Some cursed the chancellor for letting so many foreigners into the country. Others said it was a bank robbery gone wrong.

But as he walked amongst them Hicks heard most people

talking about their own lives. Dinner dates they were running late for, how much they hated their bosses and, as everywhere, many of them were lost in the digital world of their handheld phones.

It was a completely normal evening, yet to Hicks nothing seemed right. The woman he had loved had been killed only a few blocks from where he was standing. No one in the ancient city of Berlin gave a shit. Tali was dead. Life went on. Their lives went on, completely oblivious of the fact that people in their own city were dedicated to ruining their way of life.

Hicks stopped walking when he reached the corner. He didn't move out of anyone's way. He didn't excuse himself or try to shuffle off to the side of the street. He just stopped and stood where he was. The crowd simply moved around him. He drew a few awkward looks, but was quickly forgotten within a few steps.

People didn't know about organizations like the University or the Vanguard. They cared even less about those who worked for these organizations. Those who dedicated their lives and deaths so they could enjoy an easy walk through old Berlin on a nice spring evening.

They didn't know because they didn't want to know. People liked to avoid the bad and awkward things to focus on the good. The banal. The next celebrity divorce. The newest series on Netflix.

He envied every one of the oblivious bastards.

He crossed the street and stepped to the side, next to an office building. He took out his handheld and called Jason.

"I'm sorry about Tali," Jason said when he answered. "I know you two were close. Please let me know if there's anything

I can do."

Hicks couldn't afford sentiment. Not yet. "You can start by getting Demerest on the line. Make sure you scramble my location and listen in. He already knows I'm in Berlin, but I don't want him tracing the call and leading him to the Penthouse."

Jason paused. "You've been dealing with him directly until now. May I ask why the change?"

Hicks was too tired to be angry, so he was honest instead. "Because he was tracking the phone he gave me and I destroyed it. There's also a good chance I might not make it through tomorrow's meeting with Tessmer, and I want you to be able to brief my replacement on where we stand."

"You'll survive tomorrow," Jason said. "Whether you meet Tessmer or not. You always find a way to survive."

But after losing Tali, he wasn't sure he wanted to. "Yeah. Lucky me. Now get Demerest for me. I'm switching to my earpiece so I can check my handheld in case Tessmer texts me about tomorrow's meeting."

Hicks tapped the icon for the prisoner's phone and tapped out a text message while he waited for Demerest to come on the line. In English, he wrote:
WHERE AND WHEN TOMORROW?

Demerest came on the line. "I heard you lost someone today, son. I'm sorry."

Hicks shut his eyes. He hoped that was the last time anyone would offer condolences about Tali. He needed results and facts, not more grief. He knew grief would come soon enough, and it wouldn't be pretty when it did. But he couldn't let that genie out of the bottle yet.

"Did your contact at the German security police get

anything from the men Tali killed?"

"Not a damn thing," Demerest admitted. "None of the men had any cash or identification on them. All of them had their fingerprints removed. We're running their DNA through INTERPOL and the FBI systems, but it'll be weeks before they get back to us with a match, if they have a match at all."

Hicks was disappointed, but not all that surprised. The Vanguard had proven to be nothing if not efficient. "What about cell phones?"

"Brand new burner phones on all three bodies. Activated earlier that morning, never used, paid for in cash at the same store. We tracked them via traffic cameras from the spot to the store. We're still trying to trace them back further than that and that will take time."

"Time," Hicks repeated. "The one thing I don't have. I'm scheduled to meet someone from the Vanguard tomorrow."

Demerest was quiet for a couple of beats. "Delay it."

"No way. After what happened with Tali, I don't even know if it's still on. And if it is, then he's going to look to end this thing. We're too close to let him get away now."

"And you're not stupid enough to actually meet him," Demerest said. "Not like this. You burned through a hell of a lot of our good will with the Germans today, son. My contact over there has spent the better part of two days running interference for you, and he's not happy about tagging and bagging the bodies you leave behind."

Hicks grabbed the device tighter. "Careful, Carl. One of those dead bodies was one of mine."

Demerest swore. "I know that, but I can't keep going to the well empty-handed like this. I need a name, James. I need something I can have people work on to help explain this mess. It's only a matter of time before someone in the alphabet soup ties you to all of this. If that happens, the Vanguard will be the least of your problems."

It was Hicks's turn to be quiet for a moment. "I think you just threatened me, Carl."

"No, I just told you the way things are," Demerest said. "No bullshit and no sugar- coating. I can protect you if you give me a name to run through the system. A viable name, not some asshole you killed in Angola twenty years ago. I know that game and it won't fly with me. I need someone attached to these attacks. Someone vital and real. We're past the point of being coy now, son. Forget about our seventy-two-hour agreement. We're way past that shit. Give me a name. Now."

"I've never been to Angola," Hicks said. "And you've got plenty of names on the laptop my people died to give you."

"The information on that hard drive is double encrypted. It'll take our most advanced computers weeks to get everything. That's why I need a name from you right fucking now. You've already lost enough for one day, son. Don't add my good graces to the tally."

Hicks felt his handheld buzz, not from a call or an e-mail, but from a text message. He looked at his screen.

Tessmer had responded.

And for the first time in as long as he could remember, James Hicks smiled. He'd gotten his meeting. There was no reason to keep it from Demerest any longer. "The man who runs the German side of the Vanguard used to go by the alias Wilhelm Tessmer. It's an old alias that'll probably take you a day or so to run down. I don't have a current name for him, so don't bother pushing me for it. Now, if you want to make your friends in the German government happy, you're going to listen to me very carefully."

CHAPTER 29

Russischer Friedhof Berlin-Tegel Cemetery, Berlin
The Next Morning

HICKS PAID THE driver, got out of the cab, and lit a cigar. As he brought his hand up to shield the flame from a gentle breeze, he said, "I'm on the street in front of the cemetery. Give me a SITREP."

Rivas's voice came over the earbud. "Satellite confirms the cemetery is empty, except for one person standing exactly where they're supposed to be. I'm not detecting any additional heat signatures in the immediate area, so I think he's alone."

Hicks got a good draw on the cigar and pocketed the lighter. "Send me his picture."

"I would if I could," Rivas said. "I had to hack into an old NOAA satellite to get an overview of the cemetery. The closest I can zoom in is about half a mile above the target."

Hicks couldn't believe his rotten luck. "What about INTERPOL and NATO satellites?"

"They've all upped their security, so it'll take OMNI some time to hack them again. Probably in response to the Vanguard attack on New York. We'll get them eventually, but it'll take a couple of days. Probably not in time to help you."

Hicks almost bit into the cigar. "Demerest was supposed to help us after I told him about Tessmer."

"He did," Rivas said, "but none of his satellites are in position yet. He lived up to his part of the bargain. Technically. All I can give you is heat readings until further notice."

Hicks checked the street for cars or vans, or people lingering where they shouldn't. It was just another Tuesday morning in old Berlin. "Try accessing the security cameras inside the cemetery."

"I probably could if there were any," Rivas told him, "They have an old system to watch the office, but that's it."

Hicks cursed as he took a pull on the cigar. It was a mid-level Arturo Fuente stick and the draw was excellent. The infusion of tobacco into his system kept his frustration in check. It helped him focus.

He let the smoke slowly escape his nose. "Any frequencies coming in or out of there?"

"I'm using your handheld to see if it's picking anything up. I'm just seeing a cellular signal coming from the target's general direction. It looks like he's alone."

Alone, Hicks thought, *in a place full of corpses.* The irony of two professional killers meeting in a cemetery was not lost on Hicks. He didn't know why Tessmer had chosen a cemetery as their meeting place. He didn't care either. He just wanted to get it over with. "My mic will be hot the whole time. Give me reports on Scott's position as they happen, no matter what.

Understand?"

"Copy that. Checking in with him now. I'll be in touch."

Hicks took another pull on his cigar. *Showtime.*

It was just after eight that morning when Hicks finally walked through the back gate of the Russischer Friedhof Berlin-Tegel in the Reinickendorf section of Berlin. He kept his jacket open. The Kevlar lining made him warmer than he should have been. The Kevlar vest beneath his shirt added an extra layer of protection, but not comfort. If anything, it made him sweat even more.

The only comfort he felt was the Ruger hanging just beneath his left arm.

Since he couldn't rely on technology, he relied on the skills he had honed long ago. Sight, sound, movement, and instinct. The hallmarks of his craft.

The rising sun had begun to cast long shadows of the headstones across the grass. A warmish breeze moved through the cemetery, reminding Hicks that spring was almost over and summer was not far behind. He figured the odds that he might live to see it were fifty-fifty at most.

Despite the odds he felt especially sharp that morning, as though he could see every blade of grass and hear every bird in every tree. Maybe it was because he was expecting to get shot at any second.

He hoped Demerest's friend in the German intelligence service was as good as Demerest had said he was. He hoped he'd listen to Scott and follow his lead. Scott had taken down Vanguard men before. The German probably hadn't, at least not knowingly. One false step could turn a simple takedown operation into a full-blown gun battle on a Berlin street.

Hicks looked for Vanguard members as he passed by crypts families had built as tributes to their dead. Some of the tombs were more ornate than others, marble as opposed to concrete. Some boasted plaques, others had stone statues or bronze angels looking toward the heavens in eternal solemnity.

Hicks had never understood why people spent so much money to commemorate their own passing. Death was a final, ugly, and inevitable event. Some deaths were more peaceful than others, but the result was the same. No one escaped it. No number of marble stones or sculpted angels could change that.

Walking among the dead reminded Hicks of Tali. He had thought of her several times an hour, each hour, since the moment Roger had confirmed she had been killed. Hicks had seen too much of this world to believe in quaint notions of a heaven or a hell, but he hoped there was another world where spirits received rewards for the sacrifices they made to keep people safe in this world. People like Tali and Al Clay and Colin deserved that much. People he had lost. People he had allowed himself to care about.

As he walked deeper into the cemetery, more thoughts of Tali began to creep into his mind. He needed to focus on Tessmer and this mission, but for all his training and experience, he couldn't help himself. The absurdity of it was just too much, even now as he walked to meet a man who had tried so hard to kill him.

Hicks had loved a woman he had never really known. He knew her file, her skills, her specialties as a field agent, her fitness reports, and psychological evaluations. He even knew the groups-and-scores results from her monthly visits to the rifle range.

He had known everything about what Agent Tali Saddon could do on the job, but nothing about the woman she was. He had been in love with a stranger. He had willfully forgotten she a professional manipulator who had led him to believe she was actually carrying their child.

An idea he had been all too willing to believe. He hadn't wanted to believe in anything so much since the days when he had been a boy, in a time when mornings such as these, of stark sunshine and warm spring breezes, weren't clouded by fears of killing or being killed. When beautiful spring days held only the promise of the freedom of summer. A time when all the mysteries of adulthood lay over the horizon just beyond his reach, but grew closer every day.

A time when dreams were important and worth having. When dreams like being in love and having a family seemed important and possible.

A time before James Hicks had existed.

But with each passing year, he found himself moving away from the boy he had once been, and even further away from the adult he had once hoped to become. None of the dreams of his youth had come true, and in their place was the man walking through a cemetery in Berlin to meet an evil man. James Hicks, a man his childhood self could not have envisioned and would have probably hated.

He had succeeded in becoming a stranger to himself, yet another tragic death to mourn as he walked through a cemetery toward his fate. Alone.

The comforting pall of grief and loss had settled around him. He quickly shrugged it off. He blinked his eyes and cleared his mind as though waking from a sleep. He took a deep pull on his cigar and exhaled it slowly as he walked. The tobacco brought him back. It anchored him in place. *Cut this shit out right now. Concentrate on the mission, not on the losses.*

Sentimental nostalgia had no place here. Losing focus against a man like Tessmer would get him killed.

Tali Saddon and Al Clay and Colin were all dead. So was the boy who had lofty dreams of true love and noble service. No amount of grief could bring back the past. No amount of killing could avenge the people he had lost. Only information could accomplish that. Information on the Vanguard that Tessmer possessed. Information Hicks was going to get from the man, one way or the other.

Hicks was still smoking his cigar when he crested the hill, and saw a lone figure standing in front of a tall crypt in the middle of a row of graves.

Hicks brought his hand up to his mouth as if to adjust his cigar and said, "I have eyes on Tessmer."

"And I have eyes on you," Rivas responded in his earpiece. "Scott reports six men are staging outside the cemetery's front entrance. Our people are in place, ready to intercept. I'll keep you apprised of major developments. And remember, Hicks, whatever you do, don't kill Tessmer."

Hicks let the cigar smoke drift from his nose. "I'll keep that in mind."

He began walking toward his enemy.

SCOTT PEERED THROUGH his binoculars as he crouched behind the dense shrubbery at the cemetery entrance. He watched six men get out of three vans parked at various spots along both sides of the street. They gathered to smoke in the doorway of an abandoned storefront with windows that had recently been painted white from the inside. They were all wearing long coats or bulky jackets. From what he could see, each one of them appeared to be concealing an M4 under their coats.

People walked past the six men without paying them any notice.

Mueller, Demerest's contact with the German federal police, crouched next to him. He observed the scene through binoculars of his own. "These people are armed to the teeth on a busy public street. My men are ready to move in now."

"My man in the cemetery is wide open and exposed," Scott said. "We don't go until I give the order."

Mueller lowered his binoculars and glared at the American. "I give orders to my men, Mr. Scott. No one else. And I have no intention of allowing the streets of Berlin to be turned into a Wild West show. I want to take these men down immediately, while they're bunched together in the same place."

Scott kept watching the men through the binoculars. Some had lit cigarettes. They weren't going anywhere for a while. "The name's not Mr. Scott, Hans. Just Scott. And we've only got eyes on six Vanguard men so far. They usually roll in teams of either five or ten. Let's wait and see if more show up. Let's see if there are more of them in the vans. No reason to allow more of them to escape by moving too early. If they move on our position, we open fire as soon as they pass through the cemetery gates."

Mueller lifted his binoculars again. "Name's not Hans."

Scott ignored the correction. "There are six of them and ten of us. If your people are as good as you say they are, this will all be over in one squeeze of the trigger."

He heard Mueller say something in German that was undoubtedly a curse. Scott smiled. He tapped his throat mic. "Team Two, this is Leader. You boys have eyes on the prize?"

"Copy, Leader," Patel whispered from behind the painted windows of the vacant store across the street. "Six men gathering right in front of our position, blocking our camera's view. Holding for your orders."

"If you can't see them, you can hear them," Scott said. "Cobb's German is better than yours. Can he hear what they're saying?"

"Copy, Leader. Hold on."

Scott shifted his weight from one knee to the other while he waited for a response. The men lined up on either side of him were just as uncomfortable as he was. Waiting for something to happen was bad enough. Sweating under all that gear while you waited made it even worse.

Roger's voice came on the line. "Leader, this is Two. They're complaining about how this is a stupid idea. They're angry about the men they've lost. They're going to kill the American the first chance they get, no matter what the boss says. They haven't referred to this boss by name. I'll let you know if they do."

Scott was surprised by Cobb's straightforward report. He had expected him to add some commentary to what he'd heard. He was glad he didn't. "Continue listening for information on how many they're expecting to join them. Point out the shot-caller if you can. We go when they go."

"Copy," Roger said. "Team Two out."

Scott gripped his binoculars tighter as he watched the men

kill time. "Come on, you sons of bitches. What are you waiting for?"

He had a feeling he'd find out soon enough.

CHAPTER 30

THE MAN STANDING beside the crypt looked completely different than the face Hicks had seen in the mug shot in the Bonn police report.

That photo had been of a pale, bald man, painfully thin, with dead blue eyes and no chin. Wire-rimmed spectacles perched on a long, thin nose had given him a particularly harsh look.

The brown-eyed man standing beside the crypt looked more like an art dealer than a terrorist. He had wavy blond hair mixed with silver swept back from his forehead. He bore a rich tan, and his nose had since been altered to make it wider. Implants gave him a more defined jawline and chin. His neck and body were much thicker than the man in the Bonn mug shot. Heavier in a muscular way, not the way one fills out with age. If the Bonn arrest record was accurate, Tessmer was in his seventies, but looked closer to fifty.

The contrast between the old mug-shot and the man was so stark that Hicks might have walked away if it hadn't been for the eyes. The spectacles might be gone and the eyes might be brown now, but nothing could change what was behind them. Blue or brown, the gaze was the same and just as dead.

Tessmer held up a hand when Hicks was about ten yards away. "That's close enough," he said in English. His German accent bore a hint of Russian influence, especially around the vowels. He gestured toward Hicks's cigar. "I don't know how it is in America, but in Germany it is considered poor taste to smoke in a cemetery."

Hicks trailed smoke as he looked around at the headstones. "I don't think anybody's going to complain."

"One might be forgiven for believing the cigar is compensating for some kind of shortcoming."

"Wasn't it a German who said, 'Sometimes a cigar is just a cigar'?"

"Freud," Tessmer said. "He never actually said that, you know."

Hicks smoked anyway. "The truth is sometimes overrated. Speaking of which, I like what you've done with your hair. Jawline, too. Nice touches."

Tessmer rubbed his hand across his face. "The man was a true craftsman. The finest in Europe, perhaps the world. I'd offer to give you his number, but I'm afraid he's no longer practicing."

Hicks was pretty sure the surgeon was no longer practicing because he was dead. "What should I call you? I know you're not using the name Tessmer anymore."

"Tessmer will do just fine for our purposes today." He smiled, as if recalling an old memory. "I had almost forgotten about that name until your Jews began making their unfortunate inquiries about it. Serves me right for not scrubbing the Bonn records thoroughly enough. My countrymen are known for their efficiency." The smile changed. "But that doesn't matter anymore. My error has been rectified. Your Jews have been rectified, too, if you look at it a certain way."

Hicks fought the urge to reach for the Ruger and shoot the man. He smoked instead. "Heard a few of your men got rectified in the process, too. By the way, I kept your man alive. We can drop him off to you whenever you want."

"How thoughtful," Tessmer smiled. "That was just a test. I didn't actually think you'd do that. Kill him if you want. As for the others, they were just a price to pay given my sloppiness about my past. I count Yulian as part of that price, too. It was his stupidity and fear that led you to me in the first place. Though I am curious. Was the man in the nightclub an agent of yours or just an informant? There's some internal debate about that and I'd like to clear it up."

Hicks decided to lie a little, see where it got him. "We had heard Yulian was close to the Vanguard's leadership. We knew he was weak and that you had a blind spot where he was concerned. We exploited both weaknesses and now it's just you and me."

Tessmer looked at the ground. "It broke my heart to have to kill him. He had been with me so long that I had lost sight of his weaknesses. If he had only kept his mouth shut and remembered his training, he'd still be alive today." He sucked his teeth. "So many dead over one man's gaudy shortcomings. Yulian. Several of my people. Some of your people, too." His eyes slid back to Hicks's. "Your Jewess, especially. Tali Saddon, I believe her real name was. I understand you two were particularly close."

Hicks felt every muscle in his body tighten when he heard Rivas's voice in his ear. "He's goading you. Don't let him win."

Hicks forced himself to start breathing again.

Tessmer went on. "Normally I avoid killing women, even when those women are Mossad agents, but I'm afraid she forced my hand. Quite literally, too. She practically backed into the knife as she was about to flee." The German laughed. "One of the easiest kills of my career." He stopped laughing. "One of the most satisfying, too, given the circumstances."

Stifled rage made Hicks's hand tremble as he took another pull on the cigar.

"Though I must admit," Tessmer went on, "that giving her the decoy laptop was very clever on your part. Tell me, was the cripple in the coffee shop part of this or just a coincidence? There's a sizable bet among my men as to whether he was part of this. I'd like to know."

Hicks's voice quivered more than he would've liked. "I didn't think Communists believed in betting."

"I have to allow my men some fun. Killing your Jewess took some of the fun out of the hunt. Like me, they prefer to avoid killing women whenever possible."

"You didn't mind killing women when you released a bioweapon in New York."

"A plot you ably put down, didn't you?" Tessmer said. "I'll admit I never thought it would succeed, but I thought it would do far more damage before the Americans caught on. That was entirely Bajjah's idea, by the way, though I suppose I deserve my share of the blame for agreeing to fund it. My Chinese partners had more faith in the plan than I did, but all boats rise and fall together on the same tide. If I am to accept any of the credit for our many successes, then I must accept blame for the odd loss or two." He shrugged again. "If any good has come from all this bloodshed, it's that I have learned one cannot be too complacent when it comes to personnel or technology." He held open his hands. "Who says old dogs cannot learn new tricks."

Hicks smoked his cigar. "Old dogs usually get put down."

Tessmer's smile dimmed. "Some die of natural causes. In the wild, for example, like the wolf or the bear." He patted the façade of the crypt. "Plenty of dead dogs in here, though. Imperialist pigs and capitalists for the most part. The von Hayek family. My family, my real name, in case you're wondering, is Werner von Hayek. The government made us stop using the 'von' in public records after World War I, but my grandfather insisted we keep our original name on the family crypt."

Hicks hoped Rivas heard that and was already running it through OMNI before sharing it with Demerest.

Tessmer looked at the structure as if seeing it for the first time. "Gaudy, isn't it? I can't tell you how many times my father dragged us to this damnable place before the Wall went up. Always kept a picture of it on his mirror after that. He is buried here, too, as is my mother. Rather embarrassing for a KGB agent to have a family so devoted to religion, but one can't choose one's parents, can one?"

Hicks took another pull on his cigar. His instinct about Tessmer had been right. He was a man who liked to talk. And the more he talked, the more Hicks learned. "Hope someone's got the key to the crypt handy. Might be needing it soon."

"Oh, I don't think it will come to that." He took his hand away from the crypt and gestured toward his left ear. "My people tell me you came here alone. I must admit I was surprised by that. Americans are not usually fond of following directions."

"We make up for it by being direct. So let's cut the bullshit and skip to the part about why I'm here."

But Tessmer wouldn't be rushed. "I'm surprised you didn't bring at least one person with you as a precaution, in case you were walking into a trap. Isn't that the motto of your United States Marines? Semper Paratus? Or is that the Boy Scouts?"

"That's the Coast Guard, not the Marines."

Tessmer snapped his fingers. "That's right. Forgive me. Yes, of course. I should know that. After all, I've seen that phrase somewhere before. Recently, too." He made a show of rubbing his chin as he appeared to think. "Let me see, now. Where have I seen that phrase? Semper Paratus?"

The German's eyes brightened as he snapped his fingers again. "Of course! How could I forget? It's right over here." He pointed to a headstone next to the von Hayek crypt and began to back up. "Yes, there it is. Come, take a look for yourself."

Hicks didn't move. He looked at the area where Tessmer had been standing and where he was backing up. There were no obvious trip wires between them. They were so close that any kind of explosive or IED would kill them both. Rivas had reported the satellite had confirmed the cemetery was clear, so he wasn't being set up for a sniper shot.

In his ear, Rivas said, "Stay where you are, James. Scott reports Vanguard forces are about to approach the main entrance of the cemetery. This doesn't feel right."

"Come," Tessmer beckoned him. "It's quite safe, I assure you."

Hicks took the cigar from his mouth with his left hand,

keeping his right hand free. He took a wide, slow arc to the exact spot where Tessmer had stood. No farther.

It was far enough.

He saw a white marble headstone with only three lines engraved on it.

Stephen Henry Bumgarner
Lieutenant, United States Coast Guard
Semper Paratus

Stephen Henry Bumgarner was James Hicks's real name.

CHAPTER
31

SCOTT WATCHED THE six-man group break apart and begin approaching the cemetery. One of the men crossed the street to the third van and pounded on the side panel as he passed it. The leader of the other five men pounded on the side panel of each of the two vans on their side of the street as he walked to the cemetery.

Mueller said, "This does not look like good news."

Scott kept watching. The side doors of the three vans slid open and four men spilled out from each. Twelve new men, all dressed like and undoubtedly armed as well as the original six.

Eighteen men in total.

At least now Scott knew what they were up against.

Scott glanced at Mueller as he tucked his binoculars into his tactical vest. "Now you know why I waited. Have your men select and call out their targets. I don't want one asshole getting shot ten times."

While Mueller hit his own throat mic and spoke to his team, Scott reached out to Team Two. "Two, this is Leader. Hostiles on the move and inbound. We're eight men short, so you'll need to pull double duty and cap the stragglers from behind."

"Copy, Leader," Patel said.

Scott repeated that to Mueller, who said, "Just like we've practiced. My men are ready, but we're still eight men short."

"Don't worry."

Scott brought up his Mossberg .500 as the first six men passed under the iron gate of the cemetery. From his peripheral vision, he watched the barrels of six of Mueller's men track their targets as they moved down the path.

He watched for the remaining twelve men to get closer to the gate. They knew what they were doing. They had spread out. They moved slower as they hung back, not allowing themselves to bunch up for an easy target.

The more they lingered, the tougher the shot on the first six men would be.

But the last twelve weren't through the gate yet.

Without looking at Mueller, Scott whispered, "Open fire."

Mueller gave the order and every rifle fired a single round at the same time. Suppressors diffused the sounds of gunfire.

The six men furthest down the path dropped, all from headshots.

Five of the men in the second batch died just past the entrance of the gate.

Scott did the math as he moved into position.

Eleven down. Seven left.

He brought up his suppressed Mossberg and fired high into

the last group entering the cemetery. At that range, the blast took down two up front in a cloud of red mist. The boom of the shotgun sounded more like a crack.

Five left.

He racked another cartridge as the five survivors began to bring out the M4s from beneath their coats. Scott fired, the blast catching one man dead in the center of the chest while the impact caught another target in the arm, causing him to spin around. One shot from Mueller put him down for good.

The remaining three had turned to run back toward the nearest van outside the vacant store.

They were already out of range of the Mossberg and too far away for Mueller's men to risk hitting.

Scott watched the store door open. Patel and Roger stepped into the street and mowed down the men with silenced M4s of their own.

All eighteen men dead in less than twenty seconds.

Scott racked another round into the Mossberg as Mueller's men broke out, checking the dead.

Patel and Roger jogged across the street toward the cemetery as the few people on the street began to back away from the scene.

"You get everyone?" Patel asked as he joined Scott.

The man he'd hit in the chest groaned as he tried to pick up his head. The Kevlar body armor had absorbed most of the blast, but the impact had probably broken every bone in his chest. "All dead except for that one."

Roger Cobb drew his Glock and fired into the man's head as he passed him. "Now you've got a clean sheet, don't you, Scott?" He tucked the sidearm away and ran down the path.

"Where the hell are you going?" Scott yelled after him.

Roger didn't break stride. "James still needs us!"

"It's just the two of them. He'll call us when he's ready. He can handle it."

Roger yelled back, "That's what I'm afraid of!"

Scott realized Roger was right. He handed the shotgun to Patel and took the M4. "Get our van and bring it around to the back entrance of the cemetery. We'll meet you there."

CHAPTER 32

STEPHEN HENRY BUMGARNER.

Hicks hadn't thought about his real name in decades. Seeing it engraved on a headstone made it surreal.

He felt Tessmer watching him, waiting for him to react.

Hicks wouldn't give him the satisfaction. He took a pull on his cigar instead. "That's cute. How did you find out? One of your hacker boys back in the Kremlin?"

"Of course not," Tessmer said. "I haven't had anything to do with those bureaucrats in years, especially after Vladimir signed a Triple Five finding on me. I'm sure you don't know what that is. Not many outside the service do. Not many inside the service know it, either, come to think of it. It's the equivalent of a Shoot-to-Kill order. Any agent is duty-bound to kill me on sight. He doesn't like me any more than you do." Tessmer looked at the ground. "I was his commanding officer for a time, back in our

KGB days. I could have had him shot."

Hicks tried to play it cool, watching the wind carry away his cigar smoke as Tessmer walked down memory lane. But seeing his real name had rocked him to his core. The previous Dean had assured him that his former life had been buried deep. Hicks had seen how deep. There was no way Tessmer could have found it by chance, but there it was, etched in stone for all the world to see. Name, rank, and branch of service. "You didn't answer my question."

Tessmer looked up from the ground as if lost in thought. "Sorry. Just ruing generosities from my past. As for how I found your true identity, I discovered it the same way I discovered the location of your Manhattan facility. You already know how I found it, you just don't realize you know."

Hicks felt his temper spike, and glared at Tessmer. "I'm getting damned tired of your games, Ace."

Tessmer met his glare. "Then quit playing games and think. There's only one link between you and the 23rd Street facility. One link in the whole wide world and I found it. You already know the answer. The question is whether you're man enough to face it."

Hicks stopped breathing. Through all the blood, and all the gunfire, and all the death of the past three days, he had been looking for who had been behind the strike. He'd cared more about the way the attack had been carried out, not how the location had been discovered.

There was only one link between the facility and Hicks, but that was impossible. "No."

"Yes, I'm afraid so. I won't tell you it was easy. We had been tracking rumors of a shadow organization within Western intelligence organizations for quite some time. We thought we were up against a task force from MI5 or INTERPOL. Maybe even the Americans or a contractor who had decided to act on their own. I had many leads over the years, but if my Soviet training taught me anything it was that patience pays off. A few months ago, our systems picked up a series of encoded emails about one of our operations sent over an unsecured server. Helped us find a mole within our Singapore organization. The pattern proved interesting enough for us to crack the code. We traced the email back to the source, and found the user had recently sent several emails about intelligence-gathering methods. Nothing that pertained to us, of course, but enough for us to dig into who owned the device. The emails were sent to a desktop in Savannah, Georgia. A man who, according to his emails, was in the last stages of a fight against cancer. A man named Al Clay."

Hicks was shaking his head before Tessmer said the name. "Impossible."

Tessmer went on. "I'm sure you must have noticed his cancer treatment had caused a considerable degree of dementia. This condition made him sloppy when using his devices. He appears to have used the wrong device to send secure emails, probably due to his medication. He probably used his own desktop because he didn't want people like you to find out how sick he really was. We couldn't track all his activity, of course, but once we located him, we kept him under surveillance. We followed him to Sloan-Kettering, where our people discovered he possessed a secondary device. It appeared to be a normal handheld device, but looks can be deceiving."

Hicks's eyes narrowed. He was talking about the Dean's

handheld device.

The same device Hicks was using now.

The same device he had been using for weeks.

Hicks felt the cigar fall from his hand. "Bullshit."

"Even our finest technicians failed to analyze it, at least not without fear of destroying it. Clay was incapacitated, but not totally unaware of his surroundings, so we still needed to be careful. We continued monitoring Clay instead. That's when we followed him when he was discharged from the hospital to a curious set of brownstone buildings on 23rd Street."

Tessmer paused, seeming to enjoy the look on Hicks's face.

Hicks felt sweat begin to run down his back.

Tessmer stated the obvious. "That's how we found your facility, Stephen. Al Clay led us right to your front door without even knowing it. Oh, he tried to be careful, of course. Changing cabs several times, heading in different directions. It was all so cute, but pathetic, too. Like an old boxer who refused to admit the game has passed him by."

Hicks felt his left hand ball into a fist.

Tessmer went on. "We didn't know what the 23rd Street complex was. Not at first. We knew his condition was terminal and thought he had simply gone to visit an old friend to say goodbye. But the more we looked into who he might be visiting, the more questions we had. The whole thing seemed too perfect. Too bland. So I placed your building under passive surveillance. It took us a few days, but we were able to tie into the security system of a building across the street, and angled the camera your way. It recorded everyone who came and went. Of course, I eventually got your picture. It didn't take long for our sources to match you to the CIA description of the person of interest in the Bajjah disappearance."

Hicks felt the blood roar in his ears. His breathing became shallow. More sweat broke out across his back.

The Dean had led these sons of bitches right to his front door. The Dean had betrayed him without even knowing it.

"That's when I knew you and that building must be important," Tessmer went on. "We tried to get in, but never succeeded. We tried to find a way to knock out your external cameras, but could never lock on to the network. We didn't know you had gone to Toronto until much later. More digging into your trip showed you were with the girl who had been shot. Cameras showed she had given you something, though what we didn't know. But we bided our time, watching and waiting, ready to strike if and when we needed. When I received the alert that someone was beginning to dig into my Tessmer legend, I knew you must have obtained such information in Toronto and I decided the time had come to strike."

Hicks felt himself begin to slump. Everything that had happened in the past week—the explosions, the deaths, Tali—all of it had been because his dying mentor had paid him one last visit before he killed himself.

The man who had placed such a high value on safety and protocol had ultimately been responsible for hurting the one thing he loved most. The University. Hicks looked up at the sky. The irony was so thick he would have laughed if it wasn't so fucking tragic.

"Who was Al Clay anyway?" Tessmer asked. "An asset? A retiree who kept his hand in the game? We never could quite figure that out."

Hicks closed his eyes. At least he'd managed to keep some of his dignity from the bastards. "My friend."

Tessmer seemed to mull that over for a moment. "I'm not sure I believe you, but it's of no importance now. Nations rise and fall, so why should men be any different? We have both lost much since this entire mess started, Stephen. I'd like to change that starting here. Today."

Hicks wasn't sure he'd heard him right. "What?"

"That's the reason I wanted us to meet today," he explained. "To form a partnership. Or at least some level of understanding between our two organizations. I don't know much about your organization, but I know it poses a significant threat to mine. I'm old enough to know the days of conflict between nations have passed. Smaller bands of zealots pose a far greater threat than troops and battleships and stealth bombers. The world has downsized, and so has the nature of combat."

Hicks was still reeling from the news that the Dean had been compromised. "What the fuck are you babbling about?"

"I'm not babbling," Tessmer said. "Merely stating the obvious. The conflicts of the world have grown smaller with fewer players, but with greater implications. That's bad for the militaries of the world, but presents unique opportunities for organizations like yours and mine. The lumbering mobilization of vast armies has passed. Smaller organizations like ours hold the keys to who lives and who dies these days. I propose we reach a simple, mutually beneficial arrangement whereby you continue to fight the Vanguard and the Vanguard continues to fight you. But we coordinate that fight in order to minimize the damage we will cause each other's organization."

Hicks heard the words, but they didn't make any sense. "You're insane."

"No, just practical," Tessmer admitted. "The strike on New York failed to achieve its primary objective, which was to kill you while sparking an international conflict between Iran and the United States, but it isn't a total loss. The Vanguard has laid the necessary ground work to give the United States a perfectly valid excuse for attacking Iran, which is all we really wanted in the first place. Killing you was something of a bonus. The resulting conflict, be it overt or covert, could be of great benefit to our respective organizations. Arms will need to be supplied. Intelligence will need to be gathered. There is plenty of work to go around for all of us. Remember, out of chaos comes opportunity."

"Your Chinese friends know your plan?"

"No, but they will benefit from it regardless. Our respective organizations can go on fighting each other as we have for the past several days, with biohazards and raids and bombings. Or we can work together to rig the game in our favor. Keep the respective governments off balance just enough to make sure we still have a seat at the table. You have your beliefs and I have mine. Sometimes you gain the upper hand, sometimes the Vanguard wins. With proper planning, loss of life, resources, and revenue can be kept to a manageable number so long as our respective masters are served."

The shock of Tessmer's words was finally beginning to wear off. "Revenue? I thought you were a Communist."

Tessmer laughed. "I am, as are my Chinese partners. But unlike my friends in the Far East, I am a realist who understands we need money to achieve our goals. I am content with a certain amount of achievement while my Chinese friends seek to spread the revolution to every corner of the globe. My sources at the CIA are buzzing about some new information they have uncovered from an untapped source. I believe it must be the information on the laptop you stole from our facility. The laptop your Jewess died to protect. My Chinese partners want me to present your head to them at our next meeting. That's not an exaggeration. The Chinese are renowned for their cunning, but they have a great propensity for brutality."

Hicks's right hand moved closer to his belt buckle, closer to the Ruger. "So why don't you try to take it?"

"Because your death would be as pointless as my own. Our deaths would accomplish nothing. Both of us would be replaced in a matter of hours, if not sooner. That is why I propose a strategy that allows each of us to remain the white whale of our respective Ahabs, keeping each other just far enough out of reach to continue our usefulness to our causes."

Tessmer pointed at the crypt and the gravestone. "Let us stop this nonsense before we end up here, among the dead and the forgotten. We all end up here eventually. Why hasten it over the whims of some near-sighted imbeciles who seek to use us to further their own causes? Field men like us have always held back what they tell their handlers. All I propose is that we continue to do so in concert, in order to maintain our relevance and indispensability."

Tessmer gestured toward the crucifix on one of the gravestones nearby. "To paraphrase what that man once said, 'Give unto Langley and Xinjiang what is theirs, and give unto us that which is our own.' What do you say? You know I'm right."

Hicks caught the reference. "Your partners are in Xinjiang?"

And for the first time since they'd met, Tessmer didn't look quite so cocky.

Tessmer's left hand moved toward his jacket.

Hicks pulled the Ruger and fired. The .454 caliber slug evaporated Tessmer's left knee on impact. The German bellowed as he collapsed onto the grave he had arranged for Stephen Bumgarner.

Hicks saw the Glock in Tessmer's right hand. He walked over and stepped on the hand, ignoring the man's screams as his bones gave way. The bones of the same hand that had killed Tali.

He aimed the Ruger at Tessmer's head. "I knew you'd hang yourself if I let you run your mouth long enough."

Hicks heard Rivas screaming in his ear, "Don't kill him!"

Hicks pulled the ear bud free and cast it aside, but could still hear his name echoing through the cemetery.

"You goddamned fool!" Tessmer roared up at him. He feebly grabbed at Hicks's leg. Hicks put more pressure on the hand trapped beneath his boot.

"You killed my friends. You tried to kill me." A column of bile filled Hicks's mouth. He turned his head and spat it against the façade of the von Hayek crypt. "You killed people I loved. You…"

Hicks felt himself get lifted off the ground and thrown backward, hitting the crypt before slamming to the ground. It took a second for a web of pain to spread from the center of his chest to the rest of his body. He realized he'd been shot, but two layers of protective Kevlar had prevented the bullet from puncturing his chest.

He felt a weight in his right hand and realized he hadn't lost his grip on the Ruger.

He ignored the pain and lay flat against the ground, hoping the gravestones would give him some kind of cover. He brought up the Ruger, waiting for something to shoot at.

The first thing he saw was two hands high in the air. "It's Roger. Don't shoot. You're safe. The area's clear." Roger tucked Tessmer's gun into his vest and began tending to the man's wounds.

Hicks let his arm drop and gave in to the pain. "Then who the fuck shot me?"

"I did." Scott came up next to Roger, M4 at his side. He picked up the earbud Hicks had discarded and handed it back to him. "Rivas gave the order to shoot when you took this off. I'll apologize if it'll make you feel better, but I'm not sorry."

Hicks's anger at being shot deadened the pain. "I would've shot him in the head if I'd wanted to kill him."

"Been in the same position as you. Didn't always handle it as well as you did. We just wanted to make sure you didn't do something we'd all regret later." Scott held out his hand to him. "Now get up."

Hicks took Scott's hand and let him pull him to his feet. His chest hurt like hell. He'd never been kicked by a horse, but imagined it would feel pretty much like this. "You said the area's secure?"

"Demerest's German friends held their own," Scott said. "Eighteen dead, none left alive. The Krauts aren't happy they won't be interrogating anyone, but that's too bad."

"And good for us." Hicks winced as he tucked the Ruger back in its holster. Roger was already applying a crude field dressing to Tessmer's ruined leg. "He going to make it?"

"Not if Patel doesn't get here with that fucking ambulance," Roger said as he cut away Tessmer's pants leg. "Where is he, Rivas?"

Hicks hadn't put the bud back in his ear, so he didn't hear Rivas' response. Scott relayed the message for him. "He'll be coming through the back gate, two minutes out."

"The knee is completely gone and the leg is barely attached," Roger said, "but I think I can stop the bleeding with what I have in the van. After that, maybe the Barnyard has some resources that can keep him alive."

"We're not turning him over to Demerest or anyone else," Hicks said. "Not yet."

Scott pointed at the cemetery entrance. "Patel's here."

Hicks turned and saw the white cargo van speeding up the same path he'd walked not ten minutes before, back when he had been remembering his boyhood dreams and before he had been confronted with that boyhood self by a man he had come to kill. A man he hadn't killed because of the man he had become. The circular irony of the entire event would have made his head hurt if his chest didn't already hurt so much.

Patel pulled the van to halt at the row where they were. He kept the motor running as he jumped out from behind the wheel and ran around to the side to open the sliding door.

Roger tied off the bandage on Tessmer's wound and called out to Patel. "Get over here and help us load him into the van. We..."

He stopped when he saw the name on the grave where Tessmer was lying. "Jesus Christ." He looked at Hicks. "James, how...?"

Hicks didn't want to talk about it in front of the others. He grabbed Tessmer by one shoulder and beckoned Scott to take him by the other. "Patel, take his legs and keep the left one elevated. I don't want this son of a bitch bleeding out before we get anything out of him."

The four of them loaded the wounded man into the back of the van. Roger climbed in first with Hicks close behind, pulling the door shut. Patel got back behind the wheel while Scott got in the passenger seat.

Patel threw the van into reverse and backed down the path, brought the van into a hard right, slammed on the brakes, threw the vehicle into drive, and hit the gas. They passed under the gated entrance to the cemetery and rejoined the busy flow of morning Berlin traffic.

Hicks kept pressure on Tessmer's leg while Roger tried to stop the bleeding. His watch said it was just past eight fifteen in the morning. The entire incident had taken less than fifteen minutes. A lifetime for some. Not long enough for others.

He looked at Tessmer, who was struggling to stay conscious. *Don't die, you son of a bitch. Not yet.*

CHAPTER
33

AFTER THEY GOT Tessmer situated in Roger's space at the Penthouse, Hicks decided he should let the rest of the world know what had happened.

He was about to pull off his Kevlar vest, but when the pain in his chest spiked he decided to leave the damned thing on. He eased himself down onto the couch in the living area, pulled out his handheld, and dialed Jason.

"I'm glad you're okay," Jason said. "I monitored Rivas's feed via OMNI. Thank God we didn't lose anyone. Will Tessmer make it?"

"Roger's working on him now. Patel's in there with him. Tessmer's left knee is gone, but if they can stop the bleeding, he might live long enough for us to get something out of him."

"I'm glad you didn't kill him," Jason said.

"Not yet, anyway. You'd better connect me with Demerest.

Same security protocol as before. He'll definitely trace the call, and I don't want his people kicking in doors looking for Tessmer. I've had enough excitement for one day."

"Calling now," Jason said. "One moment."

Demerest answered the call. Hicks could tell by the echo it was on speakerphone. "What the hell happened? The Germans are furious that it turned into a bloodbath, and they have nothing to show for it but dead bodies. And I haven't been able to get shit out of your people all morning. What happened with Tessmer?"

Hicks had no intention of telling him Tessmer's real last name was von Hayek. He hadn't been able to run the name through OMNI yet, and didn't know what it might turn up. He'd done a good job of keeping the CIA at bay. Giving them Tessmer's real name could lead them to drive the Vanguard underground. He wanted to know as much as he could about the organization before he told the world.

Hicks stalled for time. "Why am I on speakerphone?"

"Sarah is here with me. Just the two of us, I promise. The Germans found a lot of blood at a gravesite, but no body. Do you have Tessmer?"

"I've got him. He's wounded, but I think we can save him."

He heard Demerest cheer.

The Trustee said, "This is very good news, James. Better than you know. We have our boogeyman. This is going to go a long way toward getting the Russians and the Israelis to calm down."

"Now we can get to work on the son of a bitch," Demerest said. "Time is of the essence, son. Are you ready to copy an address?"

"No," Hicks said. "I've got him and I'm keeping him. You've got his laptop, you've got his network, and in a little while, I'll probably be able to give you the location of his counterparts in China. You're going to have to move quickly to track them, because when they find out what happened at the cemetery, the Chinese faction will probably disappear."

Demerest didn't sound happy. "I want Tessmer, son. I want him right fucking now. That's non-negotiable."

Hicks ignored him. "The answer is still no. Keeping him for a while is the cost for the information we get out of him. You'll get him when I'm through."

"Unacceptable," Demerest said. "I need him in custody as soon as possible. I need him in a box with trained interrogators who know what they're doing. People who—"

"Have to obey the law," the Trustee interrupted. "And worry about congressional oversight and findings. James is right, Carl. We don't have that kind of time and you can't afford that kind of liability." Her voice changed. "James, you have your deal. You can hand over Tessmer whenever you're done with him, preferably alive. Now, why are you calling? I know it's not to keep us in the loop."

"Before I shot him, Tessmer gave me a location in China," Hicks said. "I don't know anything about China, and you people know everything. I need Agency intel on whether it's a viable location."

Hicks knew he could have OMNI hack agency files to get a handle on the region, but the files wouldn't contain everything. One phone call from Demerest to the people staffing the Agency's China desk and he'd have more information in ten minutes than OMNI could gather in a day.

"Fine," Demerest said. "I'm not happy, but I can live with that. What region are you talking about?"

"Xinjiang," Hicks said. "And don't waste time thinking it's a ruse because it's not. The son of a bitch tried to shoot me right after he said it, so something's got to be there. I need to know what could be there and what is there, and we need to start looking now. If it's some mobile base, they might already be pulling up stakes."

He heard Demerest muffle the phone, as if he was talking to someone nearby.

The Trustee said, "You ever work in China?"

"No," Hicks admitted.

"Well, I have," she said. "Xinjiang's been a hotbed of separatist activity for years. It's close to Mongolia, so it's a region that has a little bit of everything. Muslim extremists, underground enterprises, the works. The Chinese government usually gives them just enough rope to hang themselves, allowing these various deeds to go unpunished while keeping an eye on whatever comes out of the region. Given what Carl's people found on the laptop you gave them, I would have expected the Vanguard to be based in Hong Kong since that's where most of their money is. But Xinjiang makes sense. If you want to be far away from prying eyes, then that's the place to be."

Demerest came back on the line. "My China desk is putting together a report for me now. You can read it on the plane."

Hicks had heard a lot of strange things that day and thought this might be one of them. "Plane? What plane? I've got a prisoner to interrogate. I just can't drop everything and get on a plane to China."

"To Beijing, to be more precise," Demerest said. "There's an international humanitarian delegation leaving out of Berlin for Beijing in three hours. You're going to be travelling with them. Our Berlin office is scrambling to get you all the necessary papers as we speak. You'll be a public relations officer assigned to go along with the rest of the crew. Upon arrival, one of our people will meet you and take you to speak to the army colonel in charge of the country's anti-terrorist unit."

Hicks knew he was disoriented, but none of this was making any sense. "I've never worked in China, but even I know they don't just let foreigners walk around without a shadow. There's no way they'll just let me wander off on my own."

"There is when they want to get rid of the Vanguard as much as we do," Demerest said. "One of the colonels in charge of their anti-terrorist unit is a wannabe defector. He's been on our payroll for years. Seems he's become disenchanted with the politics in his homeland and wants a new life in the West when he retires from the army. We're reaching out to him now and getting him to arrange for some doors to be left open, so to speak."

Every instinct Hicks had was telling him not to go. He was exhausted and in no shape to get on a plane. And nothing about this plan felt right. "An operation like this needs time to set up properly. Hell, I don't even speak Chinese."

"You won't have to," Demerest said. "All you need to do is keep your mouth shut and play along. All my people already in Beijing have someone eyeballing them whenever they leave the embassy. And this information is too big for me to send in an email to my colonel. Ending a threat in Xinjiang would be great for his career, and even better for us."

"We're not talking about your ass here," Hicks said. "We're

talking about mine."

"I know, but the colonel will know how to handle it. No one from the Chinese Army is going to show up with an official car to greet you at the airport, but they'll allow you into the country just this once because it benefits them. If this was just a normal intelligence matter, I could just pick up the phone and call my counterpart in China. But since this is off the books, I need someone to do this personally and quietly. The laptop you captured showed the Vanguard hasn't only infiltrated the CIA. They've infiltrated the Chinese government, too."

Hicks realized going to Beijing might not be a bad idea after all. "I'll need a second set of papers for one of my men. Rahul Patel. Jason will give you his particulars. He speaks Mandarin."

The Trustee added, "Xinjiang is a big place with plenty of caves and valleys to hide. Unless we get something more specific, the Chinese could waste a lot of time and weaponry blowing up empty caves while the Vanguard sneaks out the back. We can't afford another Tora Bora here. Let's hope Roger can get something out of him before you land in Beijing."

He looked at the monitor and saw Roger sitting in a chair next to Tessmer's bed. Roger was checking the patient's body, then wrote furiously in a notebook. Whatever he was writing, it wasn't about how to make the Vanguard's co-leader more comfortable.

"Don't worry," Hicks said. "I think we'll have something soon."

CHAPTER 34

Werner von Hayek was aware of the pain before he realized he was actually awake. Muscles in places he didn't know he had burned hotter than any fire he had ever known. He thought he could feel every crease in his brain, and each of them pulsed and pounded with a new agony.

He would have cried out if he thought he had the strength. The pain was so encompassing that the simple act of giving voice to his agony was beyond his comprehension.

And then, just as suddenly as the agony had begun, it evaporated, replaced by something he could only describe as peace. Past and present lost all meaning, if they ever had any meaning at all. Only now mattered. This very second. Any inkling of memory or identity vanished, and he was completely present within himself, too afraid to even give the state much thought in fear that he may lose this bliss.

That bliss was ruined by a single name.

"Werner von Hayek," declared a voice that sounded neither like God nor the devil, but of man. A voice that belonged very much to this world.

"I know you are conscious and I know you can hear me." It was an American voice, speaking passable German. "Open your eyes and say hello."

Against his own wishes, Werner felt his eyes flutter open. A man was looking at him. A fair-skinned man with blondish hair and the bluest eyes he had ever seen. A face that would have looked almost feminine had it not been for those eyes, harsh in their clarity and certainty.

Werner realized he could not feel much, but what little feeling he had ran cold, though he couldn't explain why.

"There you are," he said in English. "I knew you could hear me."

On reflex, Werner said, "You know nothing, little man."

"Ah, but I do. I know everything about you, Werner. Everything you were, everything you are, and everything you are about to become." The face moved closer. "What you are about to become is far more important."

Werner tried to move his head but realized he could not. He could tell he was sitting at an incline, as if in a hospital bed. He was in a room of complete whiteness, but not an ephemeral white. His mind cleared a bit more and he saw the walls and ceiling were padded. He saw something in the far corner of the room, something covered by another white sheet. Was it a chair? A lamp? A piece of machinery?

He realized he was not in a hospital room at all.

He was in a cell.

His hearing began to return and he heard a cacophony of beeps and machines coming from somewhere behind him. He looked down and saw a white sheet covered him from the neck down. He tried to turn his head again, but this time felt the restraint across his forehead. "Where am I?"

"You're with me and I'm with you, and we're going to have a wonderful time together." The man cleared his throat before saying, "Werner von Hayek. Former colonel in the KGB. An impressive career, I must say. You were Putin's commanding officer once upon a time. My, that must have been something."

Against his will, the man's words made his mind begin to work again. He spoke without thinking, without control. "Putin was a puppy. So desperate for power, he'd do anything I told him to do."

"As will you, in time," the man told him. "Guess that's why he booted you from the service when he rose to power after the Wall fell. You had quite the nasty reputation. 'The Butcher of Bavaria' was what they used to call you back in the Kremlin. That must have stung. You'd worked so hard to be a good party member, a worthy Russian, only to have your high-borne title thrown back in your face. Poor Werner. You got them back, though, didn't you? The Vanguard gave you that much. Supporting the enemies of your enemies. Arming the Ukrainians and all the other separatists who rebelled against a government you never believed to be legal or valid."

Werner wanted to respond, but he remembered now. Werner wasn't his name and hadn't been his name for a long time. It was something else now, though so many memories flooded his mind he couldn't recall the name he used now. "Who are you? How do you know so much about me?"

He could not pull away when the man caressed his cheek. "How cute. Your memory is coming back. That's good. It will make our time together that much more productive. And we can reach our destination that much quicker."

The hand eased away from his face. "You remember what happened to you, yes? At the cemetery? Your family's crypt?"

Amidst the flood of memories, Werner saw a series of images rush to the fore. A forgettable man with dark hair, standing with him at his family's crypt. Another German? What was his name? Bumgarner, yes? But that wasn't the name he was using now. It was something else, something shorter. Hicks, wasn't it?

Memories of the pain came, too, and the gunshot and the screaming and the…

"Good," said the man. "Your vital signs show full cognitive ability is being restored. Now we can begin."

The man pulled the white sheet away. Werner realized he was completely naked and saw remains of his left leg, missing completely from the knee down. The bandages white and clean as if they had always been there, but he knew they hadn't. He remembered the gunshot and the agony, and began to scream again. The sounds from the machines behind him rose in quickening beeps and whirs.

But the blond man didn't try to quiet him. He simply sat in a chair at his bedside and observed him, much like he himself remembered looking at other people in rooms like this in Kiev and Moscow and other places.

This man was as indifferent to his screams, his suffering, and pain as he had once been when the roles had been reversed.

But this was different. Werner could see this man was absorbing his fear, and for the first time since he was a boy,

Werner von Hayek felt fear.

He stopped screaming and decided to do something. He tried to move but realized he was strapped down to the bed. He could feel the straps across his chest and on his wrists. He struggled against them, but found no purchase and stopped.

He began to gather himself, for along with the memories, his training returned. He had been prepared for this. He had been trained by the best counter-intelligence people in the world. Now that he knew what this was, he could fight it the way he had been taught.

He managed to imitate a laugh, though it came out hoarse and raspy. "You are wasting your time, little man. You will never get anything out of me."

"Ah, but I already have. Xinjiang, remember? You mentioned it when you spoke to my friend in the cemetery. You said that's where your Chinese counterparts are based."

Werner stopped laughing. He had forgotten that until now.

"But, as you know," his captor went on, "Xinjiang is a large place, chock full of nooks and crannies where an operation like yours can easily hide."

"And that's all I will ever tell you," Werner spat. "And if you do happen to get me to tell you more, it will be too late. They're probably already gone by now, and anything you do to me will be a waste of time. So why don't you save yourself a lot of bother and put a bullet in my brain and get it over with now?"

"Perish the thought," the man said. "Don't sell yourself short. Or me, either, by the way. Yes, you've had training, but that was a long time ago. You were a whole man then and much younger. You're in good shape for seventy, but you're still seventy, and I have a whole host of ways to get a man of your stature to cooperate."

Werner clenched his jaw, fighting the panic that began to settle in. "Never."

"Never is a long time, and we have all the time in the world. More than you know."

Werner did not see the man move, but felt intense pain spike in his left leg, intense enough to make his eyes roll back in his head as he strained against his bindings.

His captor's voice cut through the agony. "That pain you felt when you first woke up was induced by me. The peace you felt was courtesy of a tiny bit of morphine I introduced to your system. The pain you're feeling now is thanks to a special concoction of mine that enhances the tenderness of your wound. I'd like to tell you that the pain will go away, but what you're feeling right now is the least amount of pain you'll feel in our time together. That is, if you choose to be difficult."

Werner heard the man move, and as quickly as the pain came, it went. The man said, "This is who you are now, my friend. Peace, then excruciating agony that will last for as long as I allow it. Each time will get worse, more intense. Don't worry about your heart giving out, because I won't allow it. I've given you a stimulant so that you won't pass out, either. You are entirely under my control and resistance is pointless. Yes, you have been trained to resist, but, my dear Werner, no one ever trained you for me."

The man came back into view and Werner tried to spit at him, but he didn't have enough saliva. He didn't realize how dry he was. How cold!

His captor clasped his hands behind his back. "Now, I know all of this is a lot to take in all at once, so I'm going to give you a little time to rest before we begin talking about Xinjiang. I want to hear all about exact locations, defensive measures in place, how many people are stationed there, and what goes on there. And while you're thinking about ways to lie to me, consider the amount of pain you've felt so far and realize it is but a sample of the pain I'm prepared to inflict on you if you decide to be difficult. Ask yourself if your partners are worth the agony or if the truth is worth the peace you feel when you cooperate."

His captor looked away. "I've got to admit there's a part of me that hopes you hold out for a bit. You hurt a lot of people I love and there's a certain price to be paid for that, don't you think?" He bent closer to Werner and smiled. "I know I think so." He patted Werner's right leg and said, "But there'll be time for that. Rest so we can begin our journey toward the truth together."

Werner watched the monster move toward the door, only to pause before the covered thing in the corner. *What is that?*

His tormentor said, "I almost forgot. I know how terribly lonely interrogation can be. Locked up in a cell, all alone with only your thoughts to plague you, wondering what will happen next. I want your stay with us to be as pleasant as possible, so I've asked a friendly face to join us."

The man pulled off the sheet and revealed his man Henrik sitting in a chair. His eyes vacant, his chest barely rising and falling. A thin line of drool overflowing his bottom lip onto his bare chest.

The man reacted to the look on Werner's face. "Why so sad? We promised to keep him alive and we have. Hicks didn't lie to you then. And I'm not lying to you now."

He folded the sheet across his arm. "I'd suggest you two

get reacquainted, but I'm afraid it'll be a bit of a one-sided conversation. Lobotomy patients aren't known to be conversant." That smile again. "See you in a bit."

Werner was screaming again when Roger Cobb closed the door behind him.

CHAPTER 35

Beijing, China

Hicks felt a familiar rush when the lock slid open. He hadn't picked a lock in a while and was glad he hadn't lost his touch. "We're in."

Rahul went in first while Hicks replaced the lock pick in its nylon pouch and put it away. He went inside and shut the door behind him, quietly relocking it once he was inside the apartment.

Patel stood in the middle of the living room, looking the place over. "Christ, what a dump."

Hicks couldn't argue with him. It was almost noon, but the smog in Beijing made it look closer to evening. Better lighting would not have improved the surroundings. The living room had a threadbare couch, a flimsy wooden bookcase filled with all the right tomes the Party would expect a high-ranking military officer to have. Demerest had told him Colonel Li Jie Tian had been wise enough to keep his contraband reading buried on his family's farm in the south, where the Party had searched on a regular basis, but never found.

The colonel may have been a traitor, but he wasn't incompetent.

"Check the place for bugs, but don't disturb anything," Hicks said as he went into the bedroom. "We already know as much about this guy as we need to. Sniffing around his stuff will only piss him off and we need him on our side."

In the bedroom, Hicks found the bed unmade and articles of clothing cast on the floor. All of it was on the left side of the bed and all of it was male clothing. He would have felt better about Colonel Tian if they had something to hang over his head. A gay lover or a married woman. A porn fetish or syringe full of heroin on the nightstand. Hell, even a sex toy or empty liquor bottles would have been enough ammunition to force him to cooperate. But Demerest had warned him that Colonel Tian was simply a run-of-the-mill civil servant who had grown discontent with the Communist ideology and wanted a better life in the West. The first step toward securing that life would start today when he came home at the end of his shift.

Hicks opened the drawer of the nightstand and removed the NP-28 semi-automatic pistol he was told would be there. It may have been a Chinese knock-off of the Colt M-1911 A1 .45 caliber pistol, but it fired real bullets and was therefore a threat. He didn't want the colonel getting his hands on it when he found two strangers in his apartment.

Hicks checked the chamber and the magazine and found them both full. Flying commercial meant he'd had to leave his Ruger in Berlin, but the NP-28 would fit the bill. He found two extra clips deeper in the drawer and pocketed those, too. Better to be safe than sorry.

Back in the living room, he found Patel working his handheld. "I'm not picking up any signals coming from the apartment, but with the smog as bad as it is today our connection to the satellite is spotty."

He had already told Jason to improve the University's technological reach into Eastern Europe and Asia. It would take money, which they had, and time, which they didn't have. If this trip turned out as well as he hoped, the Vanguard might be set back several months, maybe even a year, but they wouldn't be destroyed. There were too many facets of the organization spread around the world. Taking out the people at the top would weaken the Vanguard for a while, but its business was too lucrative to be sidelined for long. As the previous Dean had often said, "Where there's a cash flow, there's a way." And the arms deals brokered by the Vanguard were lucrative enough to keep them in business for a very long time.

Hicks had no delusions about destroying the Vanguard in a single week. But he already knew more about them than he had only a few days before. And would know still more about them if Demerest's Beijing plan worked.

And that plan hinged upon one very important event. That Colonel Tian didn't make Hicks shoot him when he walked through the door.

Hicks sat in a wooden chair facing the door. It was far enough from the window so he couldn't be spotted and far away enough from the door to keep Tian from seeing him immediately.

Patel put his handheld away. "And you're sure he knows we're supposed to be here?"

"No, I'm not sure because I didn't order it done myself. Demerest said he got word to the colonel to expect to be contacted today. I don't think he's expecting two Westerners to break into his apartment, which is why I have this." He put the NP-28 on his lap.

"Hope you don't have to use it."

"Would kind of make this whole trip pointless if I did. And getting out of the country will be damned near impossible as it is. Killing a colonel would make it even worse." He looked up at Patel. "I just hope your Mandarin is as good as you say it is, or shit will get real complicated, real fast."

"If this goes bad," Patel checked his watch, "it won't be because of the quality of my Mandarin. I just hope Roger can get Tessmer to give us a precise location. Talking to the colonel is one thing. Giving him something to hit is something else."

Hicks checked his handheld. Still nothing from Roger. "He'll get him to talk by the time the colonel is ready to mobilize. Just focus on getting him to cooperate. Roger will handle the rest."

Patel checked his watch again. "Four minutes until he's due, assuming he's punctual."

"He is. Silence until further notice."

The two of them spent the next two hundred and forty seconds waiting to see how their trip to Beijing would turn out. Hicks hoped the colonel had gotten Demerest's message. Messages had trouble reaching Assets even in the best of times in the most open societies. China was one of the most closed societies in the world, where everyone spied on everyone else. The military was not immune. If anything, they were held under even closer scrutiny by a Communist Party that distrusted those charged with defending their way of life.

But as he sat in that dusty, dingy apartment in the center of Beijing, Hicks realized that these were the first two hundred and forty seconds of absolute quiet he had enjoyed since he had been woken from his sleep by the proximity alert back in New York. He didn't count the drug-induced euphoria Roger had put him in. Every moment since had either been running away from something or running toward something. These moments were the first in days where he had absolutely nothing to do but sit and wait to see what happened.

So much had already happened. So much had already been lost on both sides, to where the balance was almost even.

But Hicks didn't want balance. He wanted to smash the scale into a million pieces. And the colonel in charge of China's anti-terrorism efforts would help him do just that.

Both men looked up when they heard the key in the door. Hicks gripped the NP-28 but kept it flat on his lap. If Patel did his job, that was where it would stay.

Colonel Tian rushed into the apartment, shut the door, and leaned against it. He was breathing heavily, his face damp with sweat. He kept his eyes closed as he stood flat against the door, trying to control his breathing. It looked like Demerest's people had gotten word to him after all.

Either that or the colonel was having a bad day that was about to get a hell of a lot worse.

Since Demerest's file on Tian said he didn't speak a word of English, Hicks signaled Patel to start the script.

"Colonel Tian," he said in Mandarin, "we mean you no harm. We are here to…"

The colonel's eyes opened. He looked at the two men in his apartment. He answered Patel in clipped tones and gestures that told Hicks that he was a combination of pissed off and scared.

"He's not happy," Patel translated. "He said coming here was stupid. That it could get us all killed."

Hicks had heard enough. "Remind the colonel that the Party is watching him, not his apartment. Assure him we weren't followed or watched." He waited for Patel's translation to catch up before he said, "Then ask the colonel if he'd like to be a general."

Colonel Tian looked at Hicks.

Hicks smiled. Advancement. The true international language. "I thought you'd understand that one." He motioned to the chair opposite him, offering the colonel a seat in his own apartment.

The colonel sat. They were off to an excellent start.

CHAPTER 36

THE MAN WAS not happy.

It had been over a day since he had heard from the German. There were scattered reports of some kind of a confrontation in Berlin, but his sources had been unclear. He did not know if they were discussing the raid of the Facility or of the stabbing on the street or something new. Nuances between the barbarian tongue and Mandarin often left many important details lost in translation. And if the Man had learned anything in his long life, it was that details always mattered.

All he knew for certain was that the German had allowed a laptop to be stolen from the facility, and had failed to retrieve it. The German had drawn far too much attention to his organization in the past few days, making him something of a liability. They may have started this enterprise together, but neither man intended on allowing the Vanguard to die with them. Eventually, both would have to be replaced, but that time had come sooner for the German than for the Man. Fate had made it so.

Fate and superior planning. The German had always preferred a more cosmopolitan lifestyle than the Man. Spend enough time with the enemy, the Man had learned, and one begins to act like them, perhaps even admire them. He doubted the German had gone over to the other side, but he had become softer and more lenient than he should have been. He had taken the American too lightly and misjudged his abilities. This, the Man was certain, had led to his downfall. Whether he was in the custody of the West or not was of little importance. The German was done. His replacement had already been selected and agreed to the position.

The Man turned his attention to the events taking place on his wall of monitors. His base in Xinjiang was far too large to relocate, so they had begun to harden their defenses. They were deep in rocky terrain that was nearly impossible to see from the ground or air. Even satellites had been unable to locate it thanks to counter-surveillance techniques that further obscured the camp from above.

Still, the Man had learned that prudence was the better part of valor, and given the German's disappearance, he had begun backing up the Vanguard's systems to dozens of other sites around the world. Xinjiang was still the nerve center, but the German's miscalculations about the security of the Berlin facility had called for a recalibration of resources.

By his most conservative estimates, the German had been out of touch for at least twenty-six hours. His capture had not appeared in any official database, so if he was in custody, one of the clandestine services had him. Their sources in the CIA confirmed they did not have him, so it must have been Hicks or the British.

The German's death would be a major blow to the Vanguard's mission, but his capture could be crippling. He knew enough about the organization to completely destroy it. Passwords could be changed. Money streams rerouted. Delivery schedules altered and cutout men replaced.

But the knowledge the German possessed of their institution, their way of doing business, was second only to his own. Combine that with the information stored on the laptop that had been stolen and it gave the enemy a glimpse into the Vanguard's inner workings. It…

He looked up at his monitor when he saw an alarm sound briefly before it was replaced by an alert that both sensors were down.

The Man stared at the monitor. He had been around advanced warning systems for more than half his life. He had never seen them throw two entirely different signals at almost the same time. Unless…

He went to his keyboard and remotely activated the air raid alarm for the camp. Although ninety percent of the camp was well underground, attention must be paid.

From his keyboard, he toggled one of the monitors to show the camp's radar system tucked discretely throughout the valley. But the feed was already off-line. He toggled to all the many surveillance cameras he had installed throughout the camp. Each feed was completely black, with neither sound nor static.

The Man pounded his desk, cursing his blindness and his sons for not calling him from the camp by now. He picked up the phone and dialed them directly, but the line rang busy.

Too much was happening at once for this to be a mere blackout.

He had just called to one of his assistants into his office when all the monitors changed to a wide-angle shot of his camp in foothills of Xinjiang. It was a shot taken at ground level and showed the camp in full detail. The communication huts and the armory and the facility where they stored all their various vehicles.

The Man stood as the screen flickered to black Chinese lettering on a white background. The characters spelled out one word: *Watch*.

The screen flicked back to the image of the camp. The Man saw his people moving between the structures as they carried out their daily tasks on behalf of the Vanguard. The fools. Hadn't they heard the air raid warning? Why weren't they taking shelter underground?

From the left side of the screen he saw columns of dust kick up just before the camp, dust he knew had come from strafing fire from an airplane. The Man yelled at the monitor as he watched thousands of rounds rake the camp, tearing through buildings and people and structures with the ease of a needle piercing fabric.

The Man watched the image, hoping at least some of his people had survived the assault. A few staggered out into the open, only to be cut down by yet another strafing run from a second fighter jet that passed overhead.

He watched them flop to the ground, their bodies jerking from the impacts of bullets. He looked to see if he could recognize any of them as his sons, but could not. The image on the screen was too far away.

The Man's assistant finally appeared in his doorway. "Find out when this image was taken. Get someone to the camp immediately. I need to find out…"

He lost the ability to speak when a stunted mushroom cloud rose from the base.

The camera jostled from the shockwave, but remained in focus.

The Man lowered himself into his chair. His sons and some of his people could have withstood the strafing attacks. They could have even withstood the impact of several Hellfire missiles striking the site. But he recognized the last plane that dropped the final ordinance. It was a Chinese bomber that had dropped several bunker-buster bombs on the site.

Technology the Vanguard had stolen from Western defense contractors and sold to the Chinese.

Technology that had been used to kill his sons, for he knew they must be dead. No one could have survived that amount of firepower. The underground network of tunnels had been deep, but not deep enough to withstand such an explosion.

He had other sons. The Vanguard had other people, other facilities. But this blow left the Man gaping as his organization's highest achievement burned before him. Its loss would be felt by the Vanguard for years.

He vowed those responsible would feel the loss much sooner than that.

The screen switched again, this time to white English lettering on a black screen. It took several moments for his assistant to translate it. And when he did, he flinched as he held it up for the Man to see.

You killed my family. Now I have killed yours.
You hunted me. Now I hunt you.
You will live with this sorrow for as long as I let you.
You will die when I choose.
Await me.

The Man's assistant flinched when he crumpled the paper and threw it on the floor. "I want that burned, never to be read by anyone again. I want the footage of the attack removed from our servers and destroyed. All of our people are forbidden from seeing it or discussing it under penalty of death."

The assistant grabbed the paper off the floor and tucked it behind his back. "Yes, sir, but I am afraid there is a problem."

The Man balled his hands into fists until the old knuckles cracked. "What problem?"

"The footage was not sent to us directly. The footage we watched was from the site where it was posted. It has already been viewed by thousands of people. Our allies were able to purge it from Chinese sites almost as soon as it appeared, but the rest of the world is a different matter."

The Man slammed both fists down on his desk. "We have crippled nuclear missile silos and shut down the electricity for entire countries and you tell me we cannot take down a video from YouTube?"

The assistant bowed. "We are already doing that, sir, and we are making progress. I simply wanted you to know the severity of the situation. Our enemies knew what they were doing. They had a plan to embarrass us. We are in the process of undoing that damage."

The Man knew the only way to halt embarrassment was to

avenge it. Vigorously.

And that was what he was about to do.

"Continue to take down the footage. Keep me informed. Have my car brought around immediately. I have work to do."

CHAPTER 37

Xinjiang, China

Hicks jerked the wheel to the right, narrowly missing a massive hole in the ground. According to OMNI they still had a few hours before they reached the Mongolian border, and it was going to be dangerous driving most of the way. He wanted to get there before nightfall.

"Slow down," Patel said as he held on to the roll bar. "You're driving like a maniac."

"Goddamned right I am." He hit a flat stretch of desert and hit the gas. "We just blew the shit out of the Vanguard's main facility, Ace. They'll be sending someone to take a look at it, and they won't be happy when they get here. I'd like to put as much distance between us and that base as soon as possible before they get here."

An unseen divot jolted the Jeep. "Just don't wreck us in the process. I'm pretty sure Triple A doesn't make calls in this part of the world."

He steered around another hole on his left. "You're sure you scanned this vehicle after Colonel Tian left it for us?"

"I did," Patel said, "and the colonel was true to his word. Not so much as a GPS signal to trace its whereabouts from whatever motor pool he stole it from."

Hicks was glad for that much. He had enjoyed his taste of anonymity in the four minutes he had spent waiting for Colonel Tian at his apartment. He hoped things stayed that way, at least until they reached the extraction point.

He knew Demerest and the Trustee had wanted a report on the strike as soon as it had happened. If Colonel Tian hadn't already told them about the mission's success, they had probably seen the footage of the strike on the internet. They wouldn't be happy about getting the news of the Vanguard's destruction the same time the rest of the world got it, even though no one else would appreciate what they were looking at except them.

But Hicks didn't care about what they liked.

He had fulfilled his end of the bargain. His way. And he intended to keep doing things his way for a long time to come.

They hadn't goaded the Vanguard out of hiding.

They hadn't uncovered the Vanguard facilities.

They hadn't forced Werner von Hayek to give them the exact location of the Vanguard's base in Xinjiang.

They hadn't lost people in the field.

Hicks had. *The University* had.

Hicks took a small incline a little too fast and the Jeep went airborne for a couple of seconds before slamming back down to the ground. For a moment, he thought the engine would die or he'd cracked an axel, but the vehicle continued to make good time.

"Christ," Patel said. "This thing jiggles worse than a cheap belly dancer."

Hicks stole a glance at his passenger as he dodged another hole in the ground. "That's the second joke you've cracked in a couple of minutes. If I didn't know any better, I might think you're getting a sense of humor."

Patel held on. "And if *I* didn't know any better, I'd think you were becoming human again. Haven't seen that side of you since you pulled me out of my cousin's bar back in New York."

Hicks kept his eyes on the road. "Don't mention that day again, understand? I don't like my people talking about their failures. It doesn't accomplish anything."

Patel braced for the jolt from another divot. "I guess that makes me one of your people now."

Another rock jarred them. "Guess you didn't get the email. The job's yours if you want to keep it. The Vanguard's not going to take this lying down. We're going to need you, believe me."

"Then I accept, as long as you realize we didn't end anything today. If anything, we only stirred up more trouble."

Hicks saw the ground level out again. A flat road with just a thin layer of sand drifting across it. He threw the Jeep into high gear and hit the gas. The sooner they made it to their Mongolian extraction point the better.

"I know." The wind picked up and the new speed blew sand in his eyes, making him squint. "I'm counting on it."

THE END

ACKNOWLEDGEMENTS

Thanks to my agent Doug Grad, my publisher Jason Pinter, and my attorney Eric Brown for their continuing faith in my work.

Thanks to my friends whose encouragement kept me going through challenging times: Pam Stack, Marc Cameron, Reed Farrel Coleman, Joe and Justine Clifford, Eric and Christy Campbell, Joel Eisenberg, Dr. Paul Rinaldi, Rory Costello, Ed Chaczyk, Barbara Howe, Kim Hunter, Rick Ollerman, Leah Canzoneri, Steph Post, Ryan Holt, Chris and AJ, Theresa and Larry, and the kids Mary Kate, Emily and Daniel Bida.

Special thanks to the wonderful staff at the Nat Sherman Townhouse and the boys who help keep me sane: Buddha and Marie, Joe Joe, Mickey Two Fingers, Gentle George, Billy Judo, LFDom, Tony Bangtails, Bangkok Greg, Professor Dino, Davey Mats, Tommy Mets and Lefty.

As always, thank you to my Aunt Rosie and my mother-in-law Arcenia for being constant sources of goodness in my life. And to my wife Rita for everything.

ABOUT THE AUTHOR

Terrence McCauley is the award-winning author of two previous James Hicks thrillers: *Sympathy for the Devil* and *A Murder of Crows*, as well as the historical crime thrillers *Prohibition* and *Slow Burn* (all available from Polis Books). He is also the author of the World War I novella *The Devil Dogs of Belleau Wood*, the proceeds of which go directly to benefit the Semper Fi Fund. His story "El Cambalache" was nominated for the Thriller Award by International Thriller Writers.

Terrence has had short stories featured in *Thuglit*, *Spinetingler Magazine*, *Shotgun Honey*, *Big Pulp*, and other publications. He is a member of the New York City chapter of the Mystery Writers of America, the International Thriller Writers and the International Crime Writers Association.

A proud native of The Bronx, NY, he is currently writing his next work of fiction. Please visit his website at terrencemccauley. com or follow him at @terrencepmccauley.